IT SMELLS TROUBLE

❧

ANDY GALLO

IT SPELLS TROUBLE

Copyright © 2023 by Andy Gallo

Cover Art © 2023 Alexandria Corza

www.alexandriacorza.com

Published by Gallorious Readers, LLC

P.O. Box 1654 College Park, MD 20741, USA

> This is a work of fiction. Names, characters, places, and incidents either are the product of author imagination or are used fictitiously, and any resemblance to actual persons, living or dead, business establishments, events, or locales is entirely coincidental.
>
> This book contains explicit sexual content.

Cover content is for illustrative purposes only and any person depicted on the cover is a model.

All rights reserved. This book is licensed to the original purchaser only. Duplication or distribution via any means is illegal and a violation of international copyright law, subject to criminal prosecution and upon conviction, fines, and/or imprisonment. Any eBook format cannot be legally loaned or given to others. No part of this book may be reproduced or transmitted in any for or by any means, electronic or mechanical, including photocopying, recording, or by any information storage and retrieval system, without the written permission of the Publisher, except where permitted by law. To request permission and all other inquiries, contact Andy Gallo, P.O. Box 1654, College Park, MD 20741, USA; visit www.andygallo.com; or send an email to andy@andygallo.com.

❈ Created with Vellum

It Spells Trouble: Mages and Mates
Book Two

Mage Jannick Pederson thought it was a simple assignment: help the gryphon leader find some missing human children and then go home. A noble cause, even if he didn't much like the abrasive jerk. So why didn't someone tell him he'd be working *closely* with the leader's son instead? That hot piece of perfection could make even happily-single Jannick give up his no-strings-attached ways.

Gryphon shifter Conall Arwan has simple goals for his life: get his PhD in pediatric shifter social work and stay off the radar of his disapproving father. When his father orders him to work with a hot but arrogant mage to find missing human kids, all Conall sees is how it pushes back his graduation date. Again. And even if the mage unexpectedly turns out to be not *so* bad—and maybe even a little sweet—there's still no future for them. Conall's dad has plans for him and they don't include getting involved with a sexy, infuriating mage.

But fate has other ideas.

It Spells Trouble is a 75K word fated mates romance with a hearty dose of steam and a guaranteed happily-ever-after. This book is part of the Mages and Mates series and includes a plot to destroy the world, a desperate decision with far-reaching consequences, and one pissed off gryphon father.

Each book in the series can be read alone, but they are better read in order.

For my husband Michael.

Forever will not be long enough.

Fifteen years ago, you encouraged me to write again, and ever since you've been my biggest supporter. Giving me the freedom and courage to write is just one of the many reasons I love.

-Andy

Chapter One

JANNICK PEDERSON

A Homehearth Suites Hotel? I shook my head. When was the last time I stayed in a three-star hotel? Yes, that was extremely arrogant and made me the king twatwaffle of the day, but it was true. One of the perks of being a member of the storied —and insanely wealthy—Hollen family was I didn't do three-star hotels. Or drive myself to said subpar hotel in a Chevy Malibu. They could have at least gotten me a Cadillac.

Official business didn't allow for such perks, not that there were any better hotels in Hagerstown, Maryland. I'd told the travel staff to find me the best place, and if it exceeded the per diem, I'd pay out of pocket. I forgot about the car.

I pulled up to the entrance and waited before I realized no one was coming out. There were no valets, no doormen, only those push carts with the high bar to hang things waiting outside the doors. I sighed and turned off the car. Slinging my laptop case over my shoulder, I went in to see how low the bar had been set.

If I hadn't been in such a pissy mood, I probably would've

realized the place was fine. My half-brother Bart wouldn't even have blinked. Hell, he and Cael (his mate) probably would've been pleased.

"Hello. Checking in?" Toby the front desk clerk was cute—in a preppy, college kid way. Though if he was working at 3:00 p.m. on a Tuesday, he probably wasn't in college.

Gack! Could I channel Grandpa Pederson any more if I tried?

"Yes." I smiled, hoping to lose my Pissy Pederson Pants. He smiled back, so I mostly succeeded. "Jannick Pederson."

I handed over my license and credit card.

"Yes, Mr. Pederson. We have you in one of our king deluxe suites."

The way he said it suggested not many people splurged for the "deluxe" accommodations. "That's great. Thank you."

He typed a few more things, keyed my card, and handed me everything still smiling. "Pull around to the back; you can use the side entrance. The elevators are back that way."

"Thanks again."

"My pleasure."

Part of me wanted to ask if he really meant that, because I had the "king deluxe suite" all to myself. Of course, that would be highly inappropriate. If I should happen to find him on a hook-up app, however . . .

Nope. I wouldn't see him there because I wouldn't *be* on a hook-up app. This was work.

Being an adult sucked.

I had to keep those thoughts quiet. Bart always asked why I didn't quit if I hated working so much. I didn't need the money. The truth was I didn't hate work, just parts of it, part of the time. Plus, Dad being the head of the Mage Council, it wouldn't look good if his kids didn't work for the betterment of the mage community and the world.

I put my luggage down in my room and flopped onto the

couch. It wasn't terrible. Nothing like a real suite at the Ritz or the Rittenhouse in Philly, but I wasn't suffering, either.

Entering the small kitchenette, I used the little one cup maker to get some coffee. While it whirled and spritzed, I pulled up the assignment on my tablet. Another reason my family wanted us all to work—it meant they could send us to meet with alphas and clan chiefs. Hard to complain about being disrespected when the head of the council sent his child in his place.

This was only my second solo mission representing the council and the family. As much as I complained, I tried to take my job seriously. Or as seriously as my childish personality could muster.

Aodhan Arawn, alpha for the gryphons, requested the Mage Council send someone to help them investigate the disappearance of several human children from gryphon territory. Technically this was a human issue, but Aodhan took the disappearances personally since they happened in his area. He also suspected magic.

Gryphons were among the most magic-sensitive beings who weren't mages. His suspicions held more weight than the facts most beings presented.

Gryphons were also prickly as hell. Dad had warned me before I left: Arawn was abrasive and condescending. His sons weren't much better. The best way to deal with them was to project strength, not back down, and to be respectful.

I was fine with the first two bits. No one pushed me around, except maybe my grandmothers. Unfortunately, I was a lot better at snark than diplomacy. This was going to be an interesting week.

My email to Aodhan let him know I'd arrived and could meet before dinner if he had time. I was polite and deferential, but direct and to the point. Look at me adulting.

Setting the tablet down, I decided to use the oversized shower I saw on my walk through. Whining about the lack of amenities was not strength and respect. If it had decent water pressure, it would go a long way to washing away the attitude I'd had when I arrived.

I needed to keep my eye on the prize. The sooner I finished the assignment, the sooner I could leave this backwater town.

Chapter Two

CONALL ARAWN

"Let's go, Conall," Dad said, as he entered without knocking. I was used to it. As alpha and my father, he ruled the roost. This time, however, it was more personal. I was studying. He didn't approve of my getting a PhD, let alone in pediatric social work. In his opinion, all the things a gryphon needed to know were passed down through the generations.

So were the abusive ways some species treated their children. The fact the Assembly had enough votes among the various shifter clans to pass a law codifying outlawed practices for raising our young proved there was a need. Predictably—shamefully—the gryphon alpha voted with the handful of delegates who opposed the law.

This "mission" he'd assigned me was meant to distract me from my studies. The longer it took to resolve, the more likely I'd have to skip another semester. He did this at least once a year, so my three-year plan had stretched into five. Now maybe six, if I couldn't wrap this up fast.

"Yes, sir." I saved my work, grabbed my coat, and followed him out to the garage. "Did he answer your reply?"

"I didn't respond." Dad got in the driver seat of the large SUV. It projected power, in his mind at least. Others saw it as overcompensating.

"Don't you think we should tell him? What if he's not there?"

"He came here at my request. Where would he go?"

Those two sentences summed up why gryphons weren't especially liked by other species. Even minotaurs had inched past us after decades of rehabbing their image. Not that I had much use for humans, mage or not. Bit by bit, they'd destroyed the habitats of most species. Even western Maryland was starting to get too built up for our kind.

"Any number of places. Wouldn't it be preferable to let him know we're coming than to sit around waiting for him to return?"

"If he keeps me waiting, he'll regret it."

Because *that* would piss Dad off to the point we'd accomplish nothing. My degree—and by extension, my freedom—depended on this being a very productive meeting.

"He's not part of our pack, Dad. He's a representative of the chancellor of the Mage Council. You invited him here, so he's not under your jurisdiction."

"Hmph."

It was pointless to argue with him. He was never wrong, just like my two oldest brothers. He also didn't care because once he left, dealing with the mage would be my problem.

Anger at being trapped into a life I didn't want threatened my control. I closed my eyes and took deep breaths. One day it wouldn't work, and I didn't want to think of what would happen then.

As much as I wanted to escape, I didn't want to be expelled. Life without my pack was something I couldn't comprehend.

I ignored the little voice that challenged me to think beyond the narrow confines in which I'd been raised. Thinking life would be better was a fool's dream. Better to do the alpha's will than to be cast adrift.

Chapter Three

JANNICK

The shower had lived up to expectations—it improved my mood as well as my opinion of the place. I wrapped a towel around my waist and checked my tablet for a response. Seeing none, I went in search of my coffee.

It was barely warm, of course. I glanced at the three remaining pods and frowned. Two decaf and one regular. I might need to speak to Toby again, after all.

Someone knocked on my door. Impure thoughts of the cute guy anticipating my needs and coming to my caffeine rescue lasted a half second under the continued pounding. No hotel staff cared enough to make that much noise.

"Yes? Who is it?" I should have told whomever to wait so I could get clothes on, but that tiny part of my childish brain still said it might be Toby using a manufactured reason to talk to me.

Of course, it wouldn't be him, but I'd only get one chance to wow him with my stunning self, so I walked to the door in just my towel.

The answer to my inquiry was louder thumping.

"How rude," I muttered as I summoned my power stone. "If you pound on my door again, I will electrify it and call security. Who's there?"

A growl seeped through the door. If I had three chances to guess who this was, I'd only need one. More reason to stick to my guns and demand an answer.

"Alpha Arawn and his son, Conall Arawn."

Ding, ding, ding. I won the prize for guessing right.

I considered asking them to wait while I got dressed, but he didn't deserve the courtesy. Also, he'd probably break down the door if I didn't open it now that he'd answered me.

Keeping my stone out, I opened the door and stared into the angry face of Aodhan Arawn, royal douche canoe. It took him a heartbeat to notice my lack of clothes, and his pissy "you ruffled my feathers wrong" face turned into a frowning snarl.

"Excuse my informal appearance. I didn't see the email you never sent letting me know you were on the way." I waved them in with my stone hand. "Come in while I get dressed."

Chew on that. Part of me wanted him to attack me. My shields were up, and I'd added a heat element that would burn him good. The adult part of me realized that wasn't the best idea, so I let my stone flare. They didn't need to know I was an alpha three mage, only that I was strong enough to fry their magic resistant hides if it came to a fight.

Now that I'd projected strength, I'd see how it affected my ability to be respectful. What a great start to the mission.

***

I took an extra couple of minutes more than I needed. Totally petty, but I needed the time to mentally prepare. Father and son were by the window. I'd been too busy posturing to notice the younger Arawn. Tall, sandy hair, lean muscle but not beefcake big, and handsome. It was his eyes that drew me, though. They were a forest green, but they had a hint of weariness and resignation.

Until our gazes met. Then it was all hard and growly.

"Can I get you something to drink?" I asked, remembering Dad's third rule.

"No," Aodhan said. "We're not staying long. We're going to the homes of three of the families who had their kids taken. Maybe you and that pretty rock of yours can figure something out."

I shouldn't have felt so fussy. This was the point of our meeting. Something in the way he spoke to me, however, grated on me like nails on slate. "Let me get a drink, and we can talk about what to do first."

Quicker than I could follow, he had his hand on my arm. "I said we're going now."

It was sloppy of me not to reengage my wards after I dressed. I wouldn't make that mistake again. Pushing power out of my body, I forced his hand away.

"Touch me again and I'll burn your hand off." He snatched it back as if I *had* burned him, but I hadn't added the heat spell—at least not yet. "Let's get something straight. I don't work for you, and I don't answer to you. If you have a problem, call Chancellor Hollen. My father."

"Hollen's your dad?" Conall asked.

Their ignorance of my lineage, surprising as it was, didn't excuse the alpha's behavior. Fixing my gaze on Aodhan, I said, "Look it up. I was chosen for precisely this reason. You aren't going to boss me around, and I'm not scared of you. I fought and killed a demon prince with my brother and his mate. You don't want me? Fine. Dad's next pick will be my oldest sister, Deputy Inquisitor General Avelina Hollen. She's a *real* joy to be around."

We had a stare off, and I had to remain aware of the younger one. He didn't seem as bad as his father, but he was going to do whatever his alpha told him.

"Now," I said, pretending to lower my protection. "We can sit down and discuss things and plan what to do next. Or I can walk you to the door, spend the night in this nice suite, and go back to Philly in the morning."

One thing was certain, I could recount everything that happened to my father under a truth spell long before anyone would put Aodhan's call through. I'd put his odds of speaking to Dad in the next two weeks at less than zero.

I debated telling him that, but this is what Dad meant about strength and respect. I'd given him two options and let him choose, but I didn't threaten him. Maybe he knew I could reach the Mage Chancellor sooner than him, but if I didn't say it, he could pretend he chose not to report me.

The younger Arawn put his hand on his father's arm. I assumed he was trying to talk him down because Aodhan looked ready to spit fire or shift and take his chances against my magic.

He'd lose that fight.

Finally, he grunted. "Let's talk."

Chapter Four

CONALL

Typical arrogant human. Name dropping and bragging. He didn't say it, but it was clear there was a threat behind his sit-or-leave option. I'd like to see how tough he talked if we took away his fancy little stone.

Dad didn't help the situation. As predicted, not letting Pederson know we were coming caused a problem. He compounded things with his stupid refusal to identify us when asked. Finally, just to put a cherry on this shit sundae, he grabbed the mage. He's lucky he didn't get his hand singed off.

Maybe it was because Pederson looked so young. Dad was expecting a senior inquisitor, not a member of Chancellor Hollen's family. That obviously threw him off his game.

Me too.

Pederson meeting us at the door in a towel did all kinds of wonky things to my libido. My brain might not like humans much, but my dick liked this particular one. His toned body with its dusting of light brown hair could land him on the cover of a fitness magazine.

"Would either of you like something to drink? I haven't checked the wet bar, but I assume it has a typical assortment."

His manners were forced, but so much of diplomacy was observing the niceties while you planned to destroy your enemy. Dad and I needed to be careful. The Hollens were dangerous.

"Water would be appreciated," I said, drawing a glare from my father.

"What are you doing?" he asked.

Only habit kept my expression from giving away our conversation. Dad made sure his kids had good poker faces in public.

"Being polite. I have to work with the obnoxious ass. You're making it harder by being difficult."

"Watch your tone. Even you don't get to talk to the alpha like that."

My tone was fine, it was his bruised ego talking. He was showing the only other person in the room who was boss. Pederson had established he was the bull of the woods. The chancellor of the Mage Council was arguably the most powerful person in the world. Even the leaders of the superpower nations respected his power. Dad might be abrasive, but he wasn't stupid.

Neither was Chancellor Hollen.

"Alpha Arawn?" Pederson asked in a fake respectful tone. "Would you like something?"

More proof the human came prepared. He'd sized up my father and already figured out how to play him. I'd be sure to be on guard around him.

"Water will be fine." He sat in a chair separated from its twin by a low wooden table. I stood behind him, as befit his position.

We waited, and Dad refused to look at me. He'd lost face having to back down. His stoic demeanor now was his attempt to regain the high ground, even if it was just an illusion.

Pederson was back in less than a minute; he made sure to serve my father first, before handing me mine. We locked eyes for a moment longer than needed.

"Thank you," I said.

He nodded and took the seat across from my father.

"Alpha Arawn, I've reviewed everything you sent to the council. Am I correct that most of the abductions have occurred from the home?"

"That's our belief." Dad sipped his water. "No one saw them disappear, or we wouldn't have requested the assistance of an inquisitor."

I raised an eyebrow, waiting for Pederson to respond to Dad's subtle barb. Instead, he returned his attention to his screen.

"Since I can see your pack has done a thorough investigation, have they noticed any patterns other than that the children were left home alone?"

Pederson came prepared. He or the Mage Council had done their homework on the alpha. Having established his power and willingness to wield it, he shifted to praise and respect. That would have worked with most alphas, but Dad wasn't typical.

This wasn't the beating of chests and displays of strength most powerful beings engage in when meeting another apex being. Dad wasn't content to be an equal. He didn't rule because people respected him, they obeyed because he punished dissent. Brutally.

By treating him as an equal after staking the high ground, Pederson thought he was creating a working relationship. He wasn't. Unless Pederson bared his neck and submitted, Dad would spend all his time looking for ways to reassert dominance.

"No, but as you noted they are targeting children without parental supervision."

"The youngest was seven and the oldest thirteen?" He swiped his screen. "And all were human."

Dad relaxed in his seat. Competence was something he respected, and Pederson had shown some deference. Hopefully, it was enough to get us through this meeting. "Correct. And none were mages, either."

Pederson tapped the screen a few times before placing it in his lap. "I asked my sister to check if this was happening in other places. There are four similar events. All within the same time, plus or minus a month, as yours. This came just before I left home, and I haven't had time to examine the data fully, but my sister and her staff bullet-pointed some key facts that match your circumstances.

"The children taken were all human, they were about the same age, and the abductions all occurred in areas designated to a specific species." He handed the tablet to my father. "Each of the five areas belong to packs less inclined to interact with humans. Gryphons, boars in Europe, kirin in China, yeti in North Central Canada, and the hyenas in Africa."

I had to respect Pederson's diplomacy skills for how he couched our status among the races of the world. Being lumped in with boars, kirin, yeti, and hyenas spoke to how low our species had sunk.

"You think that's significant?" I asked.

"Of the five areas, only Alpha Arawn thought it significant to report. My guess would be they chose areas where they felt the alpha wouldn't care as long as it didn't affect his pack."

I cringed at the subtle dig. Dad, however, didn't notice. Why would he? The statement accurately described his attitude.

"Have you alerted the other alphas?" Dad asked.

Pederson shook his head. "We only just noticed the pattern. That and it would be better coming from you than us."

It would also raise Dad's standing among the other species. The Mage Council was as sharp as everyone said.

"Can I get a copy of this report?" He handed the tablet back.

"Of course." Pederson tapped it a few times and set the device down. "It's sent."

"Thank you."

He nodded. "That was all the general data I have. What can you tell me about the families?"

With that, they launched into the background of the missing children's parents. I studied Pederson as he spoke with Dad. He was smart, competent, and polished. And smoking hot. If he wasn't a human, he'd be perfect. I needed to ignore those thoughts. Pederson wasn't just human—he was also a mage.

The good news was the data he'd brought meant this wasn't strictly a gryphon problem. The Assembly would almost surely take over once they learned the Mage Council had gotten involved. This assignment would be taken away from me and either Dad or my eldest brother Kelton would take over. Dad would be so busy he'd stop trying to derail me from my degree. For that alone, I wanted to kiss Pederson on his full lips.

I closed my eyes to clear that image from my brain. He would be gone in a day or two, and I could forget him. He looked up, as if he knew I'd been thinking about him. His lips quirked a fraction and then his gaze returned to my father.

Only a day, two max. I could resist a human that long.

Chapter Five

JANNICK

If I took off my snooty, five-stars-only nose, I could admit this hotel wasn't terrible. It was clean, the furniture wasn't worn out, and the amenities were good. Maybe Cael was right when he said one of those extra two stars was so they'd be too expensive for all but the top one percent.

The front desk clerk, an older woman named Debra, seemed shocked I didn't plan to sneak Conall into the free hot breakfast the hotel offered all guests. Fortunately, all king deluxe suites came with four complimentary meals. No five-star hotel I'd ever stayed in offered even one free meal.

I left the hostess Conall's name as my guest and got a raised eyebrow before she showed me to a table in view of the entrance. After texting Conall to let him know where to meet me, I ordered coffee and reviewed my emails. The most surprising was still Aodhan's telling me he would drop off Conall but was not joining us. Not having to deal with the alpha was a boon, but it was weird.

Why didn't Conall drive himself? Personally, I hated driving, but most of that was I'd had a driver most of my life. I'd come to count on using the time to do things other than focus on the road.

Like check out the hot gryphon who worked his grumbly, growly raptor vibe so hard.

Speaking of said being, I spotted Conall a half second before he saw me. I smiled, raised my hand, and waited for him to circle the other tables. As I stood, my brain went blank on whether gryphons shook hands, but I went with what I knew.

"Good morning, mage." Conall took an effort to shake my hand.

I hated such petty shit, but if he wanted to play that game, I could give better than I got. "I get you don't like mages, or humans, or maybe it's just me you don't like, but if you can't be civil and use my name, I'd rather you not speak to me, *gryphon*."

My tone was condescending as hell, and I didn't care. They had the wrong mage if they thought they could treat me like a vile but necessary ally and I'd still help them. The silence dragged on, but I'd said my piece. If he wanted to play the fool like his father, I'd make my report, head home, and wait for Dad or Avie to give me new instructions.

"You're incredibly arrogant," he said.

It was a start. At least he didn't call me "mage." "Funny, that's my opinion of you and your father. You need me and my skills to do something you can't, yet you treat me like I'm something you scraped off your shoe."

"You started this with your disrespect to the alpha."

"No. I responded to the disrespect your alpha showed me. He made a conscious decision not to answer my email. Then he showed up unannounced at my door and refused to identify himself.

"I had no idea who was at the door and exercised appropriate caution. My family has more than a few enemies. Twice someone summoned a demon to kill my brother." I let him stew on that for a few seconds and then added, "Then the alpha disrespected me by putting his hands on me in an aggressive manner. I was incredibly restrained in my response to that violation of my person. Given the less-than-friendly manner I'd been treated with, I'd have been justified responding with force instead of a threat."

He glared at me with venom. "Had you hurt the alpha, that would have ended badly."

"You don't get it, do you?" I kept my gaze locked on him. This was going to be a short trip after all. "Your father requested help from the Mage Council. My father sent me as his personal representative to assist you. In turn, your father assaulted me. If I was you and your father, I'd be more concerned that I don't lodge a demand with the Assembly to prosecute him for assault."

Politics wasn't my favorite subject, but even I'd read how the gryphons weren't well-loved among the Assembly. Voting to allow continued child abuse will do that to your species. Attacking the chancellor's envoy might be just the opening the Assembly needed to discipline Aodhan and replace him with a less abrasive alpha.

Conall broke our stare off and reached for the carafe of coffee. "I did advise we contact you first to let you know we were on the way."

That didn't surprise me. Conall seemed more even-tempered than his father. Still an arrogant prick. "And yet you defend his ignorant behavior."

"He is the alpha. My loyalty is to him."

If he thought he'd adequately addressed my comment, he wasn't as smart as I thought. Many are the evils done in the name of following orders. "Even when he's wrong?"

"I don't expect a human to understand how honor is the foundation of a pack."

His smug, we're-better-than-you attitude pissed me off. "Don't lump me in with your prejudices. I understand how a pack works. I've lived and worked with shifters my whole life. One of my best friends is a polar bear, and my cousin Dylan is mated to the son of the minotaur alpha. This is unique to your pack. Your father demands absolute obedience. It's why he thought he could order me around."

The expected pushback never came. Conall kept his gaze on his cup, and I studied his face—the strong jaw and perfect nose. Why did he have to be this handsome and such a pigheaded fool?

"If this didn't involve innocent victims, with more almost sure to follow, I'd pack up and go home. Instead, I'm going to eat breakfast in silence with a gryphon who hates my guts, and then see if I can't help find the missing kids."

Plucking the napkin from my lap, I dropped it on the table and stood to get food.

"I'm sorry, Jannick." He peered up. "Thank you for helping us."

I couldn't hold in my shocked expression. It took me a moment to compose my next thoughts. "Thank you for that, Conall. Would you believe I came prepared not to be bullied and chose my battles with your father to establish my position?"

For the first time since we'd met, he smiled. It wasn't joyful or face consuming, but it was a start. "I never would have guessed that."

* * *

Breakfast wasn't friendly, but it was cordial. We both wanted to find the children and prevent future abductions. It was neutral ground that led to civil conversation.

I'm sure he didn't miss my eyes popping out when he said he was getting a PhD in pediatric social work, with a specialty in adolescent beings. Not that he didn't seem like a decent being, but his father was one of eight alphas who opposed the new laws.

"How does your father feel about that career choice?" I asked, before stuffing a forkful of cheese and bacon omelet into my mouth.

"He's supportive."

I didn't know Conall well, but he was a shit liar. "Is he?"

"Yes. He points to my studies as one of the steps the pack is taking to combat child abuse."

Which meant Aodhan Arawn disapproved like the asshat he was, but he wasn't above using it to score points with the Assembly. "It's a good thing you're doing. How's it going?"

"Slow." He took a bite of toast. "My position as son of the alpha means special projects like this come up, and they force me to push back my graduation date."

I didn't need Cael's empathy to hear the disappointment in his words. It made total sense given the alpha's view on the topic. "I understand. I hated school, but my brother Bart is an academic. I saw firsthand how the need to get the degree and get out to use it burned inside him."

"That's a good way to put it. It's not the degree I want, but the chance to make a difference."

I took a drink before I asked why being the son of the alpha didn't allow him to help others. The answer was obvious, and I didn't need to antagonize him. "I'll do my best to wrap this up as fast as possible, so you can get back to your studies."

He smiled and it made my heart skip. Damn, he was hot.

"Thank you."

Chapter Six

CONALL

My opinion of Jannick went up considerably once Dad wasn't there to push everyone's buttons. He was smarter than he portrayed himself. School wasn't his thing, but from our conversation I gleaned he'd graduated with good grades. The poor self-assessment came from measuring himself against his famous brother.

I'd spent too much time the night before doing online research about the Hollens. Bartholomew Hollen was a prodigy who'd lived up to expectations. There was talk he'd be the first arch-mage in a millennium. He also spearheaded the attack that thwarted a demon lord's attempt to breach the Great Ward.

It was an impossible comparison, and one Jannick had no doubt dealt with his entire life. But unlike my siblings, Bartholomew shared his success with his brother. There were numerous articles about the brothers winning competitions in school and in each snippet, Bartholomew credited Jannick for their success.

Warin and Nik—my brothers closest in age to me—were nice

enough to me and our sisters, but they wouldn't have given me more credit than I deserved.

"Do you want to drive, or give me directions?" Jannick asked as we exited the hotel.

Pulled from my thoughts, I answered without considering the dynamic between us. "It depends. Are you planning to sit in the back if I drive?"

Jannick kept his focus in front of him and clicked the key fob. The taillights of a white, domestic sedan flashed. "I had planned to sit up front, but if you don't want me that close, I'll sit in back."

We didn't know each other well enough for him to get my sense of humor. The question was, why did I act like he would? "The front is fine. It was a joke. I asked to see if you expected to be chauffeured."

He stopped walking. "Can we call a truce? Please? I get it. You don't like mages, especially the Hollens. I'm not trying to be best friends, I just want to work with you to gather as much information as possible."

So much for clearing things up. Either he was overly sensitive, or I'd lost my touch. Probably both. "My initial comment was rude, and the explanation wasn't any better. This is too important for us to be fighting."

"No worries. As the dirty bastard of the family, I'm good at letting insults roll off my back."

He said it jokingly, but I didn't know *him* well enough to respond. Dipping my head, I made for the driver's door. "Sorry to hear that."

"It's all good. Especially if we forget I mentioned that whole bastard thing."

I might have honored his request if I thought he meant it. Why raise it in one breath and ask me to forget it with the next? "Did this happen at school?"

He rounded the car and playfully wagged a finger at me. "You didn't forget like I asked."

I huffed out a laugh. His antics conjured the image of my nanny scolding me for nicking an extra cookie. "Come on. That's like saying, 'Don't think about the teacher naked.'"

"Ugh!" He over-dramatically slapped his hand to his face and ran his thumb and index finger across his eyes. "That's so wrong."

This was the most relaxed he'd been since we met. It felt good to put our frigid start behind us. If humor was how he built relationships, I could run with that. "I take it the teacher you're thinking of wasn't attractive in or out of clothes. Was it your third-grade art teacher?"

"You're pure evil, Conall Arawn. And I shall have my revenge in this life or the next."

Our laughter filled the car with more positive energy. "I don't think that is the quote."

"It's close enough." He gave me a fake sneer. "Seriously, can we go back to me being a bastard?"

We still weren't friends, but we'd found a happy medium. It made me hopeful we'd resolve this faster than I'd expected, so I could get back to my studies. At least that's what I told myself. "I didn't realize I was traumatizing you so much."

"I wouldn't call it trauma, but most of my elementary school teachers were older women." He shuddered. "It offends my gay sensibilities."

The offhand way he mentioned his sexual orientation didn't feel like he was asking for mine, but I wasn't going to out myself in response. Turning at the light, I pointed us toward our first stop. "I promise never to mention your elementary school teachers being naked again."

He growled playfully and I smiled.

"Do you know any of the families involved?" he asked.

The pang of regret that we'd pivoted back to work-talk

lingered too long for my liking. Our only reason for being in the car together was to find the children.

"No. The alpha doesn't have human friends."

"Oh. Right," he said in a low voice. Keeping his eyes glued on the road, he pulled out his phone.

I'd just killed any fledging connection we'd been developing. It shouldn't have bothered me, but it did, and that made no sense. We weren't, and never would be, friends.

There was nothing, however, I could say that would sound sincere. Through my studies, I'd come to appreciate that actions mattered. Pretty words didn't help the children. If I wanted his respect, I'd need to earn it.

I ran my thumbs over the steering wheel and concentrated on getting us to our destination.

* * *

We didn't say ten words the rest of the way, and it was affecting us both negatively. If the result of our work didn't matter so much, I'd have left it alone. But lives depended on us, so that wasn't an option. At least that's what I told myself.

I turned the engine off and put my hand on his arm. He looked at it the way he'd stared when my father touched him. "I'm sorry."

His expression didn't change, but neither did he tell me to remove my hand. "For what?"

"The comment that froze you out. I grew up with so many prejudices." I dropped my hand. "I'm trying to unlearn them so I can be good at my hopefully-soon-to-be new job, but I'm not where I need to be."

"It's fine. We don't need to be friends."

He was right. But inexplicably, his words left me unsettled. "Maybe not, but it would help if we were friendly. Like you said, lives are at risk. Whatever makes us less effective isn't helping those kids."

"You're right." His head dipped and he nodded several times. "We have the same goal. Thank you for reminding me."

I wished I hadn't created the need to remind him, but I was learning. Jannick had already taught me not to let wounds fester. So far, confronting issues head-on had helped us find common ground. Now, all we needed to find were the missing kids and the people behind their kidnapping.

Chapter Seven

JANNICK

We left the third house, and I was drained; Bart was right when he said finesse is harder than force. I got a firsthand reminder why trying to wield my talent with a scalpel sapped my energy more than big showy blasts of magic.

It didn't help that Conall was a distraction. A hot, yummy one I wanted to strip naked and taste all over. The brooding I-dislike-humans vibe he wore at first should've been a permanent turnoff, but oddly, it barely registered.

"Would you mind driving back?" I asked. "That last one kicked me in the teeth."

He nodded and held out his hand for the keys. My fingers touched the skin of his palm as I pulled my hand back and something passed between us. It wasn't a jolt or even a mild shock—it was soft and almost warm. There wasn't a click, but it was as if something inside me snapped into place.

We both looked up at the same time.

"Did you . . .?' he asked.

"No, I'm too zonked to play games. I thought it was you."

"How could I do . . . that?"

Curious. He was more confused than angry. We'd certainly come a long way in twenty-four hours. "I've no clue. I don't know what 'that' was."

The keys dangled from his hand. When I looked up, he said, "Mages," and then winked.

I smiled back. Maybe it had been the work, or dealing with grieving parents, but we'd come to more than a working truce. He supported me when needed and did most of the talking to the parents after we introduced ourselves.

Unfortunately, we hadn't learned much. There were hints of magic, but they weren't much stronger than you'd expect in any house that used an enchanted item. It took more digging to determine the type.

In the first house, I couldn't decipher if it had been ambient household magic or something specific to the child's room. The mother swore they didn't use enchanted items. A quick sweep of the house confirmed there were no other traces.

The second house had more "noise," but I found traces that matched those in the first house. Upon closer inspection, these bits of magic were camouflaged. Someone had disguised what they'd done as common background residue.

I tried to drill down, but they imploded the instant I tried to pierce the veil. Despite losing the evidence, it confirmed the kidnappings were a well-thought-out plan. It required talent to create a stealth spell on such minute bits of magic and *significant* talent to booby trap the masquerade.

Using what I learned, I was able to trap the bits in stasis at the third house. My hope was to slow down the implosion to catch a glimpse of what was beneath before they dissipated. Those spells within spells taxed me the most but also provided the big payoff.

"Thank you for driving. The last bit of magic was incredibly detailed and wiped me out."

"Did you learn anything useful?"

Conall's failure to acknowledge my effort deflated me. It didn't matter he'd zeroed in on what mattered most, it still deflated me. He wanted us to solve this problem so I'd go back to Philadelphia, and he could go back to his life. Tiring myself out in the name of the cause was what he expected. I screwed on as good a face as I could manage.

"Not a lot. I don't know who took them, where they are, or why, but I can confirm someone used magic to kidnap the children."

"How were you able to determine that?"

My ego hadn't gotten past him not asking if I was okay. I checked myself before I told him I was fine. It wasn't like me to be so needy, especially with someone I'd just met; Conall wasn't even a friend, let alone more. What right did I have to expect him to be concerned for my well-being?

I didn't. And truthfully, only a mage would know the effort needed to pull off what I did.

"Are you sure you want the answer? It's a long, boring explanation of a cloak-and-dagger game the person behind this is playing."

"Is there a short version? I don't want to be lulled into sleep." He smiled, and it softened the edges of my irritation.

"There is, but it's still boring."

"Wow. Such difficult choices." Tapping his lips with a finger, he stopped and pointed at me. "Let's go with option two; shorter, but still boring."

I chuckled and any remaining annoyance vanished. We might never be friends, but we wouldn't part as enemies when I went home.

Doing my best to keep it brief but understandable, I only needed most of the ride back to the hotel to explain everything to Conall. "You can tell the alpha he was wise to contact the Mage Council. I won't say the local inquisitor couldn't have found it, but I doubt it."

"Brag much?"

A day prior, those would've been fighting words. Having spent the day alone with Conall, I didn't take any offense. "Maybe a little? I'm not close to Bart, but there aren't many magi in the department who are higher than an alpha three."

"Forgive me, but is that a high rank?"

I clutched my pearls. "You mean you didn't study mage ranks before I arrived? I'm devastated."

"Mages are humans—or elves, who most shifters see as human. The alpha wouldn't debase himself to study something uniquely human." He looked at me and shrugged. "I don't mean to be offensive, but that's the truth."

Honesty, depending on the delivery, was appreciated. Conall's acknowledgment of his father's prejudices didn't hurt, it was just sad. And stupid. It paid to know who you made an enemy of and not stick your head in a bucket of bigotry.

"Fair enough. Most beings assume all magi are equal, but we're not. There are four classes—alpha, beta, gamma, and delta—and five tiers within each class, except delta. Delta's a catch-all for those with minimal talents. Bart is one of less than a half-dozen alpha ones in the world, and he might be the best of them. The vast majority of magi fall between beta three and gamma two."

"Which means an alpha three is very good."

"It's in the top ten percent, but that's my overall rank. There are four disciplines, and they average the scores in each to come up with a final score. My best two are combat and practical magic. I'm almost an alpha one in both. This assignment needed someone with strong practical skills, which is why my father asked me to come."

"He asked you?" He looked, and sounded, surprised. "As in you could've said no?"

Conall, like most beings, only saw the Mage Chancellor persona Dad put on in public. Politics required the chancellor project power, much like the alphas he met with. As a parent, Dad was nothing like Aodhan Arawn.

"Yes. If I had a good reason, Dad would have found someone else. Otherwise, he'd probably have sent me anyway."

"That is not how the alpha does things."

Another reason the alpha was held in such low esteem by every non-gryphon who met him. Pointing out Conall's father was an asshole served no purpose, so I moved on. "My rank would be higher if I wasn't an alpha five in creative magic."

"What is creative magic?"

It spoke to the depths the gryphons had fallen to that Conall knew so little about magic. "It's the ability to piece together bits of magic into different things, change one thing into another, and at the highest, to create things out of nothing. Some examples would be piecing two or three spells together to animate a mannequin, turning lead into gold, or creating a rock."

We approached the hotel, and only then did I realize how badly I'd screwed up. "You don't have a way home."

"I can call a ride-share."

Did they even have ride-shares this far out in the country? Okay, so that was arrogant, but it didn't sit right with me for Conall to wait for someone to fetch him. Not after all the work he'd done. "That's silly. Either take the car or I'll drive you."

"You don't need to do that."

No, I really didn't. We weren't friends or even coworkers. We also weren't enemies, and he was a decent being. He deserved better.

"You drove all day. It's the least I can do."

My stomach chose that moment to rumble. Lunch had been nothing inspiring, and it had been hours earlier. I glanced at him, hoping he hadn't heard, but of course he had. Shifter senses were superior, even in human form.

"Hungry much?" Conall said with a smirk.

It lacked the arrogance he'd had when we first met. Rather than smack it off his face, I fought the urge to kiss him.

"What gave it away?" I wanted to ask him to dinner, but despite our civil conversation the last few minutes, he hadn't shown any indication he'd welcome such an offer. "Is there a decent place to eat nearby? Last night I got the worst pizza ever."

"Wow, don't hold back. How do you really feel about the food around here?"

If I didn't know better, I'd have thought he was flirting. He wasn't; he might not hate me anymore, but he didn't like me. I was a human, and I'd humbled his alpha. "No, Philly pizza is worth the trip by itself."

"I'll take your word for it." He turned into the drive and stopped in front. "To answer your question, I'm not sure exactly what's nearby."

To my surprise, he sounded sincere. "I'm sure one of the casual chains will be fine. Let me go in and wash my face and I'll drive you home before I go foraging."

"What kind of food do you like? I know a few places, but they're not that close."

There was a small hitch in his voice, like he was nervous. Like he was flirting. I stopped letting my dick think for me and concentrated on the question.

"I'm not a fussy eater, but I mainly prefer simpler food. Grilled meat with vegetables and potatoes or rice."

"I know a decent place, if you don't mind taking me home after we eat?"

Maybe my dick wasn't wrong. "That'd be great, but are you sure?"

"I wouldn't have offered if I wasn't." He shrugged. "You've been good company. I don't mind at all."

Definitely flirting. Which shouldn't have thrilled me nearly as much as it did. "Thank you. I hate eating alone."

Chapter Eight

CONALL

This was probably a bad idea. Dinner alone? It looked like a date.

It wasn't a date. I'd offered so we could talk about what to do next. The sooner we wrapped this up or had enough information to hand it off to the Assembly, the better.

Jannick wasn't as arrogant as I'd thought, but he was still one of the privileged Hollens. The way he treated the alpha proved how they viewed us. He admitted he came looking for a fight to put the alpha in his place.

Except he didn't start any of it. He'd reacted to Dad's bad manners. He also worked hard to save kids he'd never met.

My head was spinning. I didn't like him and even if I did, he was a mage who lived in a city. Nothing there for a gryphon. We needed fresh air, open skies, and the comfort of the forest to be happy.

"Do you mind if we go up to my room?" Jannick's voice snapped me from my thoughts.

His room?

The idea should have made me suspicious of his intentions, but it didn't. "Sure. Is something wrong?"

"I need to submit a report before we eat. If I don't, my sister will blow up my phone asking for it an hour ago. I'll make it quick." He sounded apologetic. "If you want to go, I totally understand. I'll take you home before I do my write-up."

That didn't sound like an arrogant human telling me what he'd do. If I was honest, he'd treated *me* with respect and even when he was angry with my attitude, he didn't beat his chest and tell me he was the superior being.

It was also a good idea. "That works. I'll use the time to update the alpha. If *I* don't, he might send out a squad of gryphons to find me."

* * *

When we got to Jannick's room, I excused myself to call my father. Three minutes into our conversation, I wished I hadn't.

The alpha had spent the day reliving his brief meeting with Jannick. His sense of being slighted was strong. I tried to deflect us away from that conversation by telling him we were going to eat together. Talk about not knowing your audience.

"What's this about? Are you thinking with your head or something else?"

"There is nothing salacious in our having dinner," I said, with enough indignation that even I believed it was absurd. "We're going to discuss what we learned today and make plans for tomorrow."

"That's a great idea." My eyebrows shot up. If he liked the idea, that wasn't a good sign. He paused, which was another bad omen. Finally, he made a sound, and my dread deepened. He'd made a decision. "After dinner, you should spend the night with him."

Disbelief robbed me of my voice. My father never wanted to

know about my personal life. Nothing good was behind his suggestion. "You can't be serious." I said it loud enough that I had to check to see if anyone was around.

"I am. I don't trust him."

An anvil settled in my stomach. "Why not?"

"I had our people find out more about him."

Of course he did. He never expected the chancellor to send his son. It upended his expectations. "Did you think he was lying?"

It came out a bit defensive. Hopefully Dad would read it that I was still upset about being told to spend the night with Jannick.

"I needed to find out who I'd make an enemy of if I made him pay for his disrespect."

This conversation couldn't be happening. Did he expect me to kill Jannick for him?

"Dad, do you know what you're suggesting?"

"I'm not suggesting anything. Chancellor Hollen likes this one. If the boy died or was seriously hurt, Hollen would send that daughter of his with an army of inquisitors to find out what happened. I'm angry, not stupid."

My relief lasted for a second. If he didn't want me to hurt Jannick, what did he want? "I'm confused. Why do I need to stay with him?"

"Something's not right. The chancellor wouldn't send his child just to investigate missing humans."

What he really meant was *he* wouldn't send his son if he were Chancellor Hollen. Not for human kids. The idea of service for the greater good didn't register with the alpha. In his mind, there had to be something in it for the Mage Council.

"You asked for help. The chancellor sent Jannick because he's a strong mage."

Dad snorted. "There's more to the boy's visit. Whatever it is, Hollen needed someone he trusts implicitly. I need you to be there so he doesn't embark on any side trips without you."

This was stupid. His anger clouded his thinking. "I don't need to stay with him for that. You can have him tailed."

"Don't be an imbecile. You think he can't hide his movements?"

The asshole side of my father, the side I hated most, reared its head. If you didn't agree with him, no matter how wrong he was, you were an idiot. Or worse, disloyal. "He could keep his actions from me, too. All we'll know is he's covering his tracks. We won't know where he went or what he's after."

"That's why you need to keep him entertained when you're not investigating the missing kids."

My brain took a moment to process what he'd said. Entertained? What did he—

"Wait! Are you suggesting I *sleep* with him?" It didn't matter that I already thought he was hot. Sleeping with him needed to be a choice I made, not something forced on me. "That's repulsive."

"Stop being so dramatic."

The words struck harder than a slap to the face. I'd known about my father's low opinion, but he'd never explicitly derided me for being gay. We'd reached a new low with this conversation.

"Sleeping with someone for any ulterior motive is prostitution." My voice shook, so I closed my eyes to steady myself. "As the person forcing me to do this, what does that make you?"

The sharp intake of breath confirmed I'd made my point. If Chancellor Hollen learned Dad had forced me to sleep with his son for some sketchy reason, he'd file a formal complaint with the Assembly. It would also make him a very powerful enemy.

"Tell me you don't find him attractive."

I knew what he was doing. Dad could truth-read any member of the pack. Fortunately, I didn't need to lie. "I do, but he's an arrogant asshole who insulted you. I'd never sleep with him."

I braced myself for whatever he'd come up with next. "Fine, don't sleep with him. But find a reason to stay in the same room for the duration of his stay."

Dad's paranoia couldn't be explained by distrust or even Jannick's insults. Something else was bothering him.

"You have no evidence Chancellor Hollen sent Jannick to do anything other than help. If anything, he complimented you for being the only alpha to recognize a problem and call for help."

"I heard that fake respect. The boy thinks I'm stupid and can't see through him. My instincts tell me there's more to sending his son than just helping. As alpha, I'm asking you to do the pack a service."

Now he had me. It wasn't an order, but it had the same effect. "I'll try my best, Alpha."

"I know you will, son." The line went dead.

Chapter Nine

JANNICK

The restaurant Conall chose was nice. It also fit with what I'd said I liked to eat. Peel back the hard layer he surrounded himself with and the being beneath was compassionate and thoughtful. Nothing like the father I'd lumped him in with when I arrived.

We'd been given a booth with a window. Our waitress arrived promptly, took our drink order, and faded out of my consciousness. I took a minute to read the menu, and two minutes later we had our drinks, made our dinner choices, and had run out of things to do before our food arrived.

According to Conall, his father liked the idea of us working late. I couldn't say why, but I didn't believe that was exactly what Alpha Arawn had told his son. His body tensed a bit, and his jaw tightened whenever he mentioned the alpha. His father probably wasn't close to any of his kids, but if the being beneath the hard shell was Conall's true self, Aodhan would not approve. It was a weight Conall couldn't shrug off his back.

I wanted to help, but what could I do? I barely knew him.

Empathy also wasn't my strength. Bart had always been my conscience, even after we graduated college. But my brother had a new mate and a world of responsibility heaped onto him; he didn't have time to be my moral compass.

I also needed to check my reasons. Would I have wanted to comfort him if he wasn't smoking hot? I wanted to think the answer would be yes, but how bad a person did it make me that I didn't know for sure?

Conall yawned. "Excuse me. I didn't realize I was this tired."

Guilt welled inside me. I'd arrogantly assumed I was the only one worn out from the day's activities. He should have gone home instead of joining me for dinner. "Eating should help."

"Projecting much?"

My gaze grabbed him and when he smirked, I couldn't hold back a smile. "Maybe? It always helps me when I use a lot of magic in a day. Other mages say the same."

"But I'm not a mage."

No, he wasn't. He was a hot gryphon shifter who didn't see my family as a means to improve his standing in the mage community. "Thank God."

"Why do you say that?"

He perked up at the prospect of what I was going to say. Only it wasn't that interesting.

"Most mages want something from me or my family. I rarely make it through a meal without being asked for a favor or assistance. Usually, they steer the conversation to a topic and then pretend to 'remember' something they thought maybe I could help with."

"Isn't that what I'm doing?"

It took me a moment to understand the question. Maybe I really was tired, but the truth was Conall was distracting. Handsome, strong, but also compassionate. He fascinated me, on many levels. Finally, it clicked what he meant.

"No. You didn't invite me to dinner to ask me for something in a fake offhand manner. I'm here specifically to help you."

"Technically, you're helping the alpha."

That tossed cold water on the moment. If I'd had to work with his asshole father, I'd be back in Philadelphia by now. Or in jail for killing him. "You were doing better before you reminded me."

He glanced down and rearranged his utensils. "Sorry."

My attempt to lighten the mood had landed like a cannon ball. It didn't take a genius to realize insulting a being's alpha wouldn't be well received. "It's not your fault. Clearly, I have a terrible sense of humor."

He looked up and waved off my apology. "You're fine. I was thinking of something the alpha said. He and I don't always see things the same way."

I knew there'd been more to their conversation. Whatever had passed between them, it sapped Conall's happiness. "I'm not doing this for your alpha. I'm here because my father asked me to come. I want to find the children, and get them home, and to resolve this quickly so you can get back to getting your degree. The world needs more beings who fight to protect the children."

"I'm not that important."

I wondered who was speaking—him or his father. "Yes, you are. You're going to save a lot of children and make their lives better. I'm a government bureaucrat."

"Who left his desk and comfortable lifestyle to come to the country to save children." He raised an eyebrow, daring me to contradict him.

It sounded more noble than it was. "This is the first time in my four years working for the Mage Council that I've done fieldwork. Usually, I attend meetings and/or sit at my desk."

"According to the only mage I know, what you did today, while not in your brother's league, was pretty impressive."

Warm contentment bubbled up from deep inside at the

compliment. "I really need to watch what I say around you." Now it was me who yawned.

"I hear food will help with that."

"Whoever told you that is a crackpot."

Our salads arrived, and we quickly devoured them. I should have eaten slower because we were back to needing small talk to fill the time.

"Do you have any sisters?"

"Didn't you say you were gay?"

How did we get to this topic? I'd deliberately avoided this topic so he wouldn't think I was flirting and bail on me and the mission. "Yeah. What does that have to do with my asking about your sisters?"

"Either you need to eat more, or I need better material." He smirked and shook his head. "I was pretending you were steering the conversation to where you really want it to go so you could ask me to pass them love notes."

This was a bad sign. I was so worried about my reaction to Conall, it affected my ability to have a normal conversation. "That was really good. Props to Conall for having the sharper mind."

"Tonight at least." He took a sip of water, and I did the same. "I have three sisters and four brothers."

"Only eight? That's a doddle."

"Oh, right. You have twelve siblings, if I remember right."

We'd never talked about my family in much detail. He really had done his research. "Close. I'm one of twelve. Are you close with any of your siblings?"

The way his face flopped, I'd asked the wrong question. "I'm the youngest, and the least like the alpha of all his sons. Kelton is the oldest, and most likely the next alpha. Braylen, Warin, and Nik all work with Dad in the family business. I'm the only one in college and the only gay son. Two of my sisters got married and left before I was born. My sister Dahlia is okay, but she's bitter and unhappy. Not that I blame her. Dad won't let her leave until she gets married, but to find someone to marry, she needs to be allowed to leave."

That was spot on what I'd expect from Alpha Arawn. "Surely he realizes how impossible that is?"

"Of course, that's the point. He'd found her the 'perfect' mate, but she refused to marry the nasty gryphon. I've met him; he looks up to the alpha as a role model. As you can imagine, Dad flew into a rage. To teach her a lesson, he's made sure she'll never get married."

I held my tongue or I'd insult Conall's alpha and jeopardize our work. "Ah."

"I'm hoping once I get my own place, he'll let her come live with me." He shook his head. "I doubt it, but I can try."

Aodhan would never agree. If anything, he'd be angry Conall tried to save his sister from her "rightful punishment."

"How about you? I've heard you speak of your brother, Bart. Are you close with any of the others?"

Conall had tossed my live grenade back. "Some. Others would've been glad if I'd died fighting the demon." Or might have killed me if Bart died instead of me.

"Wow. Is it because you're . . ."

Interesting how he froze rather than call me something offensive. "A bastard? You can say it. I refuse to let them shame me with something I couldn't control, rather than judge me by what I do." I reined myself in. "Most of my siblings are fine. Leothius and Owen are the two youngest and we're tight. Those two, Bart, and I were called the four musketeers more than a few times. Otto is the next oldest after me and Bart; we get on good. He always sided with us over the nasty ones."

"It's good to have a supportive family."

I ached a bit at the longing in his voice. "It wasn't all good. Some of the older ones weren't happy I was treated like a true Hollen."

"Is that why you had to send the report to Avie?"

Stuck in my bad place, it took me a moment to piece together what he meant. "No. Avie was never one of the haters. She didn't like me much, but that's because she's so serious and I'm not. Since the fight with the demon, our relationship has improved. But she still expected my report before I ate."

"Wow. That sounds complicated."

Catching myself before I said all families are complicated, I realized he was talking as much about his life as mine. "I focus on what I can control and avoid what I can't."

"Do you all live at the family compound?"

Why did everyone assume we all wanted to live in the "palace"? "Oh, hell no. Bart and I moved out first chance we could. I think Leothius, the next youngest after me and Bart, will move out soon. Everyone else except Roderick lives there."

"Where is he in the list?"

"Second oldest after Avie. I hadn't seen him in almost ten years, but he showed up when Bart got hurt. Disappeared again a day later." I shrugged. "Don't ask. I have no idea. Maybe someone in the family knows what he's doing, or why he leaves, but they haven't shared."

Our food arrived, and we dug in like we hadn't eaten in a week.

I don't know why I blabbed so much to him. Usually, I'm very tight-lipped with people I don't know well, even with information that can be found online. I'd need to be more careful with Conall. I had to expect everything I said to get back to Aodhan Arawn.

Occasionally, I'd get glimpses of him watching me from under hooded eyes. He was definitely listening and processing what I said. But fuck. The way he looked at me made it hard to remember my own warnings.

Chapter Ten

CONALL

I spent most of dinner trying to think up ways to get Jannick to invite me over. The obvious answer was to try to do just what the alpha wanted. I tried to flirt, once, but I couldn't get the words out.

What the alpha asked me to do was repugnant, and I wouldn't stoop to it, not even for the good of the pack. Doing something vile in the name of the greater good was the slipperiest of slopes. Once you set foot on that path, I don't think redemption is possible. I'd end up like the alpha and my oldest brothers. Morally bankrupt and without shame.

Which might have been why the alpha pushed the idea.

Distracted by my assignment, I was barely better company than if Jannick had eaten alone. Several times I glanced up, and he looked like he might break our silence, but he returned to his food. Our server returned when we were finished and asked if we wanted dessert.

"No." Jannick glanced across the small table. "My bad. Did you?"

I could see he was drained, physically and mentally, but I was certain if I asked, he'd have stayed just to be polite. It made my new "assignment" that much more disgusting. "No. I'm good."

"Could you give us a minute?" Jannick said. Our waitress picked up our plates and walked away. "Are you sure? Don't say no on my account."

He'd obviously misinterpreted my slow response as being respectful of his needs. If he didn't stop, I'd lose my nerve. "I'm not a big sweets eater. Besides, you said you were tired."

"I am at that." He smiled, but it lacked his usual zeal.

Our server was back, and being experienced, she set our check down when we told her we were done.

I reached for the little plate with the bill. "Let me get this."

"I got it." Jannick put his credit card on the tray and nodded to the woman. She scooped up the check and left.

This wasn't a date, and I didn't want him to think I thought it was. "Let's split it."

"How about we let the Mage Council pay for dinner?" His grin gave him an impish quality.

I preferred this version of Jannick. He was more comfortable in his skin when he wasn't serious.

"But will you really submit the expense report?"

"Definitely. My boss is a stickler for proper paperwork and timely submission."

I waited for the punch line, but he was totally serious. "Your father sounds a lot like mine."

"Not my father. Well, okay, technically Dad's my boss, but I'm talking about the head of my department. He requires I file upon return to the office."

Here again, I'd projected my situation onto Jannick. His father, despite his position and power, was nothing like mine. "I'm sure your boss has let you slide a few times."

"You'd think." He shook his head. "Nope. He told me he needs to be harder on me so he can use me as an example. He likes to tell people if he makes me do it, they have to do it as well."

A flicker of irritation caused me to frown. Why was I upset on Jannick's behalf, especially when he could easily take care of himself? "That's a crappy management style, if you ask me."

"Probably, but as you alluded, it's hard to manage the son of the chancellor. No one truly believes Dad would be pissed at me if he got a call saying I was lazy or taking liberties."

Everyone would *know* the alpha would be angry if any of us reflected poorly on him. "From what you've said, your father wouldn't be upset."

He wagged a finger dramatically in front of me. "Au contraire. He'd be very mad. Trust me."

"Sounds like you've been on the end of that."

"Not at work, but as a kid? Let's say I was accused more than once of leading my brilliant, straitlaced brother astray."

Jannick sat back and lost the earlier stiffness. His handsome face was so animated when he told stories. Almost like he was living them all over again.

"Accused sounds like you were innocent."

He held his hand parallel to the table and wiggled it back and forth. "Maybe sixty or sixty-five percent of the time I was the instigator, but I got one hundred percent of the suspicious looks."

This sounded too familiar. If the alpha decided one of us was wrong, it didn't matter if he was right. It was shitty of them and of Bartholomew Hollen. "Your brother is awful for letting you get in trouble for him."

"Not once did he let them blame me for something he did or instigated. The problem was, he'd admit it was him, and people would blame me anyway for being a bad influence."

I smiled. I had no doubt the chip on Jannick's shoulder got him in trouble a lot. "Shockingly, I can totally see that."

"You wound me." He slapped his hand over his heart. "I

helped him have more fun, and he helped me be more serious. We were—are—good for each other, I think."

A wave of jealousy hit. There was nothing close to that in my family. "It sounds like it."

Thankfully the check arrived before he could press me for details about my siblings. Hearing about Jannick and Bart's escapades reminded me of my dysfunctional family. The alpha didn't approve of his sons being too close. They might plot against him.

Most days I could bury those negative thoughts, but inexplicably, Jannick drew them out.

We needed to wrap up our work quick before this got worse.

* * *

I yawned three times on the drive back. The first time was part of my plan to get up to his room. The others were legit. By the time the hotel loomed ahead, I needed to get out of the car for some air or I might pass out. I pulled around back and turned off the car.

"Can I ask a big favor?" I asked before we got out of the car. Butterflies I didn't remember eating fluttered in my stomach. My heart pounded with fear he'd say no, and not just because I'd have to tell the alpha I failed.

"Sure," he said without hesitation. "What do you need?"

My guilt ramped higher when he smiled. This was dirty. *I* was dirty. He genuinely wanted to help, and I was trying to manipulate him.

"Do you have any coffee? I could use some while I wait for a ride."

I worried I'd screwed up when he didn't answer immediately. He had this faraway-look on his face that I was sure meant he was thinking of a way to say no gracefully. And then it was gone and he nodded. "I'll need to stop at the front desk to get some more pods, but absolutely. I'll let you in the room first."

The invitation came across innocent enough, but my own sketchy motives made me doubt the purity of Jannick's offer. I shoved that thought aside. He didn't deserve to be viewed through the same ugly lens I used on myself.

"Thanks. I appreciate it."

I got out of the car, trying to convince myself I wasn't doing anything shameful. Keeping tabs on Jannick was not prostituting myself. Besides, if I didn't do this, the alpha would send someone unsavory to watch Jannick. This was infinitely better than letting one of Dad's toadies try to pick him up.

I told myself that all the way into the building.

Chapter Eleven

JANNICK

I keyed us in and stopped. Conall stepped forward, obviously not expecting me to stop, and we almost slammed into each other. Standing nose to nose, I stared into his amazing green eyes. A rush of desire stole my voice. I licked my lips and slowly raised my card.

"Why don't you go up, and I'll stop at the front desk."

He nodded and slipped the card from my hand. "Okay."

It was a good thing he'd been to the room before because I wasn't sure any more words would come out of my mouth. I made my way down the long hallway, without looking back, through sheer force of will.

We'd just had a moment, the kind that almost always led to getting naked. The elephant in the room, however, hadn't moved. Conall didn't like humans—pleasant moments at dinner notwithstanding.

On the other hand, he'd totally manufactured a reason to come up to my room. That didn't mean this was a good idea, but I was going to let the hand play out a bit longer.

A couple was checking in when I arrived, and I had to wait for a second clerk to come out. Conall didn't really want coffee, but calling bullshit wasn't the best move. He'd used it as an excuse, so it was best not to challenge it until after we had a chance to talk.

The entire walk back to my room I tried to find when we'd gone from "he doesn't like me" to him inventing a reason to extend our night together. Nothing popped out.

He'd thrown the latch to prevent the door from closing, so I walked in. I opened my mouth to announce I'd returned, but then I saw him. He was dozing on the couch. Maybe he hadn't pretended.

Asleep, he'd lost all the tension and worry he'd carried with him. He was beautiful. In a different world, I'd chase him as far as he'd let me, but we had to work together. And that was the easier hurdle. His father would never approve of me and his son.

I was so absorbed, I forgot about the door. It swung shut with a clank as it hit the metal arm. Conall jumped and I cringed.

"I didn't realize the door would close that quickly."

He yawned. It proved contagious. I set the pods on the counter, and he was right behind me when I turned around.

"Thank you," he said.

Conall was close enough to have kissed me, but he didn't. Two thoughts hit me about the same time: he needed a ride home, and I didn't want him to leave. Neither of us were in any condition to drive, which left calling someone for a ride. My understanding was his family's home was at least thirty minutes away. Too long for someone as tired as Conall to wait.

"Here's a crazy idea, if you haven't called someone to pick you up yet. Crash here." My heart was beating so fast, I could barely speak. "I'll use the pull-out cot, and you can have the bed."

His eyelids opened wider, but then he dropped his gaze. "I can't take your bed."

The answer thrilled me more than it should. I'd expected him to reject my offer immediately; I mean, I'd created a fake reason for him to *need* to stay. And while he hadn't agreed to stay, he also hadn't nixed the idea. "It's totally fine. I feel responsible. You drove me to the restaurant and stayed to eat. It's the least I can do."

"I wouldn't feel right. I can call a ride." He stepped back and put his hand in his pocket.

My unrealistic hopes deflated fast. Before he could reach for his phone, I decided to try again. If he refused, asking a third time would make me seem desperate.

"It's already late and there's no reason to bother your family. This room comes with a pull-out bed for just such occasions. It's truly not a problem if you stay."

His eyes narrowed, but he wasn't looking at me. Probably trying to think of a polite way to turn me down.

"If you're sure it's no problem."

Clearly, neither of us wanted our day together to end. "Nope. No problem at all."

"But I can't take the bed. Seriously, I'll be fine on the couch."

A smart person would have accepted this solution, but when my libido was involved, I didn't always do the smart thing. "If the situation was reversed, would you really send your guest to a hotel pull-out bed? We both know you wouldn't."

"Tossing that back on you, would you really take my bed? We both know *you* wouldn't."

We'd reached the go-for-it or go-home moment. Neither of us put this much effort into this conversation for either of us to stay on the couch. Plowing ahead like a minotaur, however, probably wouldn't work. "Fine. Employing the wisdom of Katarina Hollen, we can split the bed in half."

"If you cut the mattress in half, you won't get your security deposit back."

Conall tossed out obstacles but never voiced anything serious enough to derail the plan. I should've been wary of his talent at playing cat and mouse, but I ignored the warning. I needed to move us to the endgame before either of us came up with a legit reason for him to leave. "It's the Council's money, but I could create a wall with magic. It would be just as effective without causing property damage."

"Unless you plan to attack me in my sleep, you don't need to go to such drastic measures."

Done. We'd finally reached the point we both wanted but wouldn't admit out loud. "Then it's settled. If you'd like, I have an extra pair of shorts and a spare tee shirt you can borrow to sleep in. They're clean, I promise, and we're close enough in size that they should fit."

I couldn't figure out his expressions. Was he offended I offered him clothes to sleep in when he thought I'd been offering to sleep with him? Or did he just not like to sleep in anything other than his boxers?

That was a visual I didn't need if I planned to be good and stay on my side of the bed.

He blinked and smiled. "Thank you."

The front desk had spare toothbrushes in case a guest forgot, so Conall went down to get one. I used the time to change into my shorts and oversized tee. Next, I ran through my nighttime routine at warp speed. I'd just started to brush my teeth when he returned.

"They're friendly here," he said.

I pulled the brush from my mouth. "Give me two more minutes and I'll be out."

"Take your time," he said as he disappeared into the main room.

The Conall who'd come back from the desk looked fresh and reinvigorated. Hardly someone too tired to get home. If he hadn't fallen asleep on the couch, I'd have wondered if this whole evening had been scripted to get us to this moment. We'd both wanted this, even if I didn't know what "this" meant.

I should've been offended by how he tried to play me, but I wasn't fooled, and he knew it. He'd maneuvered us so we could spend the night together, and I'd obliged by pretending there was a valid reason for him to stay.

What eluded me was why either of us had tried so hard to get to this place. Neither pushed for more than sleeping on opposite sides of a very large bed. There had been openings to ask for more, and we'd let them pass. So why did we engage in this intricate dance?

Finishing up, I might have used the mouthwash a few extra seconds. My reflection stared back at me, and I shook my head. This was an instance where I needed to think, not react. Conall was totally hot, but he didn't like humans. Hooking up would only complicate things.

The face in the mirror rolled its eyes. That was one word for it.

I didn't need this to get awkward. My job was to collect as much information as I could and report back. For that I needed open lines of communication with the gryphons. Conall was my contact, so this needed to stay professional.

Spitting the blue liquid into the sink, I turned on the water to wash it down and then walked out.

"Finished," I said as I rounded the corner. And because I have the most shit poker face, I froze.

Conall stood in front of the bed wearing my shorts and tee. He appeared unsure and I knew the feeling. Awkward only scratched the surface. We weren't friends, and this wasn't a hookup, yet we were about to sleep in the same bed.

"I . . . um . . . left out toothpaste, floss, mouthwash," I said, totally not noticing the long, toned legs covered in sandy hair. Or how the thin fabric of the shorts showed more of his package than his jeans. "Use what you need."

He nodded. "Thanks."

As he walked to the bathroom, I detoured around him, grabbed my tablet, and climbed into the left side of the bed. This was going to be a long, sleepless night.

Chapter Twelve

CONALL

I tried not to stare as we passed each other. Failed, utterly. There was something about Jannick that drew me. He had a great body, and I'd seen almost all of it now. It was a classic athletic build that hadn't gotten too bulky, like some of my brothers.

It was his face, however, that most captured my attention. He had dark, soulful brown eyes that shone when he laughed. From my limited interaction with him, smiling, laughing, and grinning were his favorite facial expressions. I imagined him goofing around with his brother, joking, having fun—something I'd rarely experienced with my siblings. They weren't particularly abusive, at least not by gryphon standards, but only Nik had shown any kindness or nurturing. What was the expression about apples falling close to trees?

Unlike my brothers, I was close to my mother and three sisters. She'd tried her best to shield us, but the alpha didn't believe in a woman having a say in anything he did. I went into my current field to honor her desire for children to be treated better.

As he'd said, Jannick had left his things out for me to use. It was a gesture so foreign. Were the situation reversed, I'd have sent him home unless there was no other choice. He'd sleep on the couch, begrudgingly, and never touch my toothpaste or mouthwash.

Clearly the image of humans most gryphons harbored was self-projection, not based in facts.

Instead of touching me, his kindness filled me with self-loathing. All joy and excitement were sucked away by the alpha "asking" me to sleep with him for the good of the pack. He knew I wouldn't refuse. And I hadn't.

But I *liked* Jannick, not because I'd been told to, but because he was a good being. I clung to that as my reason for staying.

I nearly spit my toothpaste laughing at the absurdity of the thought. Brushing my teeth, I tried to wonder what it would feel like if this were real. Would my heart pound with anticipation, or my dick strain to get out? Would I be smiling back at myself instead of hating the being I saw?

I took a swig of mouthwash and swished it around before I realized I didn't need it. Nothing was going to happen. I'd lie awake most of the night wishing I wasn't a coward. Wishing I could be honest with Jannick.

One thing I wouldn't do was give in to my desire for him. After all his kindness, I wouldn't use him for my own pleasure when it came from such a corrupt place. Jannick might not leave Washington County, Maryland, with fond memories of an amazing night of sex, but he also wouldn't leave feeling dirty and violated.

I shut the light. Jannick was in bed, leaning back against pillows, reading his tablet. It reeked of domestic bliss. A simple, familiar joy mates shared. It struck me to my core, amplifying the unscrupulous feeling I tried to hide away.

He looked up, smiling like he had before. It was warmth and comfort, inviting you to share in his zest for life. This human upended every prejudice I had against his species.

His gaze lingered on me, and I couldn't stop the longing I felt for him. I didn't just want to get my rocks off, I wanted to feel a connection with him. One that lifted me up to where I could enjoy life the way he did. With him.

I forced my lips into a strained smile. "Thank you for the toothpaste and floss."

"Of course."

His eyes followed me as I climbed in the other side of the bed. It was so big, we could've fit someone between us and none of us would touch, but it felt small. Jannick confused me. I was drawn to him, and I couldn't pinpoint why. Complicating that was the alpha's "request."

As soon as I was settled, he turned off the screen and clicked off the light.

"Thank you for letting me crash." I felt like the biggest fraud, but I still wanted to thank him for his generosity. "I'll get a ride home in the morning."

"Take the rental. I want to go for a run to clear my head. Then you can come back for me, and we can go visit the other houses."

Using his car would make it easier, but he'd given me enough already. "Are you sure?"

"Truth? This is going to sound so privileged, but I hate driving. I almost had someone drive me, but they'd have to stay here, and that wouldn't be fair to them."

Worrying about someone else wasn't elitist, but neither did driving himself make Jan a regular guy. The fact he had the option to be chauffeured killed any common-man persona. "You get driven everywhere?"

"Mostly. The family has a big fleet of cars and drivers. It's safer to employ people we can vet than hire random drivers."

I'd never considered that side of his life. It made sense the

Hollens would be targets, and I felt a bit shitty I'd thought it was all about status. "Is this a constant issue?"

"It's more a worry than an actual threat. It's been years since anyone tried to abduct someone, and decades since they succeeded."

Hearing the Hollens worried about all their family members made me a little jealous. No one would abduct any of my extended family because they knew Dad wouldn't pay anything to get us back. If anything, he'd tell them it served us right for getting kidnapped.

"I had no idea."

"The family tries to keep it private." He rolled onto his side, facing away from me. "Anyway, I'll shut up. Goodnight."

"Goodnight."

Chapter Thirteen

JANNICK

The casket was open, but I wasn't tall enough to see inside. She was inside. Grandma said she was sleeping peacefully, but if she was sleeping, why wasn't she coming home?

Grandma held my left hand and the man she told me was my father held the other one. There were a lot of people I didn't know, and some of them came to talk to me. I didn't want to talk to them. I wanted Mama.

I asked to be picked up, and my father lifted me gently. When I reached for her, he held me back, clutching me to his chest, telling me it would be okay. He would take care of me. I didn't want that, I wanted to tell Mama to wake up, but he wouldn't let me.

I screamed, asking her to help me.

"Jannick!"

Something was shaking me.

"Jannick. Wake up."

I shot up to a sitting position and summoned my power stone out of reflex. "What?"

"You were screaming for help."

The fog of sleep started to clear. I was in a hotel, in bed . . . with Conall Arawn. It took me a second to realize this wasn't part of the dream. The dream I hadn't had since I was ten. Why now?

"Sorry."

"Are you okay?"

Conall still had a hand on my shoulder. His warmth seeped into me; it was strong, yet calming. "Yes."

I wasn't. It had taken years of therapy to move past Mom's death. To accept the loss and find a way to keep her alive in my heart without waking up screaming.

In the dim light, Conall was inches away, his face etched with concern. I put my stone on the nightstand and exhaled.

"I'm fine. I was dreaming about . . ." A wave of grief broke over me and I barely kept in a sob. "My mother."

Conall knelt beside me, anxious and unsure, but still maintained the contact. His touch was the only thing keeping me together. I sucked in a breath, held it, and exhaled.

"I freaked you out." My chest kept heaving like a bellows. The fear and desperation from the dream were fading, but the sad longing remained.

"Don't worry about that. Are you okay?"

I wanted to accept his compassion. Not only was he handsome and hot, he also had a good heart. It was surrounded by protective walls, but it was there. The problem was, he was an Arawn. This would also make it back to the alpha, who would try to exploit it if he could.

Digging deep, I steadied myself. Aodhan was not going to use this to hurt me or my family. "Yes. I'm fine."

"It's normal for your emotions to bubble up during times of emotional stress. At least, that's what all the textbooks teach." He squeezed my shoulder and pulled his hand back.

I missed the contact. It was like someone pulled the blanket from my pretend fort; staring into the barely lit room, I felt exposed and vulnerable. "The shrinks said the same thing."

"I'm sorry about your mother. Sometimes it helps to talk it out when you have an episode. But if it's too painful, no worries."

I didn't understand why I wanted to tell him. Yes, he sounded sincere and he'd been kind when he heard why I'd screamed, but it could be an act. We'd known each other less than two days, and the first one had been tense.

Then again, everything I was going to tell him could be found online.

"I was five. She was a doctor. The hospital was short-staffed that night and she'd worked crazy hours. It was the last patient of her double shift, and she was reading a chart on her way to them."

Tears rolled down my cheeks, and I wiped them away. It was pointless. Two new ones appeared for every one I swiped off my skin.

"I didn't mean to dredge up painful memories."

"No. It's okay. Not talking about her is worse. It would mean she didn't exist and hadn't wanted to make the world a better place." I tried to swallow but my mouth was too dry. "She tripped on the top step, tumbled down, broke her neck. She died instantly. It was all on video, not that I've ever watched it. I—"

He reached and pulled me to his chest. I resisted for half a second and then collapsed into him. Bart used to hold me like this, when it hurt too much. "She sounds like a beautiful person who would have been proud of her son."

I sniffed. When I leaned back, he lay next to me; our shoulders touched and his hand partially rested on mine. Heat radiated from him, but it was soothing, not sexual.

"It doesn't usually hit me like that. Today, however, was hard."

"What do you mean?"

I'd spent the day trying to make sense of my unbalanced emotional state. Only one thing came to mind. "The parents who lost their kids? I remember how I felt when Mom died. I'm told losing a child is worse, only I can't imagine worse."

"I didn't realize it affected you so much."

Tears welled in my eyes, so I squeezed his hand and rolled onto my side. "I've learned to hide a lot. Bart and my grandmother are the only ones I don't hide my feelings from." I expected him to move over to his side of the bed. Instead, he inched closer and hugged me.

"Is this all right?" he asked in a soft whisper.

I wrapped my arm around him. "It feels really nice."

Lying there, I ignored the voice telling me Conall was off limits. I didn't care; I was hurting and needed the contact. When the pain receded, my thoughts returned to the day.

"I don't understand these parents. Why would you leave your kid unattended? There has to be someone who can help watch them."

"Believe it or not, for some there are no other options."

Clearly, I needed to get my head out of my privileged ass. "That's so sad. I guess I took it for granted that my grandparents could watch me when Mom was working."

"Why didn't you stay with them?"

This ventured into facts he couldn't find online. Had this been his goal all along? My brain said no. Nothing he'd asked had felt malicious. Still, I picked my words carefully.

"When Mom died, the father I never knew showed up at my school and claimed me as his son. He was . . . *is* amazing. Kind, compassionate, protective. I didn't realize it at the time, but I do now."

"I take it he knew you were his son."

I'd been asked this many times, and it always rankled me. Surprisingly, this time it didn't.

"Yes. So did Miriam, my stepmother. She's such a beautiful person. Rather than be angry or take it out on me, she treated me like Bart's twin. Even when she was mad at me, she never once suggested I wasn't their child. I can't say the same for some of the siblings, which makes no sense because if Miriam wasn't mad, why were they?"

"You're very lucky."

He said it with such regret. There was a story behind those three words. "Do you want to talk about it?"

"About what?" Conall asked.

Perhaps if my emotions weren't so raw, I'd have let it go, but I spoke before I thought.

"You don't seem happy with how things are in your family." He stiffened and I realized my mistake. "Oh, God. Forget I said that."

I tried to pull away, but he wouldn't release me. "It's okay. You're not wrong. If you'd been my stepbrother, Dad would never have prioritized you over his image."

That wasn't a surprise, given the way Aodhan punished his daughter for daring to have an opinion.

"I'm the one who should apologize," he said. "When I said you didn't understand loyalty and honor, I was wrong. Your father taught you what both meant by what he did for a hurting five-year-old boy."

Dad had done that and more. He was my hero. "My father had my back when I needed it most. I'll always have his."

"It's wonderful you have that relationship with your father."

The pain of his lack of anything close with his own father hovered between us. I didn't like that I'd pushed him there after he'd tried to comfort me. "I'm not sure why I told you personal things I rarely tell anyone, but it felt right telling you. I hope I didn't make you uncomfortable."

"I'm fine. And you don't need to worry, I won't tell anyone."

His voice was soft; it soothed a part of my battered soul. I'd never shared this much of myself with anyone who wasn't family because I worried I'd be rejected. Conall's promise, made freely and without my asking, washed away the fear.

"Thank you for that, but it's not a secret. If you type my name and Dad's into a search, the first result will be him holding my hand at the funeral. Wilhelm Hollen having a secret son made headlines. Mom's death got a lot of press because of it. I'm sure your father already knows all the details."

Conall tensed against me. "He does."

I expected him to let me go at any moment, but the longer he held me the more it lulled me to sleep. Just before I drifted off, he reached down and pulled the sheet up. I rolled over and pulled him into me so we stayed snuggled together. Conall didn't resist.

I inhaled his scent just before weariness overtook me. Crazy as I knew it was, I wanted to get used to moments like this.

Chapter Fourteen

CONALL

The blinds were closed when I woke, but I knew it was past dawn. My gryphon always knew the position of the sun. I moved and my eyes shot open. Jannick's arm was around my waist. My arm was over his and I was snuggled into his big spoon. I wiggled back and his cock pressed into the cleft of my ass. I didn't need to grope myself to know I was rock hard.

I breathed in and I felt refreshed. All the fears and worries I carried with me had been held at bay, and I'd had the most restful sleep since I was a kid. Jannick calmed my inner conflict and left me exhilarated by our closeness.

The alpha's voice telling me to sleep with Jannick pushed against my serene moment, but I pushed it aside. I hadn't done this for him or for the pack. This was *my* choice, *my* desire. That it achieved the alpha's direction was coincidence.

A happy warmth flowed from Jannick into me, and my heart burned with panic. I shouldn't have felt his emotional state. That was something only mates did. I rubbed the arm holding me; a satisfied thrum filled him and pushed its positive energy through our link.

Our link! That wasn't possible.

Except it happened.

Thinking back, I easily saw the signs. My instant attraction; the small jolts when we touched; his comfort in sharing secrets with me; the need to hug him when he was hurting. That was when I bonded with him.

I tested our link. As I expected, Jannick was still free. Only in rare cases did a human bond with a shifter without explicit consent. For mages, it never happened. Their wards prevented any inadvertent linkage.

It also allowed them to walk away if they chose. I'd never love another being, but he could. He'd never have another mate, but he could still fall in love with someone else.

A rush of jealous rage saturated me in an instant. More proof. I had bonded.

I needed to get out and clear my head. Sort things out. Easing my way gently from his hug, I rolled over and stared at his handsome face. His eyes fluttered until they opened.

"Good morning. Please tell me you're coming back to bed. I had the most perfect sleep last night; I don't want it to end."

His euphoric energy was like a drug, sending me soaring and leaving me giddy. I stroked his face and smoothed a strand of hair back. "You said you were getting up to go running. While you do that, I should go home and change. Can I still take your car?"

He propped himself on his elbow. "A run sounded great last night. Now I want a few more minutes with you."

The urge to give my mate what he wanted was incredibly powerful, but I resisted. There were complications to our being mates I couldn't work out with him unwittingly exerting such control over me. I hopped off before I could give him what he wanted.

"I need to get home and get back so we can have breakfast together before we visit the rest of the houses."

"We can't see all eight today." He yawned. "Four a day is pushing it, but if we do two each morning and two in the afternoon I'll manage."

Our connection was subconsciously influencing his behavior. I peeled off the tee shirt. "We can, but didn't you want to get back to Philly yesterday?"

"That was before I slept so well last night." He smiled dreamily at me. "Maybe you should bring an overnight bag when you come back. You might be too tired to go home again tonight."

He didn't know how much his words pulled at me, manipulating me at a soul deep level. "I doubt that will happen after how well I slept last night."

I stepped out of the shorts, folded them, and put them on the end of the bed.

He clicked his tongue. "I knew I should've kept you awake longer."

The mild disappointment shattered my ability to say no to him. "Hmm. Maybe I ought to bring a change just in case you drag out the visits and it gets late."

"I would never do that." He feigned innocence. "But it's a great idea."

Jannick's mood shifted, and my heart thudded in my chest. I'd made him happy. It was a heady feeling.

I pulled my jeans on and dragged my Henley over my head. "I'll be back soon. Don't waste too much time in bed alone."

"It's like you know me."

If he only knew just how well. "I'm starting to get a picture."

He came around the bed while I was pulling on my boots. "Stay tonight and I'll add some more details."

I didn't need him to tell me anything; he was an open book

now. He was also a drug I couldn't stay away from. "How can I refuse such an offer?"

"Take the spare key card in case you get back and I'm not here." Then he kissed my cheek.

We both froze at the intimacy of the action. It had been pure instinct; he hadn't given it any thought. Time felt static, but I could see his chest moving as he breathed. Neither of us wanted to acknowledge what he'd done, but we didn't want to deny it, either. Finally, I blinked and cleared my head enough to get us past it.

"How far are you going to run?"

Jannick jerked like he'd been roused from sleep. He plucked the car keys off the desk and handed them to me. "Not sure. I need to think, and the endorphins help inspire me."

We both needed space to clear our minds. I accepted the keys and forced myself to smile. "Don't tire yourself out too much. We have four houses to visit."

* * *

As I'd hoped, the alpha and my brothers were already at work. The family owned a factory that built harnesses specifically for our gryphon form. I'd never wanted to work there, and hopefully I never would.

The large farmhouse we lived in was one of the oldest structures in the county. The original home was built two hundred and fifty years ago. To accommodate multiple generations, the family added to it many times over the centuries.

In more ways than one, my family resembled an Amish community. My grandmother, mother, and sister managed our large farm, overseeing close to twenty farm hands. Dahlia was desperate to get away, but the alpha forbid it. Female children remained until married, and since he was never going to let her get married, she was stuck here until he died.

Mom walked out of the barn when I pulled up. She eyed the car and smiled. I wondered how much the alpha shared. Her eyes twinkled as she gave me a hug. "There's a story here, I assume?"

"He didn't tell you." I answered my question. "I need to talk to you."

I wanted to brush off her worried look, but I couldn't. "Of course. Come in and I'll make you breakfast."

"I'm supposed to meet Jannick for breakfast. I need to change and grab clothes for tomorrow."

"There really is a story here if you can say you have a date and plan to spend the night and not sound excited."

Mom's amusement was mildly irritating. It wasn't her fault; how could she know? "I bonded last night."

Old lore says a gryphon mother can always tell when her offspring are in danger. Mom's smile vanished, replaced by a tic on the left side of her face, which only happened when she was afraid.

"He's Chancellor Hollen's son."

Her fears confirmed, she searched the area and hooked my elbow. "Let's talk inside."

* * *

Mom listened as I laid out what happened when we met Jannick, the alpha's command, and what happened overnight. Thank God we just fell asleep. I couldn't lie to her when I needed her advice, but how embarrassing would it have been to discuss who fucked who?

"And you're certain you're bonded?"

She couched it as a question, but I'd given her enough information to know I had. "I have, but I haven't let him. I won't let him suffer from my mistake."

Mom stood and went to get the coffee pot. "Why do you see this as a punishment?"

The attempt to sound upbeat missed by a mile. We both knew the truth. "Can you image what the alpha will do if I bond with Chancellor Hollen's son?"

She refilled her cup and mine. "He's your father. I wish you'd stop calling him Alpha."

Her admonishment was forced. The alpha was a shitty father and a worse husband. Mom stayed with him because she knew he'd keep her from her children if she left. Even she couldn't make him look bad and not suffer. "It's clear he doesn't see me as a son. What father tells his child to sleep with someone for the welfare of the pack?"

"Unfortunately, that's how he treats everyone. We're assets to use for the pack's best interest."

Mom had been my rock growing up. No matter what the alpha did, she was there to take care of us. He might punish her if she left him, but he didn't want her to leave, either. It would shatter the image of perfection he tried to project. "This had nothing to do with the pack, just him."

"But you didn't sleep with Jannick because he told you to. From what you said, the bond is calling to you both."

My cheek tingled where Jannick had kissed me. He'd done it so casually, without thinking. If I hadn't checked, I'd wonder if *we had* bonded. "I'm sure that's true, but last night and tonight are going to have to last us a lifetime."

She stared into her cup, and I knew she wouldn't be this quiet if I was wrong. "You think your father will keep you two apart to gain leverage over him."

I didn't *think* the alpha would do it, I knew it in the depths of my soul. "I won't subject Jannick to that. If he never bonds with me, he'll be able to move on. If I don't let him bond with me, he'll have a chance at happiness." *Eventually.*

"But what about you? You'll never fall in love."

My entire life I'd held out hope I'd finish my degree, find

someone to love, and grow old with them. Now even that had been wrenched away from me. "There isn't any other choice."

"There are always options, Conall." She took my hands in hers and squeezed. "You must decide what you want and what you'll sacrifice to get it. I suggest you speak to Jannick before you decide for him."

Mom had thought she'd found something special when she met Aodhan, but he'd changed and instead she found herself stuck in a loveless life. I know she didn't want that for us, but she also never saw the worst in the alpha. "He'll want to bond without fully understanding the risks."

"From all I've heard, he's an astute young man. He's also a Hollen. We can't fully understand the resources he and his family have at their disposal that might help give you both a better option. There is life beyond the pack, Conall."

The suggestion I leave my pack was something I'd never expected from her, but it spoke to how much I underestimated my mother. She *did* see the alpha for who he was. "If I leave, he will never let me see any of you again. And when Kelton becomes alpha, he'll reissue my banishment."

"The world is changing, dear." She patted my hands and stood. "Fate acts for a reason. Find out what it wants, and you'll find your answer."

I wanted to grab the hope she offered, but it was a false one. The alpha would never give up an asset as valuable as Jannick, and there were limits to the power of even the Mage Chancellor. "I need to get back. We have houses to visit."

Chapter Fifteen

JANNICK

I made it back to the hotel, a bit more winded than I expected. There were more hills here than back home, but the scenery was much better. One point in favor of country living.

Conall hadn't returned, so I walked around the building to cool down. A pair of cars were parked near the side entrance. They were so nondescript, they stuck out. No one was in them, but it raised my hackles enough that I took out my stone as I approached the back entrance.

The hallway was empty, which enhanced my suspicions. I called the elevator, and when it arrived, I sent it to my floor without me, making it stop on every other floor.

Taking the stairs two at a time, I kept my wards at full power and held a combat spell ready to release. I made it to my floor before the elevator and waited.

The bell announced the elevator a moment before the door opened.

"It's empty!" someone yelled.

"I told you we should've called first," a voice I recognized said. "Jan's not going to let you catch him unaware."

"Much as we like you, kid, we still answer to your sister."

I swung the door open with a huge grin. "Leothius! My God, what are you doing here?" I quickly closed on Leo and wrapped him in a hug.

"Eww. Sweaty," he said, squirming from my grasp. "Let go of me, you disgusting person."

Despite his words, Leo was smiling. "When did you get home from school?"

"Three days ago." He made a face like he'd smelled rotten eggs. "Which is probably the last time you bathed."

Leo had always been that kid who came home covered in mud. When he turned fifteen and discovered cute guys didn't like smelly, he'd taken a serious interest in personal hygiene.

"I took two showers yesterday and plan to take another one in a few minutes." I tapped a button on my watch. "Ten point four miles will cause you to sweat."

Stepping back, he swept his arms dramatically. "Don't let me stop you from making yourself presentable."

"We're going to go book rooms," one of the inquisitors said. "Is Leo staying with you, sir?"

"No." I said it fast enough that everyone's eyebrows went up. "It has one bed, and I don't share my bed with anyone who'd be offended if we woke up spooning."

Leo's face turned beet red. "I think a room at the far end on the opposite side. Preferably one with a bleach shower."

The agent in charge snorted. "We'll get you a room, but one of you two may need to pay the tab. The chief only authorized three rooms."

Clearly, he didn't know our sister as well as we did. "I'm certain Avie authorized one for the supervisor, one for the two agents, and one for her brother, Leo." I waited for him to correct me. When he didn't, I winked at Leo. "But since I'm springing for a room, ask for the cheapest one they have for Leo."

"I will gut you if I don't get a room as nice as yours." He turned to the supervisor. "I want the same type of room he has. If Avie balks, you heard him say he's paying."

He shook his head. "It's a good thing you like each other. I'd hate to see what would happen if you didn't."

Bart, Leo, Owen, and I had a running battle with our sister Nerea. She was twenty-seven years older than me, and when Otto, who was between us, got strong enough to fight back, she turned her nastiness on the four youngest ones. Nerea was also the loudest voice of my siblings claiming I wasn't really a Hollen.

Leo and I smirked at each other, turned in unison, and said, "Stink bomb under the door."

The man laughed. "That must've been some shitshow your parents had to handle." He left without waiting for an answer.

Despite the people like Nerea in the family, my childhood had been as good as could be expected, given my mother's death. The bond with my brothers embraced me in love and support that never wavered. "I look back on those as good times."

"Me, too." Leo gave me a side hug. "Damn, it's good to see you, Jan. I'd hoped to catch up with everyone, but Bart and Cael are off riding dragons with the Guardians, and you're off being an adult."

Growing up, I'd imagined what it would be like to be an adult. I'd thought it'd be all grand times and no rules. Until recently, it was all that and more. Then I watched Bart nearly die trying to do everything himself. All that love and support needed to go both ways; I had to leave my childhood behind. Fast.

"I know. Can you believe it?" I let us into my room, and he looked around.

"So, who's this guy you're shagging that you didn't want me to stay with you?"

Leave it to Leo to spot the signs I'd had a guest. Proof "takes one to know one" wasn't just words. "One, that's none of your business. Two, there was no shagging. Only spooning."

"Right." He rolled his eyes and flopped on the couch. "I got my slutty side from you. I know better."

Part of that was my fault. Leo saw me as a role model. But unlike him, I slept around to avoid making a connection, not because it was a badge of honor. "This time you'd be wrong. All we did was hold each other and fall asleep. It was one of best nights I can remember."

"That's crazy. Who was it?"

From the moment Leo saw how some treated me, he'd stood next to me even if he didn't know why. Conall said I didn't understand what it meant to be a pack, but he was wrong. My brothers had taught me. So why did I hesitate to answer now? "Conall Arawn. The alpha's son."

"Oh shit. Avie and Dad are gonna go nuts."

That was why this was crazy. Except, it felt right. "If they do, I'll deal with it."

"Wow, Jan. You must really like this guy."

People always talk about "deep down" as if there are levels to our consciousness. They were a euphemism for denial. Leo said out loud what I'd already known but tried to bury. "Probably more than I should," I mumbled. "Would you like a drink? Coffee? Water?"

"Coffee, if you have any."

Conall's ruse had left me well stocked with unused pods. "I have plenty. Help yourself while I shower."

Leo walked over to the kitchenette. "Is Conall joining us for breakfast?"

My chest felt tight, and I had actual fuzzy feelings. No lecture, no suggestion I was wrong. Leo accepted my decision and had my back—again. "I think so. Let me shower before he gets back."

The coffee machine whirled, and I forgot to ask if he'd be working with Avie as an inquisitor or with Dad for the Mage

Council. A topic for breakfast; Leo liked to talk, and I was famished.

* * *

With Leo waiting, I showered in record time—for me. I was working some product into my hair when I heard the door open. *Shit!*

"Who the fuck are you!" Conall yelled.

"Me?" Leo shouted. "Who the fuck are you?"

Double shit! I grabbed the towel wrapped around my waist in one hand and ran out of the bathroom. Leo had his stone out and Conall . . . Conall's hands had turned into claws.

"Whoa!" I ran between them. "Everyone chill." They each held their ground, but they didn't move closer. I pointed to Conall's claws. "You don't need those, I promise. This is my brother, Leothius. Our sister sent him to help."

I spun without waiting to see if he retracted them. "Leo, this is Conall."

"You gave him a key?" He put his stone away. "You are whipped."

Standing in a towel, what could I say to that? I was; I just hadn't admitted it yet.

Leo walked around me. "Leo Hollen." He held out his hand then yanked it back when Conall extended his claws.

"Oh." He closed his fist and when he opened it, the talons were gone. "Conall Arawn. Sorry if I overreacted."

"Maybe if Jan had warned you I was here, it would've helped."

I was never going to live this down. Leo would tell Bart. And Cael. And definitely Owen, who always felt left out as the baby of the family. Surprisingly, I didn't care. I gave him my best "do your worst" smile. "Says the brother who tried to surprise attack me at my door."

He shrugged. "You got a problem with it, talk to Avie. She

gives the orders. And crap, would you get dressed please. I already need bleach after the spooning comment."

Conall growled, and I glowered at Leo. "Why don't *you* go find *your* room, and maybe I'll invite you to breakfast."

"I'll see you at breakfast," he said and hitched a thumb my way. "He's buying."

I had to wait until the door closed before I could face Conall. "Do you want to explain why you freaked out like that?" I made my hands into claws.

He dropped his head. "I remembered what you said about having enemies. I guess I should have thought it through a bit more. I mean, Leo was sitting on the couch, drinking coffee and scrolling through his phone."

Defending me earned him major points. Not that he needed any after last night. "That's really nice of you, but no one gets into my room I don't want without blowing up my wards. That explosion would blow out half the wall."

I winked and he smiled for a nanosecond. "We need to talk."

He sounded serious, so I reacted the way I always did when things got too real too fast. "Should I get dressed first, or is it that kind of need?" I wiggled my eyebrows.

"After last night, I totally have *that* kind of need, but this is a 'you should get dressed' conversation."

My heart thumped faster, and a swarm of agitated bats materialized in my stomach. That wasn't the answer I wanted. "Right. Give me a minute."

Chapter Sixteen

CONALL

Jannick never left my sight, but he'd shut me out. He'd slammed up an impressive wall in the blink of an eye, and I couldn't feel a single emotion from him. If he wasn't getting dressed in front of me, I'd have wondered if he'd left.

The peaceful calm I'd woken to was gone. In its place, an empty longing sucked me down into loneliness. This was a preview of what my life would be like without him.

It was a grim future.

Carrying his socks, he sat on the sofa and turned to face me. "Is this dressed enough?"

He was already hurt, and I hadn't told him the worst. I nodded. "Last night..."

"If you're going to say it was a mistake, please don't." He turned his head. "Let me at least walk away thinking you had a nice night."

His answer told me he felt the same. Jannick might not realize I was his mate, but the bond already affected him. "I had a great night, but we can't do it again."

"That's a new one." Jannick exhaled and his head drooped. "The way you left, I figured you regretted it."

The flood of Jannick's emotions took me a few seconds to sort. He was hurt, disappointed. And incredibly sad. "It's not that, either. Can you let me explain before you jump to any more conclusions?"

"It's . . . Go ahead. Tell me why you . . . *we* can't do it again."

This was not going to end well. Already he was ready to fight to keep us together, and there wasn't even an us yet. "Please let me explain everything before you get mad?"

"I can't control if I get mad, but I'll try not to interrupt."

I had trouble looking at him. Even if he didn't know we were mates, his emotions affected me like we were fully bonded. "I made up a reason to stay last night. The alpha told me to sleep with you."

His face tightened. "Did he congratulate you when you told him?"

Flinching at the accusation, I tried to make sense of his emotions. The anger I expected, but not embarrassment. "I haven't spoken to him, and I won't, but if he asks I can't lie to him. Given his feelings toward my being gay, he won't ask for details, and I won't offer any. All I'll tell him is I did as he asked and stayed in your room last night."

"Is that it?" His words were clipped, his body rigid. He was getting ready to unload on me. Further explanation probably wouldn't make it better, but he was owed the truth.

"He wanted me to sleep with you to keep you occupied. I lied to you when I said I was too tired to go home. My plan had been to crash on the couch. That way I could do what the alpha ordered, but not do something that would make you feel dirty."

"Well, you failed on that score." He held up a hand and shook his head. "Right. I promised to hear you out."

As upset as he was, he still showed me more respect than I gave him. "I slept in the bed with you because I like you. A lot.

The alpha telling me to sleep with you screwed with my head. I was going to stay on my side of the bed like we discussed, but then you had that dream."

"You could've just woken me up. Instead, you pretended to care."

He was so hurt, his walls crumbled. His emotions hit me all at once, and I almost cried. I took a moment to block as much as I could. "I know you won't believe me, but everything I did and said was honest. I held you because you were hurting, and I wanted to help you."

"Why? So you could tell your father I was weak?"

Everything came back to the alpha and his abusive ways. "If it was for him, I wouldn't have told you and I would use last night to sleep with you again tonight. I'm telling you so you'll hate me."

"That doesn't make any sense. You *want* me to hate you?"

Not being able to tell him the truth made this hard. If I were as nasty a bird as the alpha, I'd have made him feel used and dirty. But I wasn't my father. "I like you, Jannick. More than I'm allowed to."

"Allowed? Your father controls your feelings?"

The way my heart was pulling itself apart, I almost wished he did. "The alpha won't let us be together once you finish your investigation. I told you what he did to my sister. If he finds out I have real feelings for you, he'll take everything away from me."

"Why? What does he get from that?"

The more I tried to dance around what really happened, the more he wanted to push back. I could feel his anger shifting from me to the alpha.

"It's all about control. He's going to decide who I mate with. No doubt it will be some abusive asshole who kisses the alpha's ass, and I'll be his payment for being a good toady."

"He can do that?" He shook his head because he didn't need me to confirm the truth. "It's so medieval."

Most beings had abandoned the old ways decades ago. Before

my father took over, gryphons had been at the forefront of change. Now, we'd been detached from the train and were sliding backward. "That's how it is. The alpha's word is law."

Jannick frowned. "I don't understand how you so easily accept being mated to an asshole who'll abuse you."

Under different circumstances, he would have stood beside me to prevent such an outcome. He still might if I asked, but I couldn't. Jannick needed to leave and never want to see me again.

"Should the alpha wish it, I'll have to mate with whomever he picks for me, but I'll never accept being mistreated. The first time he hits me or even tries to, I'll send that gryphon to the healers."

Snorting, he looked away. "That'll make your father happy."

In a strange, fucked up way, it would. "The alpha values strength. If this gryphon tries to hurt me and ends up needing medical help, he will lose the alpha's respect."

"But you're still stuck with him?"

I'd been trapped since the day I was born. "Most likely."

"That can't be right."

His anger on my behalf likely meant our bond already affected him. More reason I needed to remove myself. "There are many things that are not right that I can't control."

Jan stood and walked over to the coffee machine. He played with the pods before putting it down. "Thank you for telling me the truth. And thank you for last night. You probably already know this, but I like you, too. Maybe more than *I* should. I don't know if there's anything that can free you, but if there is, I promise to try and make it happen."

A knock on the door ended our conversation.

"Come on you two," Leo said. "I'm *morta di fame*."

I gave him a quizzical look and he smiled. "Dead of hunger. Leo spent a year in Italy with a family who said he was too skinny. That was what his host mother said when he didn't eat enough. I suppose we shouldn't keep him waiting."

It was a good time to go anyway. I needed time to think

before we talked again. The good feeling his promise to look for an answer created was tempered by the realization it was unlikely he'd succeed. Still, I needed to let him try or else I'd end up alone the rest of my life.

"Right. He looks like he's dying."

Chapter Seventeen

JANNICK

My energy sagged as I slid the card into the slot. It was hard enough trying to stop the spells from imploding; trying to do it while Leo watched had been worse. Doing it four times kicked my ass, and not in a good way.

I exhaled and swung the door open.

The real issue was Conall. After our talk before breakfast, I couldn't get him out of my head. The way he felt snuggled into me, his scent, and how content it made me just to hold him. We hadn't even kissed, and I was besotted. Me. That was crazy.

Except it was true.

When he confessed his alpha told him to sleep with me, I was angry. He'd betrayed my trust. His assurances his feelings were genuine shouldn't have cooled my ire. The fact his father instigated this should have been disclosed before he got in my bed, if he had real feelings. Telling me after the fact made it suspect. So why did I believe him?

The simple answer was I wanted to believe him. I'd spent a lot of my run thinking about him and how I'd get to do it all again soon. This wasn't normal for me.

Not only did I forgive him, I used my connections to search for ways to help him escape his alpha's control. He saw it as altruistic, but it was self-serving. I couldn't be with him if he answered to his alpha.

I flopped on the couch and laid my head back. This was why I only did hookups. No messy feelings to sort out.

My phone rang, and I debated ignoring it. Seeing who called, I really wanted to let it go to voice mail, but she was sort of my boss. Not really, but Dad had me filter everything through her.

"Hey Avie."

"Are you okay?"

I blinked and almost asked who stole my sister's phone. Fortunately, I didn't. The world might never see it, but she cared about those she loved. Until that moment, I hadn't realized I fell into that group. "Just tired. We went to four houses, and I had to walk Leo through the process."

"I'm sure I'll regret this, but that's good work you're doing. I'm impressed, but not surprised. You're gifted when you apply yourself."

A backhanded compliment, but from big sister, it made me preen a little. "Thank you. Leo's good, by the way. He needs more practical experience, but he catches on fast."

"That's why I sent him to work with you."

We both knew she'd have sent him to Bart if he hadn't been too busy playing mates with Cael, but I'd take the compliment. "Thanks for trusting me, Avie." That came out before I could stop it. It wasn't a lie, but I didn't say shit like that. My emotions were a mess, and I needed to connect with the family who supported me.

"Now I know something's wrong. And don't tell me you're tired." In my mind I saw Avie make her "I'm calling bullshit" face.

We weren't close like she and Bart, but Avie knew me well

enough. "I'm in a weird place, is all. Sorry if I offended you with my affection."

"Better, but still not Jannick." She paused and I readied myself for her broadside. "Does this have anything to do with your request to legal this morning?"

Her question was better than a lecture, but not by much. This was probably the real reason she'd called. "Maybe?"

"Crap." She exhaled. "You need Bart for this, but he's not here. What's going on?"

I didn't need my brother, I needed his mage psychiatrist mother-in-law, but she wasn't around, either. "Thanks for asking, but you don't need or want me to bare my soul."

She didn't speak and I checked to see if the call had dropped. "You still there?"

"I'm here," she said. "Thinking how to say this without it getting weird."

The entire conversation had been weird, at least by our standards, but I still wanted to hear what she had to say. "Too late. We're in uncharted territory, so just spit it out."

"True." She paused again and then exhaled loudly. "Right. Rip the Band-Aid off. I was wrong about you. Actions define us, not words. You're still a smart-ass and that is always going to get under my skin, but you're a good man. I wish I'd been more supportive."

"Avie." I caught myself before my voice hitched. Fuck, my emotions were a mess. "What I remember is you never piled on. I think if you had, things might have gone worse for me."

"No, Jan. When you were a little kid, there was no way Mom, Dad, Gran, or Grandpa would have sent you away, other than to military school. Our siblings, cousins, and other relatives who were most vocal about sending you away or claiming you weren't a real Hollen are the ones who do the least for the family. If anyone needs to worry about being cut off, it's them.

"But this isn't about that. I know something's wrong, and I

can't help you because I've never been there for you before. Why should you confide in me?"

This wasn't about trust. As much as we butted heads, she'd never been evil or nasty—unless I deserved it. "Avie. I appreciate it. Really. The problem is I don't *know* what's going on. I can't wrap my head around it."

"Is it related to Conall Arawn having the key to your room."

My brother was a dead man walking. "What did Leo tell you?"

"That I should call you. He wasn't talking because snitches get stitches." She chuckled softly. "Agent Means mentioned it in his report."

How the hell did *Means* know about that? Leo wouldn't have told him. "How was that related to anything?"

"He tied it to the working relationship between us and the gryphons," she said. "Clearly, he thought I should know you two had connected."

Dealing with Conall was hard enough without having to worry about what would be reported back to Avie. "It's not what you think, and I know why you *should* think what you think. I didn't even kiss him."

"Oh! Now I need to hear this."

The day just kept getting weirder. Since when did my sister want to hear about my personal life? "That's so wrong."

Wrong or not, it didn't stop me from telling her everything. Fifteen minutes of me baring my soul proved I wasn't right. I'd never shared my feelings and emotions with Avie, and she'd never wanted to hear them.

Avie had listened without interrupting and didn't say anything for a few seconds after I'd finished. Talk about instant regret. I could only imagine what she was thinking.

"You're not going to like what I have to say," she said finally.

I doubled down on wishing I hadn't said anything. There had been a reason she and I didn't have these talks. "If you're going to tell me to let it go, don't."

"I wasn't, but that statement convinces me I'm right. I think you found your mate."

"Are you crazy?" *Mates?* How was that possible? But even as I protested, things slid into place in my brain.

"Your grandmother said you had a mate. Tell me this doesn't sound like how Bart acted before he and Cael realized they were mates."

"It took them a lot longer to figure it out."

"That's not how it works, little brother. If you're mates, you don't need months of courtship to decide if you like each other. It's there or it's not. And once you awaken it, it's there. Those two just liked being tragic."

Avie making at joke at Bart's expense should have drawn a snarky retort from me, but I was too stunned to oblige. Her theory made sense, and it certainly answered the "What's wrong with me" question, but it was still insane. "Are you sure?"

"Not one hundred percent, but it fits with the facts."

Humility had never been Avie's thing, and for good reason. If there'd been any doubt in her mind, she wouldn't have offered her opinion. But it was still just a guess. She didn't have proof. "So when he comes back with dinner, do I just walk up and say, 'Thanks for getting dinner, Conall. Are we mates?'"

"Maybe for once, don't make a joke of it?"

Surprisingly, she said it without her usual malice, but she'd forgotten her audience. Conversations about relationships weren't my thing. Even if I was good at them, this was particularly sensitive. "I get it, but this is dropping the L-word after knowing him two days, times a billion."

"I really need to talk to the school board. Shifter sex education needs to be part of the curriculum. Trust me, as much as this is affecting your emotions, I promise you it's worse for him. He already knows."

I flashed back to our morning conversation and my heart sank. "If he does, he doesn't want me for a mate."

"He doesn't make that choice. This isn't a teenage crush that will go away."

My crushes came and went with the months of the year. This was different. Conall had planted roots in places I didn't know existed. "It's not like that. He wants me, but he said his father will never allow us to mate."

"Which is why you asked legal to find out if an alpha can keep a child in the pack against their will."

When I made the request, I didn't fully understand why I needed him. Avie figured it out in twenty minutes. "Did they find anything?"

"No, they asked me if they should do it first. I wanted to talk to you before I assigned staff; I'll make it a priority tomorrow."

She was right. Action defined us, and her unquestioned approval left me ashamed of all the shitty things I'd said about her in the past. "Avie, I'm sorry about . . . everything between us."

"Me too, Jan. You've grown into someone I admire and respect. The snarkiness? Well, you're going to have to cut me some slack."

Bart told me repeatedly if I gave her a chance, Avie would surprise. I always thought he was blind to her faults because he loved her. Turns out he was the only one who saw things clearly. "I will if you do."

"Fair enough. Listen, I need to get back to work, but I have a suggestion to find out for sure."

Chapter Eighteen

CONALL

Spending the day an arm's length from my mate without touching was torture. Most of the time he worked with his brother, but that didn't help. They bickered a lot, but it was the playful kind of ribbing siblings who were close enjoyed. When it came time to focus on work, they settled into an easy rapport. There was admiration, friendship, and genuine love. It was wonderful to see. And sad, because even with Warin and Nik I had to be guarded lest the alpha find out.

Even to my untrained eye, Jannick—Jan, as I learned he preferred—was the better mage, and Leo looked up to him. According to Jan, Leo was very good, but had no practical experience. The field exercise was designed to help him apply his theoretical knowledge to real problems.

Working with Jan, Leo, and the other mages gave me a glimpse into their lives. The inquisitors weren't cowered by the famous brothers. There was respect for their talent, especially Jan's, but they didn't shy from offering their opinions or questioning something if they didn't agree.

Where the alpha would bristle at any suggestion he was wrong, Leo and Jan listened to their colleagues and the five discussed the issue in question. The result was far superior to allowing one person, no matter how powerful, make all the decisions.

Leo and the other mages insisted Jan rest while we ordered and picked up dinner. Jan texted when we were on the way back, asking to talk to me without his brother. My stomach felt like I'd swallowed an engine block. The chance to see him alone made my pulse race, but it broke my heart at the same time.

I tried to soak in every detail of every minute we were together. When he returned home, those memories would be all I had left. They wouldn't be enough.

When I let myself in, Jan was pacing the small living room. He looked over at me and I shivered. This close, the joy only our bond could provide should have filled me to overflowing. Instead, I felt nothing. Worse than nothing. It was the soul-rending emptiness that came with death. "What happened, Jan? Are you okay?"

He heaved in a breath, tightened his lips, and stared over me like I wasn't there. "It's true."

The resignation in those two simple words crushed me with grief. "What's true?"

I moved closer, but he held up a hand to keep me away. "I shouldn't be surprised. She's usually right, but I didn't truly believe her until now."

His cold affect unnerved me. I was cut off, physically and emotionally, and I couldn't console my hurting mate. "Jan, you're scaring me."

"What's wrong?" He crossed his arms and stared at me. "Can't read your mate?"

The accusation struck like a sharp slap to the face. He couldn't know. I'd blocked those feelings. "How?"

"Nope." He swept his hand in front of him. "I'm not answering anything until you explain why you hid this from me."

His anger stung. My mate was angry with me, and I fought the instinct to comfort him. He needed to be mad. Mad enough to walk away and never come back. Unfortunately, once I told him the truth, he wouldn't leave.

"If we complete the bond, the alpha will gain control over you." I met his accusing glare. "That can't happen. Even if I lose you, I won't let him control you. Ever."

Jan's wall was still in place, but his icy demeanor melted some. "Conall, it doesn't work like that. Your father can't assimilate me, nor can he deny me my mate."

I refused to give in to the false hope that stirred inside. Maybe that was his world, but he didn't understand mine. "His word is law. I belong to him."

"You don't belong to anyone, Conall. And he absolutely can't control me. There are rules about everything where mages are concerned. The council will never cede its authority over me to anyone, let alone a single alpha."

Jan's faith in the council was misplaced. For all their power, the mage world couldn't interfere in pack business. "The alpha would control you through me. If he finds out we've mated, he'll prevent us from being together unless you submit to him."

"He can't do that."

"I belong to him." I repeated the line he'd drummed into our heads since we could speak. "Even the Mage Council can't interfere with how an alpha rules his pack."

"There are hundreds of treaties between the Mage Council, the Assembly, the Conclave, and the United Nations that govern interspecies relationships. I'm sure there's one that addresses what happens when a mage and a shifter mate."

For centuries, the Council led the way in improving quality of life for mages. Jan saw the world through his mage-tinted glasses, but that wasn't how the rest of the world lived. "I'm reasonably certain there are no treaties that tell an alpha how he can run his pack."

"The Great Ward was created by pairing a human mage with a shifter. There must be some law that governs those pairings. Avie is going to have the Council's legal division check into it tomorrow."

I wanted to believe there was a chance, but the alpha wasn't going to care about a treaty. Not where I was concerned. "The alpha won't agree to any treaty that tells him how to treat his children."

"You're an adult. Any rules regarding children would have expired when you turned eighteen."

Everything he said made sense. It gave me a kernel of hope. "I want to believe you're right, but it flies in the face of everything I've been taught."

"Waking up with you this morning felt amazing. I'm ashamed to admit I've been a huge slut. I avoided intimacy, limiting myself to only sex. One night with you obliterated all my so-called rules. Then I found out you were my mate, and my world tilted and there *were* no more rules."

"*How* did you find out?"

"One question at a time, please." His smile warmed my heart. It was for me, and only me. "Like I said, when I learned I'd met my mate, I didn't believe her."

I mouthed the word "her" but didn't interrupt.

"I can see I need to start over. Avie called me when she found out I gave you a key to my room. Like I said, I've got a bad reputation. I was so conflicted, I told her everything. My sister is driven, and sometimes a bit cold, but she's also one of the sharpest beings alive. She pieced it together. Closing myself off from you was her idea. Only someone who had bonded with me would notice what I'd done."

No matter how smart his sister was, she shouldn't have been able to connect those dots. Maybe the alpha was right and Jannick being here wasn't as selfless as it seemed. "How did she figure it out?"

"I've been unable to stop thinking about you since I woke up, I gave you my room key, I've asked legal to help you, and the other inquisitors and my brother know me. When I told her how much I like you already and it didn't make sense, she suggested I'd found my mate."

Still suspicious. "Even with all that, it wouldn't be the natural conclusion."

Jan smiled and it helped calm me. "My sister has a bad reputation, but there was nothing nefarious here. My grandmother is head of the Ocular Society. Years ago, she read me and said somewhere in the future I'd find my fated mate. Avie was there when it happened."

A small hurricane of emotion hit me all at once. He finally opened himself to me and I was nearly overwhelmed. Rather than be scared by their vastness, I plunged in and saw the depth of his feelings. It didn't change things. If anything, it made it worse, just as I feared.

"I'd hoped to spare you the pain."

"Pain?" He frowned. "I'm not in pain. I'm so happy I might explode."

Now that he'd let his walls down, I knew that without him telling me. His emotions were affecting me, and I had to bear down to keep on message. "Nothing's changed from this morning. If anything, it's more important than ever we don't bond." The hurt my rejection caused broke my heart. "I think it's best I leave now. The less we're around each other, the sooner you'll move on."

"I can't. I already know what this feels like. No one else will be able to capture my heart again." He put a hand on my cheek. "As bad as that would be for me, you will suffer so much worse. You'll be left with a hole in your heart that nothing will fill."

Had I known he knew the difference between humans and beings who mated, I wouldn't have risked coming back. "Better my heart be empty than I watch my alpha hurt you."

"The idea he can usurp a mate's bond can't be right." Jan took his hand off my face. I could still feel the warmth of his touch and his scent on my skin. "Give me a chance before you walk away from us, please? We haven't completed our bond and already I can't stand the idea of losing you. We have powerful allies who will fight for us to be together."

His voice said the words, but it was his heart pleading with me that made it so hard to resist him. "I don't want to lose you either, Jannick. But I can't bear to see him ruin you. Until we know for sure, I won't let you bond with me."

"Does that mean you're going to avoid me?"

Fear, fiery and raw, rolled off him. If leaving was going to cause him such distress, I'd need to remember how much worse it would be to stay. "Unless it will hurt you, there is nothing I would willingly deny you."

"Will you stay with me tonight?"

My heart wanted to leap at the offer, but my brain told me that was a mistake. We needed to put distance between us, not draw each other closer. "Now that you know I'm your mate, I fear what would happen if I did."

"Is this where I promise to pull out before we mate?" He wiggled his eyebrows.

The joke didn't hide his angst. Nor did it calm my fears. "You're terrible."

"I thought that was pretty good."

"Fine. It wasn't bad."

"Glad to hear I'm not bad, said no one, ever."

From the moment I got to see the real Jannick, he'd used humor to defuse tension. We were both scared for different reasons. He worried I'd leave, I was afraid I'd stay. "Haven't you ever heard the expression 'brutally honest, like a mate'?"

"Humans have far fewer mate pairings than any other species. Mages don't use clichés that remind us we're inferior in any way to anyone."

Clearly, Jannick took what I said to heart. I smiled and shook my head. "Mages."

He spread his arms wide. "Can't live without us."

I attempted to scowl, but my smile made it impossible. "Gryphons have managed for centuries, and I've made it thirty-three years without you."

"Ouch." He dropped his hands to his sides and took a step toward me. "This brutally honest stuff is going to take some getting used to."

My gaze locked on his. I couldn't leave. I knew to my core this wouldn't end well, but I couldn't resist. "Promise me we'll be careful?"

"I will, but you're the one who needs to be careful. As much as your father hates me, he won't spend enough time around me to figure it out from me."

He was right, but I had the alpha's blessing to stay with Jan until he left. Away from each other, it wouldn't be as noticeable, and even if the alpha learned of our bond, Jannick would be out of his reach. "We'll both avoid him while you're here."

"Does that mean you're staying here tonight?"

Jan's smile was a jolt of adrenaline for my weary soul. More likely, his emotions were bleeding into me, but the effect was the same. "Are we going to make sure we don't bond?"

Running his index finger across his chest, Jan drew an imaginary X. "Cross my heart."

A warm glow built inside. Jan met life head on. His playful side kept the darkness we all kept inside from overwhelming him. For all my adult life, I'd let the same pit of despair slowly devour bits of my soul. I clung to my dream of becoming a social worker to stave off the worst, but I still allowed myself to let outside forces direct my path. "With that kind of promise, how can I refuse."

"Can I kiss you, please?"

It was a bad idea, but that didn't stop me from inching my head closer to him. His need matched mine. "The others are setting up dinner. They're probably wondering where we are already."

"I don't care."

We were so close, the soft puff of air from his words brushed my skin. I slid my hand behind his head and closed my eyes. "Me neither."

Our lips touched. My body exploded with a rush of the most incredible energy; I soared to the heavens and floated in the airless void. Were I a poet, I would have said the rapture had arrived, and I was in a tranquil place where nothing hurt me.

Jan's tongue touched my lips, and I parted them. He didn't rush in but teased the edges and waited for me to respond. Our tongues tangled for a moment and then he withdrew his.

I opened my eyes and realized he'd put his hand on my nape. Our foreheads touched, and his smile matched the emotions he leaked.

"Wow," he whispered. "I don't want to stop, but I keep my promises."

Our kiss must have fried my brain cells because I almost asked, "What promise?" It scared me how easily I forgot my own admonishment. One tiny screwup and the alpha would destroy both our lives. "It's better we stop now. If we show up with puffy lips, it'll announce we've been making out."

"Assuming Leo doesn't pound on my door first demanding we stop holding up dinner." Jannick laughed. "Promise we can pick this up when we get back."

Agreeing to pour gasoline on a fire I was standing in the middle of would be smarter than kissing Jannick again. Neither of us would remember the danger, and even if we did, we wouldn't care.

"Only if you promise me the same."

Chapter Nineteen

JANNICK

The others had commandeered tables in the empty dining area, and Leo had set wards so our group could speak in private. Conall and I paused outside and waited for Leo to admit us.

We got the expected stares, but it didn't bother me. I wasn't ashamed of Conall, not even a little, and I didn't care what they thought . . . other than to tell them to stop gossiping.

"Sorry we're late." I paused long enough for their imaginations to take them where I knew they would. "I got a call from Avie."

The smiles disappeared, and they all found something interesting about the table in front of them. I held my fist out to Leo. "Thanks for having my back, little bro. No stitches for you."

"Damn right. That's not how we roll. You and Bart taught me that."

Outsiders assumed our family was a den of Machiavellian schemers, climbing over each other to get to the top. In fairness, that defined more than a few aunts, uncles, and cousins as well as a couple of siblings. It didn't, however, describe most of the family.

"Exactly." I winked and turned on Means and his team. "One of you told Avie Conall and I are sleeping together. Thank you for not supplying details that didn't happen. All we did was sleep in the same bed with clothes on the whole time."

They squirmed and it irked me. If they could tell her what they thought happened, they should be able to hear the details of what didn't happen without getting embarrassed.

"At least that's it so far," Conall said.

Leo snorted out a laugh, but I didn't join him. Team cohesion was a thing, and I needed to know if I could trust this team if trouble found us.

"I made the report," Means said. He met my gaze without flinching. "Deputy Hollen asked me to report on your interaction with the alpha's son. I told her you gave him a room key so things must be going well."

Hearing it from him helped me put it behind me. "Thank you for telling. If you need details for tomorrow's report, let us know. That way you won't have to speculate."

"Not necessary, Jan. She can ask you directly if she wants them."

Avie would, too, if she thought it was necessary. "Thank you. Let's eat and we can debrief on a full stomach."

* * *

Discussing the day's events took longer than I expected, but it was worth the time. Everyone had a slightly different take, which gave me information I could use in the morning when we visited the last four houses.

I didn't want to think beyond tomorrow because barring some great enlightenment, I'd be heading back to Philly the day after. Tonight, I wanted to focus on one thing. Or rather, one person.

Conall's announcement had put it all out there, so we didn't hide our intentions. Other than Leo's brotherly ribbing, no one commented when we excused ourselves.

He rounded on me the moment the door to my room closed. "I didn't think that meeting would ever end," he said.

Pressing me against the door, Conall kissed me on the lips. It was quick, but not chaste, and previewed things to come. "I really need to brush my teeth. Nothing says kiss me less than dinner breath."

"You plan on kissing someone?" he asked with a smirk.

There wouldn't be any more someones. Only him. "Yep. You. Any problems with that?"

"Nope, but I need to brush, too, and a shower would make me feel better."

The thought of joining him under the spray, getting wet and soapy, danced through my thoughts, but that wasn't where I wanted to have my first time with him. "Anything you want. Let me brush first, and you can have the bathroom to yourself."

"Anything?" He tilted his head to the right and leered at me.

I was surprised I hadn't even thought about what we'd do naked; normally, I had very clear ideas about what I wanted with a guy. Not with Conall. "Sure. I just want it with you."

He slid against me. "I prefer to bottom, but I feel the same. I'd do anything with you."

"In that case, I'm mostly a top, but I'd bottom for you so hard if that's what you wanted."

"Sounds perfect." He rubbed against me and his hard-on brushed over mine. "You need to go or I'm going to skip the shower, I want you so much."

Not that I cared if he did, but we'd only get one first time. We had the time to make it special. Reluctantly, I pushed myself away from him. "Be right back."

***

I paced the room, glancing constantly at the bathroom door. Did I get undressed? Get in bed naked? Keep my clothes on and let him undress me? I'd slept with dozens of guys, why was this time so fucking hard?

A little voice in my head answered for me: because this mattered, more than every other time put together. I wanted the night to be perfect for Conall.

I finally settled on just boxers. Conall was going to come out with just a towel; we weren't going to be undressing each other. I pulled the cover off the bed, drew the sheet and blanket back halfway, and flopped on top.

Conall said our bond wasn't complete and I could walk away without consequences, but he was wrong. I'd fallen so hard for him already, I'd never love anyone again. Nothing would ever feel like this.

The water turned off and my heart pounded hard. Goose pimples covered my body in anticipation. Seconds ticked by. I fought the urge to jump up and go find him.

Conall stepped round the corner and came into view. He was so much better in person than my imaginary him. Lean, with tight, wiry muscles, his chest and abs were covered in light brown hair. His damp hair looked like he raked it with his fingers.

He held the waist of the towel with his right hand and stared at me.

"You are so beautiful," I said.

The bashful smile only made me want him more. "No one who said that before meant it like you."

I wanted to feel his skin on mine. To press my lips to his. Feel his weight on me. "Come here and I'll show you just how much I mean it."

With a flick of his wrist, the towel slid down his slim hips, leaving him gloriously naked. I inspected every bit, and I thought I'd burst. He was hard, but I didn't let my gaze linger. I sought out his eyes and we stared at each other as he climbed onto the end of the bed and crawled over me.

"You're wearing too much." He hooked his thumbs under my boxers, and I lifted my hips. He slid them off and blanketed me with his body.

I shivered despite the warm body that covered mine. It was strong and comforting yet made me pulse with vibrant energy. He ran his hand lazily over my chest and abdomen. It was incredibly sensual, but lacked overt sexual tension.

I cupped his face, running my thumb across his cheek. Leaning closer, I pressed my forehead to his. My eyes were closed, and it heightened my other senses. He smelled like the open sky and pine trees. His body moved gently with each breath and the warm air washed over my chin and neck.

In life, you can't go back and relive firsts. Often, we don't think about them in the moment. We just take the opportunity presented, never realizing we're about to make a permanent memory. On rare occasions, however, we see things clearly and savor the moment rather than rushing to get to the next one.

This was one of those moments.

Conall put his left hand on my cheek and caressed my skin. Where his fingers passed, my face tingled. The feeling spread through me, and I could have lived in that place forever. He slid his fingers behind my head and gently pulled us closer.

Our lips touched for a brief kiss. The next one lingered, but it was still soft and tender. I ran my tongue along the groove in his lips until they parted. The heat from our kiss filled me with a tingling energy that extended all the way to my toes.

He hooked his leg around mine, locking us together as our tongues tangled in a gentle dance. I floated in that place between reality and dreams. All I knew were his lips, his skin on mine, and the fingers that traced imaginary patterns on my face.

We broke for air, and I pressed my forehead to his. "You're an amazing kisser," I said.

"So are you. I could spend the whole night kissing you and not leave wanting."

For being told I wasn't getting my dick wet, I was surprisingly happy. For the first time in my life, I experienced why sex wasn't intimacy. I was closer to Conall in that moment than I'd been with anyone before. We connected on a level that left me breathless. It was a sensation I'd never grow tired of.

"What do you want, Conall?"

"Fuck me?" He breathed into my ear. "I want to feel you inside me."

I rolled us over and straddled his hips. Crushing my lips to his, I plunged into his mouth and explored with an urgent need. His arms snaked around me, squeezing me tightly to his body. I could've kissed him all night, but I had other plans.

I pulled my head up and his lips slipped from mine with a soft pop. Trailing my wet, swollen lips down his neck, I planted soft kisses on warm skin. Continuing down, I detoured to his right nipple, painting a wet line down his chest.

Rolling the little brown nub between my tongue and teeth, I tweaked the left one, drawing a moan as Conall writhed beneath me.

"Jan!" he hissed, gasping a second later as I bit lightly on the hard brown pebble.

"Found a spot, eh?" His body answered for him, and I gave it another nip. "Let's see if I can find another one."

Drifting lower, my bottom lip touched his leaking cock. I paused to lick the precum from his slit, and then wrapped my lips around him. Pushing his foreskin down, I swirled my tongue around the sensitive head.

Conall bucked and I put my hands on his hips to steady him. A constant stream of groans and whimpers let me know he liked what I was doing. I swallowed as much of him as I could, running the flat of my tongue along the bottom of his shaft.

I loved the taste and feel of him in my mouth, but I had

another destination in mind. Releasing his cock with a slurpy pop, I kissed my way down his saliva coated length and tickled his furry balls with the tip of my tongue. Then I put my hands under his thighs and pushed up.

The puckered, pink flesh winked as his body clenched in my hands. I blew air over his hole, sending more shivers through his body.

"Oh God, Jan."

I did it again just before swiping my tongue across the wrinkled rosy skin.

"Fuck yeah," he whispered in an urgent plea. His hands gripped the sheets on either side of his hips.

My tongue darted forward, forcing the tight muscles to let me in. I slid my hands down until I cupped his cheeks. Using my thumbs, I opened him wider, and burrowed deeper. My nose was jammed against his skin as I strained to wiggle my tongue as far as I could.

"More!" he demanded. "Feels so good."

I gave him a last lick before I tucked my legs under me and sat back. Wetting my finger, I pressed it into his entrance. The muscle clenched around me, and I gave him a second to relax.

My dick pointed toward its desired home, but it wasn't time yet. I applied more spit to his hole and slid my finger back in, working it in and out before adding a second one. I extended my free hand toward the nightstand and the lube I'd set out flew to my palm.

"Nice trick," he said. I twisted my fingers inside him. "Shit! You gotta fuck me, please."

"I'm getting there, babe. Give me a minute. I want it to be perfect for you."

I dribbled some of the slick liquid onto my fingers and worked the lube into his ass until I could slide in and out easily. Then I pulled them out and coated my cock, pushed his legs back, and positioned the head against his hole.

I leaned in to mash our lips together; my tongue tangled with his as I slid, slowly, into his tight warmth.

He moaned into my mouth; I stopped when he tensed and waited, still kissing him, until his body loosened up. As I sank into him, I felt the heat inside him radiate through me. When my groin finally pressed against him, I let out a pleased hum.

"You feel so good." I stared into his eyes, looking for signs of distress. Seeing none, I eased out and then plunged back. A needy, filthy noise escaped his lips as my body slapped against his.

"That's it. More." He angled his hips up and whooshed out a breath when I slammed into him. "Yes. Fuck me."

The stream of demands spurred me to give him what he craved. He put his hands on my face and pulled me back into a kiss, forcing his tongue into my mouth. He got me close sooner than I wanted.

"I'm close, babe. You want me to stop?"

"No!" He wrapped his long legs around me. "Come for me, baby. I want to feel you shoot."

I buried my head against his shoulder and sucked gently. I had the presence of mind not to leave a visible mark but tasting him tipped me over the edge. My body tingled a second before I hit that moment of no return.

"Oh shit. I'm coming." I fucked him harder, and I heard his grunts as I hit deeper than before.

My body shook as I shot. He clenched his muscles around me, and I sought his mouth. His lips parted and I plunged my tongue in as my cock continued to spasm inside him. With a last heave, I collapsed my weight onto him.

Three soft kisses on his lips later, I sat up and fisted his cock. Pushing my still-hard dick up, I raked his prostate.

"Oh God, that feels so good."

"Come for me, babe," I whispered.

He wiggled his hips and pushed himself down onto me. "Right there. Yes."

His breath came in ragged gulps. "Oh God, I'm gonna shoot." Muscles squeezed, sending shudders through me as his cock fired a blast of white cum across his stomach and chest, all the way to his chin. He continued to clench and release as he came. When he finished, I released his dick and leaned forward for a soft kiss.

"That was so incredible, babe," I said.

"You stole my line."

I eased out, kissed him again, and moved to the side of the bed. "Let me get something to clean you up."

"Can't you . . . ?" He waved his hand around. "Like you did with the lube?"

"If I only wanted a dry towel, sure." I winked and headed for the bathroom.

If we didn't share a full bond, it didn't matter. There would never be anyone who could replace him.

Chapter Twenty

CONALL

Jan tossed the washcloth on the floor and snuggled into me. He rested his head on my shoulder and ran his fingers over my chest. It was the most content I'd ever been in my life. The talk about mate bonds didn't come close to capturing how this felt.

The revelation shouldn't have surprised me, but there weren't many fated mates among gryphons. Maybe there were more than we knew about, and they just kept quiet in case the alpha didn't approve.

"I love your body," Jan said, tracing a pattern only he saw. "I didn't expect you to have all this chest hair. So fucking hot."

I'd never seen it as sexy, just as part of me, like my feathers when I shifted. "Glad you like it."

"I like everything about you."

He probably didn't realize it yet, but his emotions were tied to our bond. My old insecurities reminded me Jan would have liked everything about me no matter how I looked. The new me decided I didn't care. "I love how liberated I am with you."

"Oh?" I heard the lilt in his tone. "Going to run naked through the hotel now?"

I snorted. Clothes were a human thing. Shifting left beings naked a lot and we saw nudity as normal. "Not unless you join me. I meant I can finally be myself and not worry. Under my father, toxic masculinity has become prized. If you're a gay gryphon, you'd better be a top or else you're not a real male. Male gryphons are tops, only females take dick."

His disapproval washed over me. "That's so stupid. I don't think I'm any less a man when I bottom than when I top."

"That's why they call it *toxic* masculinity. It's not healthy."

"How does that even work? Don't tops need bottoms to be tops?"

The rule had probably been meant to make sure being gay didn't work. You let another gryphon top you at your own risk. The result was almost no gay gryphon couples. "It doesn't work. Generally, we sleep with humans or other species."

"That . . . My opinion of your father gets lower every day."

I'd seen him abuse my sisters; Jan's opinion couldn't be lower than mine. "Now you know why I won't let him gain any leverage over you."

"Why is he still alpha?"

I almost growled at the question. Growing up, we'd been taught never to discuss pack business with anyone outside the family. We certainly didn't discuss it with beings who weren't gryphons. This was different. Jan was *my* pack now, even if I couldn't openly acknowledge it.

"He's strong and he rules by fear. The only time he was challenged, he eviscerated the other gryphon. Left him to die in the street and ordered no one help him."

"I swear, I'm going to find a way to get you away from this. Then I will cherish you, however you want to be. There won't be any fear or feeling of shame for enjoying something meant to be pleasing. We'll be open and free, and no one will tell us how to live."

It was a beautiful sentiment, and he believed it with all his heart, but it was a fantasy. He couldn't make good on such a promise. Gryphons had held themselves apart more than most species even before my father imposed a more xenophobic culture. Then, it had been out of arrogance. The alpha did it to keep power. "Let's enjoy now. There are no guarantees in life."

"I guarantee I will love you forever, Conall. If you believe nothing else, trust that is true."

His passion and love rolled off him in huge cascading waves. They swamped me and filled me with hope I shouldn't embrace. One mage, even a powerful one from the most powerful family, couldn't change the centuries old course of an entire species. "I believe you."

We lay quietly, and I soaked in the calm it brought my soul. Jan's fingers continued to dance lazily over my skin. I ran mine up and down the muscles of his back. The simplicity gave it an intimacy that couldn't be planned. Moments like this bubbled up unexpectedly and left the heart yearning for more.

I wanted to cry at the unfairness of life. Why show me my mate only to deny us the chance to be together?

Jan put his hand on my cheek and nudged me gently until our gazes met. "I don't have a perfect bond with you, but I know you're hurting."

"I love you, Jan. I wish I didn't because it will break us both."

He craned forward and brushed his lips to mine. "Whatever you fear, I will protect you, Conall."

The second kiss lingered longer. I ran my tongue along his lips and rushed in when they parted. His scent, still musky from our first time, roused me to fully hard in seconds. I rolled on top of him and pressed my cock against his hard-on.

We kissed and ground our bodies together until I needed air.

"The things you do to me," I whispered, dipping my head to kiss the sensitive skin between his shoulder and neck.

He squirmed under me. "Oh, God."

Now I'd found a spot. I pressed my lips and licked, arousing him further. "What do you want, Jan?"

"I want to feel you inside me," he said.

I wondered if he'd offered to bottom for me because of our conversation. It's what I'd expect from someone who wasn't my mate. But with Jan, the need was real. I thrust my groin up. "You want this?"

"Oh my god, yes." He pressed up with his hips. "Let me feel you."

This was dangerous. If I got my knot, and I surely would, the urge to bond would be strong. I pushed up to see his face. His eyes, hooded with lust, drew me in. He didn't just want me, he *needed* me to fuck him. Which made it even more dangerous.

It was a sign, a bad one, that refusing him when it became necessary would be nearly impossible. Not everyone's mate was perfect for them. Some needed a few decades to appreciate the other. We fit hand in glove.

"What's wrong?" he asked, running his hand over my cheek tenderly. "We don't have to do this if you don't want to."

I guided his free hand to my cock. "I want you like I've never wanted anyone before, but . . ." I put my hand over the one on my cheek. "Wanting you this much, I'm afraid it will trigger your bond."

"You mean you'll offer me your heart?"

I smiled at his innocence. Who'd have thought the brash, arrogant asshole who put my father in his place had such a romantic heart? "That's one way to put it. I offer to meld our souls. If you accept, it's permanent."

"This is probably *the* worst time to ask technical questions, but how is it you're bonded to me if our souls haven't joined?"

I rolled onto my side. This was a conversation we needed to

have. Jan had to understand everything if we were going to avoid an accidental bonding. "I'm not as precise with my language as I should be. I haven't bonded with you, but my bond with you is active. A bond is the connection two mates have with each other. Think of it as the desire we feel for each other. Even when it's not completed, we can feel the other in ways we can't feel anyone else. It's what allows us to find each other in the great, wide world.

"Bonding is the act of unlocking your soul to your mate. There can only ever be one specific being you can bond and merge your soul with."

"I hate the crazy English language thing where the same word can have multiple meanings." He threaded his fingers through mine. "If it means anything, my feelings aren't divided among multiple people."

It was a bittersweet feeling. I wanted him with everything in me, but I knew we couldn't be together any time soon. Being able to touch him but not have him made it so much worse. "It means everything. I'm sure you know I feel the same. If I'm being honest, I felt an instant attraction to you. Prejudice and anger prevented me from seeing it at first, but now there's no doubt."

"I wish I could say the same. When we met, I thought you were attractive, but it wasn't more than, 'Wow, he's hot.' Everything changed when I woke up this morning. I don't know if it's a mate bond, but I'm hyper aware of you."

The universe had a warped sense of humor. Jannick and I found each other because of the alpha. If he hadn't ordered me to spend the night, I doubt we would have gotten close enough to see the truth. The alpha was also the reason we had to remain apart. To make the irony complete, the alpha was unaware he'd done either thing.

I should have shut Jan out before tonight, but it was too late. There was no going back from that experience. "It's more than just aware. I know when something hurts you, it hurts me. When you're happy, I feel it and it affects me. With a little practice, we can close ourselves off."

"Does sex trigger the bond?"

He absently rubbed his thumb back and forth over my skin. The simple contact soothed me like nothing I'd ever experienced. "No and yes. If I get my knot, the urge to bond will be strong. It will be like that every time we're intimate, but after we bond, it will be a renewal, not a connection."

"If you only get a knot when you top, we can do other things until it's safe."

It hurt that I couldn't give him what he wanted, but I needed to support his attempt to be responsible. "Oh, babe, I want you so much, but imagine how you'll feel if we bond, and you can't even see me. The alpha will use your need for me to get whatever he wants."

"Being miserable apart is better than being together?"

Jan didn't understand the alpha the way I did. His world view was influenced by how his father came through for him. That couldn't be more different from what we were facing. "He will use our bond to force you to do things you find offensive. You'll end up hating what you've become, and it will poison our love. I'll watch him destroy you from within and know I was the reason. Apart, I'll know our love was real and never sullied by compromising who we are. Apart, I'll never hate myself for what I did to you."

Jan pulled us together and squeezed tight. "Promise you won't give up on us?"

As if I could ever give up on him, or us. "Never."

He kissed my cheek and snuggled his head into my ear. "Then together we'll find a way. Even if we can't see it right now, we will."

I closed my eyes and imagined this would be every night. My fears lingered, but Jannick was so certain, it made me hope. I relaxed against him and let him hold me.

Chapter Twenty-One

❦

JANNICK

For having spent a decent amount of the night in hot, sweaty sex that still had me tingling, I was surprisingly rested. After our heart to heart, we snuggled until Conall fell asleep. I held him all night, drifting in and out of a dream state, and woke up at 5:00 a.m. naked with my cock nestled in the cleft of his ass. All it took was a soft, gentle kiss for him to wake up and make his needs known. We didn't go back to sleep after that.

Not surprisingly, we were the first to arrive at breakfast. I tried to concentrate on what we planned for the day, but my mind kept returning to Conall's amazing body. We connected so well.

I still wanted him to fuck me, but I wouldn't ask again. When it was safe, he'd let me know. He reached for my hand, and I ignored the danger for a moment. The contact sent me soaring. I wasn't blind to the struggle we faced, but we'd find a solution. I had a secret weapon: Deputy Inquisitor General Avelina Hollen.

Funny how things changed so quickly. On many fronts.

"What's funny?" Conall asked.

The urge to kiss him was strong, but I held back. When it was safe, I'd never hold back. "Two days ago, I drove up here growling at being pulled from my familiar routine. Now I don't want to go back."

Conall's affect changed immediately. "If you stay, the alpha will ask questions. He'll figure it out."

I hated Alpha Arawn with a ferocity I barely recognized. "I understand, but I hope you understand this is very temporary. If I need to raise an army to free you, I will. We'll be together sooner than later. Believe it."

I couldn't pretend with him unless I shut him out completely, which was announcing I was hiding something. We both knew I had no answers yet, but I was determined to make it happen.

"You don't like being told no, do you?"

Who did, but this wasn't about being denied something trivial. Conall was my mate. No one had the right to keep us apart.

"Not really, but I *really* don't like it when I'm right."

"Oh lord." He smirked. "This is going to be a long eternity if you're never wrong."

"Christ on a cracker, this is too early for decent people to be awake," Leo announced from somewhere down the hall.

Conall looked down his nose at me. "Is it too late to beg off going to your house for the holidays?"

As if I'd ever invite Conall to the snake pit that was Hollen Hall. "We'll limit visits to every other leap year."

Leo was in full-on bear mode when he entered the dining room; his salty expression matched the irritable tone that presaged his arrival. Conall glanced at me, and I shook my head.

"If I had to guess? Grindr wasn't very helpful last night."

Agent Means and the other two grabbed a small table halfway across the room. He glanced at me and I got the message. Whatever this was, Leo needed to grow up and stop being a spoiled brat.

My brother pulled out the chair across from me and flopped into it like someone stole his puppy. "Leo?"

"Look, just stick it okay? Just because you two are—"

My hand snapped out and cut him off. "Whoa! I'm not sure why you're upset, and I'm trying to find out, but Conall and I had nothing to do with it."

"Whatever." He flicked me off with a wave of his wrist.

This was a new side of my brother. I didn't like it. "Do we need to take this outside?"

"You want to go outside and fight?" He looked at me like I'd lost my mind.

Whatever had happened, it was worse than I'd imagined. Leo knew we didn't air family business in public places. "No, I want you to step outside and tell me what's wrong without informing the whole restaurant."

He huffed out a breath, slumped in his chair, and lost his angry glare. He shot Conall a look.

"Do you want me to leave?" Conall asked.

Leo shook his head. "Jan's going to tell you anyway. I was supposed to *meet* this guy last night. He showed up and I came down to let him in. Dude looks me up and down, shakes his head and stomps off."

"Really?" Conall asked. "Is he blind?"

That improved Leo's mood. "Did you use a fake picture?" I asked.

"No, but it wasn't a face picture." He shrugged. "I chased after him and asked what the fuck, because *that* doesn't scream desperate loser."

I moved my hand up and down. "Inside voice."

He sneered at me. "Yes, Gran. Anyway, he turned around and said he didn't do stuck-up, spoiled-twink mages."

"Was he a mage, too?" Conall asked.

"I don't think so. Pretty sure he was shifter. He had that alpha vibe going."

Alpha male or not, he shouldn't have upset Leo this bad. "Was he from around here?"

"Doubt it. He mumbled something about waste of an hour drive as he got back in his car."

"Could be a lot of beings," Conall said. Leo wore a puzzled expression that matched mine. "Gryphon territory extends all over the world, this is just the alpha's personal territory. There are at least seven or eight different shifter packs within an hour's drive."

Something about this felt wrong, but I couldn't ask Avie to investigate without embarrassing Leo. "You going to be okay, bro?"

"Yeah." He held out his fist. "I didn't mean to bark at you."

He sounded better. Maybe talking it out was all he needed. I tapped my knuckles to his. "We're good, but can we eat now?"

* * *

Conall turned into the driveway of the third house of the day. I was already fried; my emotional dam had opened the night before and it wouldn't shut. Every time I watched parents struggling to show us their child's room, I was five years old again, my heart breaking as the handsome man with sad eyes told me my mother was dead. It didn't matter he promised to love me like his son, I wanted my mother. For years I'd wake up to find Bart holding me as I sobbed. I wanted one more moment with her, to tell her all the things I didn't get a chance to say.

These parents had the added grief of knowing they hadn't protected their child. They heard our names, and it gave them false hope.

Coward that I was, I asked Leo to talk to the guilt-ridden parents after we knocked. I left him and went to the room the father said was his child's. This was the tenth home and while I'd perfected the capture spell, we'd learned nothing new. The children had been taken using magic, but we couldn't trace the mage.

Conall came up behind me and grabbed my hand. "You don't need to do this. Leo can do it."

It still amazed me how much I felt from simple contact with him. In the past, I'd scoffed at the idea that mates were this amazingly special thing. Like most humans, I wrote it off as trying to have something unique. "I've dumped enough on my brother making him deal with the parents."

"That's not what's happening. This is ripping open a wound that no one should live through once. You can step back."

That was just it, I couldn't. My mother dedicated her life to helping people. I needed to honor her by not letting my grief stop me. "I need to man up and do my job. It was twenty-three years ago. They deserve better from me."

He stepped in front of me and gripped my shoulders. "It could be two hundred and twenty-three years, and you'll still be allowed to miss her."

Concern and love rolled off him. It steadied me. I swallowed and smiled at him. "Thank you. This isn't the part that hurts. I'll be fine."

He released me but didn't move out of my way. "Want me to come with you?"

My instinct said I was fine, but then it hit me: I wasn't alone. "Yes, I would."

"Not that I wanted you to say no, but what just happened?"

I placed my hand over his and squeezed. "I'm not alone. Magic isn't just about power. Focus and inner calm matter when attempting complex spells. You center me like I haven't felt since I was five."

"I'll always be here for you, Jan."

To the depth of my soul I believed those words. I held out my hand and when he took it, I felt steadier. "This time might be the same as the others, but I keep hoping each new house will be different."

Two steps into the room, I knew we'd found different.

"Can you get Leo? Tell him to come in cold. Use those exact words. He can't leak power at any level, or we might lose this."

"Of course."

He left without asking for more. Banking my power, I took out my stone. A different mage did this abduction. The last nine all had the same distinctive feel. It blended into the background so completely it barely registered. A talented spellcaster handled those.

Someone far less talented had come to this house.

"Jan." Leo's voice was barely more than a whisper. "What's going on?"

"It's different. The signature isn't tight."

Leo stopped next to me and closed his eyes. He rotated slowly until he'd made a circle. "It's so faint. How did you find it without entering the room?"

I reached behind me and Conall took my hand. "Gryphons are magic sensitive. We were holding hands, and I saw it instantly."

The snarky comment I expected never happened. "That's incredible. It's like those optic puzzles. Now that you told me it's there, it's crystal clear, but it took me a minute to find it."

"Exactly. Once you see it, you can't unsee—Fuck me." It was so obvious we missed it.

"I'm fine with the hand-holding and the sappy schmoopy looks, but you really need to get a grip on whatever you two have going on."

Snorting, I slapped him lightly on his arm. "No, you twit. It's what you said. This is a magical optical illusion. That's how the spell works."

"Say what?" Leo closed one eyelid and stared at me with the other eye. "Are you losing it?"

Here I thought I was brilliant because I'd found a way to prove something so obvious it didn't need more evidence. All the compliments just made it worse. "We were supposed to find the camouflage spell and drill down to find the spell beneath. That's the part that hides it in plain view."

"You can't know that for sure."

I was right, but it didn't matter. I carefully gathered power to my stone. "I don't need to be sure. We can see it, and that means we should be able to trace this."

"What if they meant for us to find this? It could be a trap."

I pulled back my energy. He had a point. The mages behind this had gone to extraordinary lengths to hide their tracks. At some point, however, we had to stop looking for reasons to step back. "It's that old conundrum—you know that I know, that you know, that I know, ad infinitum. We can't let that stop us from acting."

Leo stared into the room. "You're probably right. I can't see how they could rig this to hurt us. We've been manipulating their residual magic for two days now."

I was proud of how well Leo had pulled it together. He was going to exceed so many people's expectations. "Many are the dead mages who charged in without looking both ways."

"Stop getting old on me, bro." He scowled. It was a bit too over the top. "I already have one Bart."

"Learn to take a compliment when you deserve it. Trust me, it helps."

"Fine. Thank you. What do we do next?"

It was amusing to see him flustered. "We try to use the signature to track the user."

"Right." He frowned. "So simple."

I kept my attention on the magic but held up my left index finger. "No negativity. It won't be easy, but it can be done. Now let me show you what we need to do."

* * *

I folded myself into the passenger seat of my rental and pulled the door shut. That was the last house, and I hadn't found an answer. Conall's eyes were on me, concern filling the passenger compartment.

"I'm tired and frustrated, but otherwise I'm fine."

He started the car but didn't put it in drive. "I thought things went well. Why are you frustrated?"

I'd screwed up. I hadn't made a mistake, but I'd missed something and it cost us. "We need one more point to triangulate."

"Okay, tomorrow we revisit one of the prior houses."

If it was that easy, I wouldn't have been so annoyed. "We destroyed the bits we need to track. It's bad dumb luck we figured it out one house too late."

"So that's it? You're giving up?"

The words hit me like an accusation, but I felt his concern. Conall was afraid for my mental health if I failed. "No, but I need a break to recharge before I tackle what to do next."

"Sure. I'll take you back to the room."

I'd been dreading this moment. If we'd hit a dead end, there was no reason for me to stay. We'd avoided this topic because there was no solution. In the morning, I'd have to go back to Philadelphia.

"Go out with me tonight? Just us?"

He smiled. "Is this a date?"

It wouldn't change tomorrow, but for one night we could forget about the future.

"Yes, but you need to pick the place."

Chapter Twenty-Two

CONALL

The drive home had been draining. I'd expected the alpha to be there and steeled myself for the grilling I was sure to get. He'd want to know every detail and pry into what Jan and I were doing when I was staying there. I was a shit liar, so I'd have to admit we slept together. He'd revel in the news I'd knuckled under to his will, never wondering if I'd wanted to do it all along.

I was relieved when he wasn't there. My mother didn't say a word, but I knew what she wanted. I explained the last two days' events and went to get clothes for my date and the next day.

My sister's door was cracked open, so I knocked.

"Come in," she said in a stiff, emotionless voice.

"Hey, Dahlia."

She turned and relief swept over her face. "Conall." She smiled a second, and then looked confused. "What are you doing here?"

"I need to go back." I shrugged.

"Right." She frowned. "The alpha gave you an order. How's that going?"

I inhaled sharply. "Complicated."

Her brows went up. "Really?"

"I can't talk about it right now. I just came by to tell you if I'm ever in a position to help you, I plan to free you from him."

She shook her head. "Stop dreaming, baby bro. I gave that up twenty years ago. He doesn't have a heart. He's not letting either of us go."

"I know, but I've still got hope." I leaned in and hugged her. "I love you."

She eyed me and looked ready to ask a question, but just nodded.

Driving back, I realized it had probably been a mistake to tell her that, but Jannick gave me hope. I wanted to give her some, too. Maybe we'd both die bitter and lonely, but if I had even a tiny chance I was going to try and grab it.

* * *

The restaurant wasn't crowded, even for a Thursday in July. I picked it because it had good food, was out of gryphon territory, and was human owned. Our booth gave us an added level of anonymity.

"You can't listen to Leo," Jan said, when I suggested he'd had a wild adolescence. "Compared to Bart I was crazy, but we didn't get into half as much trouble as some of our classmates."

I laughed at his not-an-admission admission. "So, you did get into trouble."

"Come on, we were kids. Most of it was harmless."

The way he squirmed, I needed to hear about the adventures of young Jannick. I twirled the wine in my glass. "Which means some was pretty bad."

"Not bad as in someone got hurt, but we got into trouble now and then. Only once was it serious."

Jannick was comfortable in his skin and easily made the shift from work serious to personal laid-back and playful. I envisioned our life together filled with nights like this. "You need to spill."

"Oh, do I?" Leaning back, I smiled at the animated way he told the story of himself and his brother sneaking off campus to see a concert. A couple of times I laughed so loud, the couple nearest us shot me a look. I wanted to tell them to lighten up, but Jan was a natural storyteller and I didn't want to miss a beat.

It was easy to glean how close he was to his brother. Even in the face of dire consequences the two of them took turns trying to take the blame—Jan because he loved and admired the brother who always had his back, and Bart because he wanted to protect the brother he loved. The rest of the details were just filler. They got caught, the media was there, his parents were embarrassed, and they punished the brothers for their antics.

"It was a stupid kid prank, but we weren't just any pair of kids. Our grandfather was the mage chancellor. My family thought we'd been abducted and called in a small army of inquisitors. When it turned out we'd just snuck out, it painted a picture that we thought we were above the rules."

My classes on child development would argue this was typical of teens whose brains weren't fully developed. Even the most mature weren't immune to making poor choices. "What did they do?"

"How much do you know about my family?"

I didn't like he'd answered me with a question, but he hadn't been evasive, so I went with it. "Not much, just what I read online."

"Did you know all five mages involved in creating the Great Ward were from our family?"

I probably should have, but gryphon school focused on Leifr Cormaic. My distant ancestor was Guardian of the Eastern Point. To gryphons, *that* was the bit worth teaching. "I did not."

"Katarina Hollen was the matriarch, and it was her brother, two nephews, and a grandson who assumed the four points. Most of the great mages have come from our family. Two of the other four great mage families trace their line back to Katarina or her siblings. That has created a lot of backlash.

"About two hundred years ago, the two mage families not related to us all but declared war on the Hollens. The family banded together in a show of force that rocked the entire world, not just mages. My grandmother and grandfather led the fight after an ambush killed two of their nine children. It was vicious, but short-lived. The two families expected the rest of the mage world to rally around them to topple the high and mighty Hollens; that never happened, but in hindsight it's a shock it didn't.

"For centuries, my family acted like the kings and queens of the mage world. The attack was a wake-up call. Since then, my grandfather and father have tried to fix the systemic issues. It's not perfect by any means. Mostly what happened was the four other families got a bigger slice of the pie. There are still big issues that need correcting, but Dad is working on it."

Jan sipped his wine. "Our sneaking out was reminiscent of those autocratic days."

On behalf of my mate, I was angry the mage world found it necessary to punish two fourteen-year-olds sneaking out to see a concert to compensate for the sins of their ancestors. The fact it was fourteen years ago and Jannick wasn't upset didn't matter.

Jan reached across the table and patted my hand. "It's okay. It worked out in the end."

I tried to relax as he explained how the Mage Council appointed a human judge to decide their punishment. My emotions waxed and waned as Jan took me through the school asking they be expelled, and the court finding that stupid but still sentencing them to a summer of community service.

"A whole summer for a stupid teenage prank?"

Jan shrugged. "The way he saw it, we cost the Mage Council a lot of money by mobilizing all those inquisitors. Fining us was meaningless, so he needed something we'd remember."

The judge must have had experience dealing with juveniles. Consequences were important for kids to learn. "How'd that go?"

"Bart and I spent the summer working with Habitat for Humanity. We were the unskilled labor who got all the mindless, menial jobs. But the adults treated us well, and it wasn't so bad."

Our meal arrived before I could respond. The server set down our plates, asked if we needed anything, and faded out of view.

"How about you?" Jan asked as he cut into his chicken. "Any crazy kid stories you want to share?"

Chapter Twenty-Three

JANNICK

Despite being hopelessly in love with Conall, I knew more about what he liked to do sexually than about his favorite music, type of movie, books, or even if he liked to read. This was our first date, and in a normal world, we'd still be wondering if we liked each other enough for a second.

"For my sixteenth birthday my brother Nikandros—Nik—took me on a camping trip to teach me the ways of a gryphon."

This was the most affection I'd heard him display for a brother. "Which brother is Nik?"

"He's the next youngest. He's also the nicest. My oldest brother Kel, he'd probably be okay except Dad is grooming him to be alpha. To keep his position, Kel has to impress Dad with how Dad-like he can be. Braylen is next oldest, and he's a dick. Thank God he's not the oldest. There's hope that Kel might ease up on some things; Bray would be worse.

"After him are three sisters—Pia, Dahlia, and Sybilla. Pia and Sybil were married before I was born; I rarely see them."

I had experience with shitty siblings. The difference was, I also had some amazing ones who always had my back. "Is Dahlia the one still at home?"

"Yes. Lia helped raise me."

I didn't need our bond to know he loved his sister. She'd clearly been there for him when he was younger. I didn't know how, but if she was important to Conall, I'd save her, too. And anyone else he loved. "It sucks she's being mistreated."

"I know."

The conversation stalled, so we ate in silence. I had so many questions, but none were great dinner topics. When we finished, I tried to steer us back to something that wouldn't be so somber. "You were telling me about your sixteenth birthday before dinner arrived."

He set his fork down and wiped his mouth. "Two days before my birthday, Nik told me to pack for a trip. He'd gotten Dad's permission to teach me how to be a gryphon. Nik wasn't married yet, so he was the natural choice to teach me."

Nik was probably the only one who wanted to help his little brother. "Had you shifted before then?"

"Yes. We learn that almost as soon as we can walk. Nik taught me how to eat, sleep, and live as a gryphon. I know that sounds silly, but we spend most of our lives in human form. Some things come instinctually, but others need to be taught."

This was the first time I'd seen Conall smile when talking about his family. "It must have been a good trip."

"The best. Nik was awesome. Unlike Kelton or Bray, who would have been impatient, or degrading, he was patient and explained things when I got them wrong. He taught me to hunt, build a temporary shelter, and to eat. Which sounds simple, but it's hard to eat with a beak and talons."

I'd grown up with Isaac who used to shift for us, but I'd never have traded magic for being able to shift. Now? If I could become a gryphon and Conall and I could fly off together and just be ourselves, I'd hand in my mage stone in a heartbeat. "I can't imagine."

"He also taught me how to fly if I was in a fight."

Conall looked at me, but he was seeing something else. "That sounds . . . ominous."

Blinking, he came back from wherever he'd been. "It was necessary. He and Warin taught each other how to fight in case Kelton or Bray came for them. They weren't going without a fight. Nik wanted to be sure I could defend myself."

I didn't know how to answer him. It was wonderful his brother loved him enough to teach him, but learning to fight in case your family tried to kill you was unimaginable. "Are you worried it will come to that?"

"I don't know. Maybe? Dad killed one of his brothers and drove another out of the pack because he saw them as threats. They keep their heads down, support Dad when asked, and avoid family politics so Kelton won't see them as a threat."

Talk about sleeping with a gun under your pillow. Thank God my family wasn't that dysfunctional. It made Nerea trying to get rid of me seem like a doddle. "I'm sorry."

"We're all used to it. Dad likes to play us off each other, especially Kel and Bray. If they're busy worrying about each other, they can't plot to take his place."

No surprise that's how Aodhan Arawn, Alpha Assclown, thought to treat his children. "That's crazy."

He nodded. "It is. I've been lucky so far. Dad hasn't found anyone to pair me with that would be to his advantage. When he does . . ."

I reached across and squeezed his hand. "That's not going to happen."

"Old habit." He smiled, but it was rueful.

I wanted to hug away the sadness I knew it brought him, but I needed to do better than that. I needed to find a way to free him. "What's it like to fly?"

"Incredible. It's exhilarating to feel the wind in your face. To power dive and level out before you hit the ground, to catch a draft and soar into the clouds, and twist and turn in ways you can't on the ground. You need to think in three dimensions, not two. Up and down are a big deal. If you forget those, you'll crash into the ground."

Talking about flying animated him. I'd never wanted to be a shifter if it meant giving up magic, but I'd probably do it for a chance to fly with Conall. "That sounds so cool. I wish I could go with you."

"You can. If you wear a harness, I can scoop you up and take you with me."

The description scared and thrilled me at the same time. Before his offer fully sank in, my phone vibrated. I glanced at the screen and my pulse quickened. "It's Avie. She must have an answer for us."

"Take it." He nodded to the phone.

My stomach churned and my heart thumped so hard, I'm sure Conall heard it. "Hey Avie. How are you?"

"I'm good. Thank you for your report. I know you're mad you figured it out one house too late, but that was incredible work you and Leo did. I took the report to Dad myself. He smiled the whole time he read. He's proud of you both. Me, too."

Making Dad proud mattered most to me, but impressing Avie was a close second. "Not bad for a couple of goofballs."

"Seriously. I'm not sure how you got Leo to toe the line, but you did it far quicker than any of us could with you."

We'd had this conversation before, but this time it lacked its usual edge. This wasn't a criticism, for one. "You know that old saying—takes one to know one."

She laughed, and it was a real, humorous one rather than the sarcastic fake ones I usually received. "You've grown up a lot in the last few months."

Nothing like almost losing to a demon lord—who almost ate me—to sober a mage. "Thanks. I assume you have news?"

The line went silent, and my heart sank. "It's not good."

I'd known it was foolish to hope, but I hadn't been able to stop myself. This sucker punched me so hard I could barely breathe. "Oh? What did you find out?"

Conall looked up from his food, and he knew. His disappointment hurt the worst.

"Normally, if a mage mates with a shifter, the alpha can't claim the mage for his pack. The treaties between the races specifically exclude the five species involved in creating the Great Ward."

Which meant Conall's fears were justified. "Is there a way around that?"

"Not that we've found. This dates to right before the Ward was erected. Katarina Hollen insisted on that condition in case a Guardian pair died. She didn't know if there would be more than one pair of mates and wanted the alpha of the species in question to choose the best one."

Talk about missing the mark by the longest mile. I curled my lips because I thought I'd vomit. Breathing deeply, I blew air out my nose to regain control. "Thanks for checking, Avie."

"I've asked legal to keep looking, and I have a meeting with Dad tomorrow. He won't be happy if Alpha Arawn tries to claim you."

He wouldn't be the only one. Not that I had any intention of submitting to him. "I appreciate that. I'll call you tomorrow."

"One more thing." She paused. I checked to see if we'd been disconnected.

"What's that?"

"Whatever else, don't bond with him. Not yet. If you do, the alpha will have a good claim that you belong to him."

I wouldn't give him that chance. If it happened, he wouldn't live long enough to use me. "I won't."

I tapped the screen and couldn't look at Conall because of the tears welling in my eyes. I breathed in deep and squeezed my eyelids tight. "Legal reported back to Avie."

Chapter Twenty-Four

CONALL

Five words in and I was numb. I didn't need details to know the news broke his heart. "What did she say?"

I fought back tears as he clinically explained what his sister had told him. The Mage Council lawyers confirmed what I'd suspected. Dad almost surely knew this. He was many things, but not stupid.

"This isn't over," Jan said. "I told you, I'll raise an army if I have to."

"I know, babe." My voice was even and without emotion. I had to keep it that way or I'd shift and tear the restaurant apart. "I have a magic question."

"Um . . . okay?" He looked slightly put out by my change of subject.

My timing sucked. I'd clearly hurt him by minimizing his vow to fight for us, but we needed to do something. Something for us. "Can you summon something of mine?"

"Not directly, but I can give you the power to fetch one object." I could see his suspicions mounting. "Why?"

I hadn't meant to be so mysterious, I just needed to know what he could do before I suggested what I had in mind. "I want you to fly with me tonight, but I need something to make it happen."

"You can teach me to fly?"

I was screwing this up, and it was killing me. "No, but I can take you flying with me. I want to give you—*us*—this memory tonight, because even if you fix this or need to raise that army, we're not going to be able to see each other for a while."

He raised his arm, and the waitress appeared. A credit card appeared in his hand, and he held it out. "Can you ring us up, please?"

I didn't protest or try to pay. She took his card and disappeared. No matter how much I'd told myself the odds weren't good, I'd kept a large dose of hope Jan was right and we could be together without my father's interference. My hope had died when he took Avie's call.

I couldn't even renounce my place in the pack. Once Dad found out I was valuable, he'd get the Assembly to force me to go back. Jan wouldn't give up, but he knew in his heart it was a losing fight. I felt it.

He scribbled his name on the slip, took his card, and nodded for us to leave the booth. The hostess wished us a good night, and we both mumbled something that sounded like thanks.

At the car, Jan grabbed me by the arm, spun me around, and hugged me. "I won't . . . I can't lose you. I'll fight until the last breath. In my heart, I know we're going to be together. I don't know how, or when, but we will."

I cupped his face and pushed his chin up. The words he wanted me to say wouldn't come out. What I wanted wasn't going to happen. Instead, I pressed my lips to his. "I love you, too."

All I could see was I'd spend my life alone. I wasn't being tragic, just realistic. There weren't any loopholes, and the Mage Council would never approve of an all-out war with the Assembly over two people. Better to be apart than to let the alpha destroy both our lives.

Jan pressed something cool and smooth into my hand. I turned my palm up and his power stone glowed faintly. "Focus on what you want and where you want it delivered, and my stone will bring it to you."

He stepped back. I was humbled by his trust; a mage's stone was the most intimate object they owned. It was an extension of their soul.

Closing my eyes, I concentrated on the harness I wanted and where it hung in the garage. I don't know how, but I knew the stone found the right object. I opened my eyes and stared at the ground between me and Jan. An instant later, the thick leather harness lay on the asphalt at my feet.

I handed his stone back and let my hand linger. We stared into each other's eyes, and I studied his so I wouldn't forget them. "Thank you."

"Of course."

He understood the reality, but he refused to accept it. I latched onto his optimism and hoped it was enough. "We need to find a more secluded place. Not only do I need to get naked, if the locals see a gryphon launch skyward, it will get back to the alpha."

We weren't doing anything wrong, but I wanted to keep everything that had to do with Jan from my father. Jan scooped up the harness and put it in the backseat before getting in the car. We drove for ten minutes until I found a suitable field and pulled off the road.

We didn't speak as I helped Jan put on the harness. I fiddled with the straps until they were secure. The fit was snug, but not too tight. I pulled my shirt over my head; he held out his hand for it, folded it, and put it on the car seat. Again and again, until I was naked.

Unashamed, I stood in front of him. "I need you to move away from the car, so I can swoop down and pick you up."

"Is there anything I can do to help?"

Jan was calm. I wasn't surprised. He'd faced a demon prince and lived; letting your mate snatch you off the ground was no big deal.

"Just don't flinch, or I'll miss the strap. When I pluck you off the ground, it'll be a bit jarring. Think of a hawk swooping in and snatching an animal. The difference is, I'm going clutch these hooks, not your flesh." I grabbed the two metal U's and shook him gently.

"Got it." He leaned in and brushed his lips to mine. "Thank you."

I put my hand on his nape and kissed him harder. A second later, I released him and backed up a few paces. "It'll take me a minute to gain enough altitude to soar up after."

"I'll be in place." He smiled. "Can I watch?"

"Of course, but then you need to move into the field so I can grab you."

I spread my arms in front of me and willed my other form to take over. The magic that shifted my flesh coursed to life, and my bones broke and reformed. My body expanded and wings grew from my back as my hands twisted into talons. Feathers covered me from my head to just below my sternum. The tail tickled as it grew from just under my tailbone. I dropped to all fours and scratched the dirt with my hind paws.

Clicking my beak, I motioned for him to move into the field. Jan did as he was told, walking backward slowly, never taking his eyes off me. I extended my wings and backed up a few feet. A burst of speed propelled me forward and with a leap, I was airborne.

I flew away from Jan, gaining altitude as I moved. The full moon made the night as bright as daylight to my gryphon sight. It bathed Jan in its soft white light, giving him an angelic glow. I etched that image in my mind. That was how I wanted to remember him, so beautiful, brave, and full of love.

When I circled around, his eyes were still on me as he walked farther away from the car. I made one more circle to make sure I wouldn't crash when I picked up my mate.

Jan turned his back to me, somehow knowing I was about to come get him. Adrenaline surged through me and fueled the strokes of my wings. This would be ours and only ours, forever. We'd find other ways to fly in the future, but this was the only first we'd have. It needed to be as perfect as Jan. Tucking my wings, I began my dive.

Chapter Twenty-Five

JANNICK

My first thought seeing him paw the ground was he was fucking beautiful. He was much bigger than I expected. Not dragon big, but easily bigger than a lion with wings and the head of an eagle.

Strong, majestic, graceful. I never felt inferior to any being, but seeing him leap into the air, I wasn't worthy of someone so amazing.

I followed him in the moonlight as he grew smaller and harder to see. He circled to gain altitude, but even when I lost sight of him, I knew where to look.

Hiking slowly so I didn't stumble, I eased away from the car and into the open field. Blood pounded in my ears as I strained to hear him approach. I closed my eyes and imagined him bearing down on me. My brain screamed at me this was foolish and dangerous. One fraction of an inch off and I'd be pierced multiple times. I'd bleed out long before we could get help.

I steadied myself. Conall said not to flinch. He wouldn't have suggested this if he thought he'd hurt me.

A loud fluttering behind me was the only warning before I was snatched off the ground with surgical precision. I whooped like I had when Bart and I rode every rollercoaster in Six Flags, only this was so much cooler. The wind pummeled my face as Conall beat his wings to gain speed.

I was flying. Fucking flying! "This is amazing!" I shouted.

"*Speak to me with your mind.*" Conall said inside my head. "*In this form I can hear you.*"

As mages we learned to communicate through our stones, but only with each other. "*Like this?*"

"*That's perfect.*"

We crossed a huge field, and he dove. The rush of watching the ground rush up at us only to have him snap out his wings and send us soaring up was an adrenaline junkie's drug. He leveled off and headed for a set of low mountains ahead of us. I couldn't tell how fast we were going or how far we'd come, but it didn't take long for the mountains to loom large.

I fumbled for my stone and when it touched my palm, I enhanced my vision as much as I could. Conall no doubt still saw better than I did, but I could make things out a little clearer. The mountains were covered in evergreen trees.

He banked to his left, and we flew along the ridge for a minute before he circled around. In front of us and forty feet down, there was a large open patch in the trees. It ran down the mountain, and eventually I saw the cables for the ski lifts.

Conall skimmed along the towers until we came to the open space at the top. He tilted back and raised the front of his wings. We slowed quickly; little eddies of dust swirled below my feet.

"*I'm going to release you,*" Conall said a moment before I fell the last two feet to the ground. I dropped to a crouch to absorb the impact and stood once I was stable. Conall flew a few feet ahead of me and landed gracefully.

I jogged up to him, and he spread his wings around me.

Accepting the invitation, I moved closer, and he wrapped me in a cocoon of feathers.

"That was amazing," I said. "Thank you for sharing that with me."

"We're not done. We still need to go back."

I pressed my head against his chest and heard his heartbeat. Enveloped in his warm embrace, I was surrounded by his scent. It was similar to what I smelled when we were in bed, only more. It was air, pine needles, earth, and sun. If that was even a scent.

He unfolded his wings and backed up. Two seconds later, Conall stood before me as naked as when we started.

"Did you want me to get your clothes?" I asked.

He shook his head. "I'll need to take them off again to go back. Does my being naked offend you?"

"As if. But I'm overdressed."

He raised an eyebrow. "That's easy to fix."

With quick, agile fingers he unfastened the harness. By the time he tossed it aside, my cock was straining to get out of my pants. He was in a similar state, minus the clothes. He put his hands on my shirt.

"Is this okay?"

"Always," I whispered.

Slowly, he unbuttoned my shirt and pushed it off my shoulders. Running his hands over my chest and abs, he hooked the fabric and tossed the shirt to the ground. I kicked off my shoes as he unbuckled my belt. A second later he pushed my pants and boxers down and helped me step out of them.

I reached down and fisted his cock. He did the same with mine. "I want you, Conall. Please?"

He knew what I wanted, because he froze. "Jan . . ."

"I promise you, I won't bond with you. If you do the same, we won't. But I want to feel you. Please?"

"I want that so much."

He sounded so conflicted, I almost took it back. Almost. "Avie warned me not to bond with you until we resolve this. I'm horny and I want you, but I'm not stupid. I understand what I'm asking."

I held out my hand and called my stone. When it slapped into my palm, I summoned a blanket and some lube.

"Promise me," he whispered.

Knowing how much it scared him, I wouldn't let it happen. "I promise."

We spread the blanket and lay facing each other. I ran my hand over his skin, something I loved to do.

"It feels so nice when you do that," he said.

"Good, because I love to touch you." I leaned closer for something else I adored. My lips grazed his, and I felt it all the way to the soles of my feet. An energy thrummed through me like a drug. It sent me soaring, and each touch shot me farther into the sky.

He cupped my nape and pulled us closer. Our lips touched and he pushed his way into my mouth. A moment later he rolled me over and blanketed me with his body. I rarely let anyone take control during sex, but this dominant side of him was a total turn on.

He kissed me hard, pushing his tongue in places he hadn't gone before. His hands gripped my head, moving it how he wanted me for maximum access. A knee pushed my legs apart and he ground his body into mine.

"Conall." I dragged out the last syllable. "You need to fuck me."

"Yeah? You like when I'm in charge?"

He never showed this side of himself. It unlocked something in me I didn't know I wanted. No. This wasn't a side of me I hadn't realized, this was something I only wanted with him.

"Yes."

Chapter Twenty-Six

※

CONALL

Jan totally giving himself to me ignited an aggressive streak I rarely let out. I preferred to bottom, and I liked my tops in charge. When I topped, I wanted that same control. And Jan gave it to me without hesitation.

I kissed him again, but I didn't think either of us would last very long, so I limited the foreplay. Without breaking contact, I found the bottle of lube on the blanket. I bit his lower lip and Jan's body shook. His body responded to everything I did to him. Through my connection with him, I knew when I approached a spot.

I feathered soft kisses down his neck and made my way down his torso, stopping to bite his nipple gently. Like me, that was a spot for him. He jumped under my weight. I looked up and we made eye contact before I nipped him again.

"Shit, Conall. Do you know what you're doing to me?"

I swirled my tongue once around the little nub and drifted lower. "Absolutely."

Unsnapping the lube, I dribbled some on my fingers. I rubbed my index finger against his hole and slowly slipped it inside. Jan writhed and sucked in air. He hadn't had anyone inside him in a long time, so I used extra lube and worked in a second finger, twisting and moving them around. This had to be perfect. It had to last him a lifetime.

I drew my fingers mostly out and dripped more slick liquid onto them. I slid in and out, feeling his body respond to my touch.

"Please, Conall. I'm ready," he whimpered.

Despite his pleas, I was giving him exactly what he wanted. What he needed. Only the level of trust we shared let him be vulnerable enough to let someone else be in control. "I'll tell you when you're ready, babe."

I twisted quicker and he lurched. "Not yet." I coated my hand with a generous amount of lube and slicked my cock with a few quick strokes. Rubbing the rest on his hard-on, I held his cock and aimed myself at his hole.

When my head was lodged in place, I eased forward. Jan hissed and clenched as I cleared his ring; I pressed on without stopping and felt my shaft brush over his prostate. He shuddered and tossed his head back.

"Now you're ready."

"Oh God. That. More."

The words were breathless whispers. "Shout it out, babe." I raised my voice for emphasis. "No one can hear us."

"Give it to me!"

I yelled and pulled out, shoved back hard. "Like that?"

"God yes! That. Fuck me!"

It was exhilarating, to shout as loud as we wanted. There were no constraints. I leaned in and kissed him hard as I plunged in harder. Connected as we were, I knew I wasn't hurting him. This was what he wanted. What *we* wanted.

Completing our bond would've made us equal parts of a whole all the time. It wouldn't happen, but for one night we'd know what it felt like to be complete. Pushing that from my mind, I focused on the now. It would end too soon anyway.

"More." He didn't shout, but his voice carried up the mountain. "Give it to me, babe. Don't hold back."

Like me, he was cramming a lifetime into this one moment. I fucked harder, roaring toward my orgasm. I wanted to make it last, but it would never be long enough. I kissed him and shortened my thrusts. The slower, more sensual pace brought me even closer. My body tingled; every cell burned with the joy of our coupling.

He grabbed my head in his hands and held our mouths together. Our tongues danced around, and Jan didn't need my words to know. He squeezed his muscle just as the first blast left me. I slammed down and he wrapped his muscular legs around my waist to keep me in place.

A bright light exploded in my head and instinct forced me to seek my mate. I needed him to complete our bond. With a primal lust, my cock expanded, locking me into my mate's body. I sent out an urgent plea for him to bond with me and slammed into an unyielding wall. Twice more I tried to shatter the barricade keeping me from what was mine. I growled and smashed again into the fortifications in my path.

"Conall! Stop." Jan grimaced and a jolt of pain stabbed me.

My brain cleared like I'd been dunked in ice water. "Jan." I stroked his face with my hands. "I'm so sorry, babe. Are you okay?"

Filling his lungs, he exhaled. "Fuck you're big when you get your knot."

I laughed and touched my forehead to his. "That wasn't what I meant, but does it hurt?"

"Only when you laugh." He kissed me again and grabbed his cock. "It's the most amazing feeling."

He stroked himself a few times and his dick erupted. Gulping air, his body contracted around me with every shot. The pressure on my hypersensitive cock sent shivers thundering through me. We shuddered, nanoseconds apart, until his body stopped convulsing.

The immediate rush after sex receded and guilt replaced ecstasy. I'd hurt Jan trying to force him to mate with me.

"Stop!" He put two fingers on my lips. "You warned me what would happen, but I begged you to do it anyway. I'm not mad, not one bit. That was amazing. So much better than I imagined." He ran his hands over the mess on his body.

He pulled me down, and we hugged on top of the mountain while I was stuck inside him. Neither of us spoke. Words wouldn't improve this moment. The fear and sadness he held down told me everything. He knew exactly what had just happened, and that it wouldn't again.

Locked together, we lay quietly. This would end soon enough; I wasn't going to waste even a second.

Chapter Twenty-Seven

JANNICK

The car pointed toward home, but my heart protested. I belonged with Conall. He was my home, but forces beyond our control slammed the front door shut.

Conall left in the middle of the night, as we discussed. If he stayed, we'd end up dragging out our goodbye; the chances his father would hear about us made that too risky. Leaving in the wee hours would convey he'd slept with me to satisfy his alpha. At least that was our hope.

"You okay, bro?" Leo asked.

I shrugged. I couldn't say if I'd ever be good again without Conall. "No?"

"You two are mates, aren't you?"

My stomach gnarled in an anxious twist. "Does the whole world know?"

"Doubtful, but they don't know you like I do." Leo shifted his leg under him and leaned against the door so he could face me. "I'm not an expert on this, but isn't this supposed to be the single greatest thing in human existence?"

It was, and it could be if the universe didn't hate me. "Yes, but we didn't complete the bond."

"How can that be?"

It was a question I was going to ask over and over. "When your mate's father is the alpha and happens to be a narcissistic petty autocrat who will pervert your bond to his own ends, you don't dare give him the power to destroy not only you and your mate but untold others."

"Wow, Jan. Don't hold back."

I thought I'd been restrained, which proved I wasn't bitter in the least. "Believe it or not, he's much worse than I just said."

"It sounds pretty insane he can do that."

Nothing about finding my mate and being kept apart made sense. "Avie told me point-blank I shouldn't complete the bond until she and Dad could figure some way around the alpha's control."

"Shit. That's fucked up."

I knew he was trying to help, but I just wanted him to be quiet. Silence was the worst thing for me, but I didn't care. My soul was in pain. "I know, but Avie wouldn't have said anything unless it was serious."

"What are you going to do?"

I'd asked myself that a dozen times since I woke up alone. No good answer presented itself. I had to hope Avie and Dad knew something I could use. "Stay positive and not give up."

Leo didn't believe me, but he let me keep my fantasy a little longer.

Chapter Twenty-Eight

CONALL

I slept late, and not just because I was tired. Starting the first day of the rest of my life alone was something I didn't need to rush. Jan talked a good game, but he didn't block me from his feelings. We weren't going to see each other any time soon.

Through my link to him, I knew when he woke up and realized he was alone. It worried me; our bond shredded the walls he'd used to keep his grief from crippling him. He couldn't love me if he shielded his heart, but once his defenses were gone, he needed me.

And I wouldn't be there.

The house was empty when I left my room. I should have used the time to catch up on my schoolwork—my studies always centered me and gave me hope. Not today. Cracking open a book seemed pointless.

I made a cup of coffee and put some bread in the toaster. Jan's melancholy hovered at the edges of my thoughts. I needed to block him, not only for my well-being but also to keep my negative emotions from feeding his. Maybe later I'd listen to logic.

Looking out the kitchen window, I saw Mom directing the farmhands. I'd need to wait until she came inside to make lunch to talk to her.

"Con?" Dahlia said from behind me. "Are you okay?"

My impulsive actions from the day before had come to haunt me sooner than I expected. Dahlia wouldn't tell Dad anything, but if she'd noticed already, I wasn't going to keep my mate a secret for long.

"Just tired from the last few days." I took a plate from the cabinet, and when I turned Dahlia held out a jar of the blueberry jam she and Mom made.

"When you were little, you called it bluebees. You loved your bluebees."

There were a lot of things I'd loved when I was a kid. Reality had a way of sucking the joy out of most of them. "You and Mom made the best jam."

"I remember holding you and playing with you as a baby. Your eyes sparkled like you were ready to conquer the world. I was jealous of your innocence, but I knew it wouldn't last. Except it did. No matter what Dad threw at you, the spark never died." She unscrewed the lid and set the jam next to my plate. "Until now."

I felt her eyes on me, but I didn't dare turn. What could I say? She'd suffered in silence for decades. It hadn't even been twenty-four hours since Jan left. "I'll be back to normal once I catch up on school."

"Of all the things I despise about Dad—and there are so many it's hard to keep track—the thing I hate most is how he programmed us to distrust each other. It's how he keeps us cowered and under his control."

In school, I'd learned about abuse. The victim rarely admitted they were abused until it was too late. Denial and excuses were common, until they were separated and could see things from safety.

I'd known Dad was abusive—we all did—but I hadn't seen the

big picture until now. How he treated us had just been an extension of being the alpha. In truth, it was much more. "That's—"

"Don't give up, Con." She squeezed my hand. "Be the example for the rest of us."

She patted my shoulder and left the kitchen.

I wasn't as strong as she believed. When there was hope I was driving toward, I kept my head up. But the light was gone. Extinguished by forces outside my control.

And it wasn't coming back.

Chapter Twenty-Nine

JANNICK

Waves crashed against the shore and water ran up the sand to swallow me. Inches before it reached my feet, the tide yanked it away from its prize. Nature was cruel that way—teasing us with something perfect, only to take it back before we could grasp it.

I'd always loved the beach; I'd hoped coming here would help. Not make me forget but remind me of my place so I could move forward. The sea didn't care about names or titles, who we loved or even if we loved. It was here before beings, and it would be here when we were gone.

Instead, I saw the futility of always grasping for something but falling just short. Just like the sea. After high tide passed, each subsequent wave ended farther away until, finally, it started again. Always stretching for a prize just beyond its reach.

At the edge of my consciousness, I felt him. The pain and sadness. I could heal the hurt if I could touch him. But I couldn't. So close, but inches too far.

It had been ten days, and the shadow of my empty future grew. I couldn't live when I was hollow inside.

Seawater touched the edge of my shoe. The answer to everything crept closer.

"Jannick?"

Even the shock of Dad's voice couldn't move me. "Hi, Dad."

"Bart and Cael are making lunch. Come join us."

Bart must have called him. My depression scared him more than fighting a demon. He loved me, and it hurt him that he couldn't help. I swallowed because Dad knew why I stood here. "I can't, Dad. I just can't."

A hand grabbed my shoulder and spun me around. I was five again, and this amazing man had come to save me when I was lost. But he couldn't save me this time.

He pulled me into a hug. "We can fix this."

"No, we can't." The tears came first, and I struggled to breathe. I gulped air and panted, trying to control the sobs. "Please let me go."

"I can't do that, Jannick." He squeezed me through his pain. "I won't lose you."

His sorrow mirrored mine, but a broken heart could only heal so many times. "I barely . . . Losing her . . . almost broke me. This . . ."

Losing Conall shattered the broken heart I'd barely kept whole. When my mother died, Dad had held me in silence as I cried out my pain and loss. I remember voices and him telling them to go away. If I'd needed it, he'd have held me forever. He'd let me know I wasn't alone.

This time, he couldn't fix me like that.

"What . . . did I do . . . that was so terrible?" I asked. "Am I so horrible that I can't love someone?"

"No, Jannick. Don't ever think that." Dad sniffed. "You've grown into the person I always knew you'd be. She . . ." He swallowed hard and his breath hitched as it came out. "She would be so proud."

We stood in the sand, grieving for a little boy's broken heart. Again.

"My beautiful little boy." He shook as his arm squeezed tighter. "I promised you I would never leave you, and I won't. No matter what it costs, I will find a way to fix this."

I sniffled to clear my nose. "You can't, Dad. I love you for offering, but this is beyond even you."

"Then I'll go down trying, Jannick." He stroked my hair. "There is no love like a parent's for their child. It breaks my heart to see you in such pain."

My fragile control broke, and the tears came in endless streams. The salty air whipped around us, stinging my cheeks. We stayed that way until the tide had reached well past us. Dad's expensive shoes were ruined.

I pointed to his feet. "I'll buy you new ones."

"They don't matter." He kissed my head and swallowed loudly. "Jannick, I'm so sorry I failed you."

I pulled back, stunned by his admission. "You've never failed me. Never."

He squeezed a last time, put his arm around me, and turned me toward the house. Gently, he started us forward. "I let this go too far. I should have seen how much you were hurting."

His ruffled hair made me laugh for a second. "Good thing there are no cameras here. Your image would never survive all the hairs out of place."

"Why do you think we own the island?"

I inhaled deeply and blew it out. "How did you meet Mom?"

I'd never asked because I didn't want to pick at a scab. But she was on my mind, and he'd mentioned her. Dad didn't miss a step, but he'd gone quiet. I'd have thought I'd upset him, except he never moved his hand from my shoulder.

"I wondered if you'd ever ask me."

I stiffened at my insensitiveness. He'd done this amazing thing for me and I trashed it by reminding him of something he kept secret from the world. "That was wrong. Forget I asked."

"Oh no, I'm not mad. Miriam and I discussed this. What would we say? When would we tell you? I'm surprised you never raised the issue."

That must've been one of the most awkward conversations they'd ever had. "I didn't think of it when I was little. As I got older . . . well, not everyone was happy I was part of the family."

"Your grandparents, Miriam, and I weren't happy with *those* members of the family."

And that was why I'd never asked. "You've been the best parents I could imagine. I never wanted to remind you that I was a mistake."

"Which means I should have told you a long time ago." He stopped walking, dropped his arm, and faced me. "First, you were never a mistake. I didn't sleep with your mother. There was no affair. No sneaking off behind Miriam's back. You were very much planned."

My face became the new image of gobsmacked for the dictionary. "What does that mean?"

"As you learned, your grandmothers are close. I knew your mother from the day she was born. I watched her grow up and become the beautiful, caring person you should have known." A tear rolled down his face. "Your mother was asexual and found it hard to find a person to share her life with. After several failed relationships, she decided she wanted a child without having a partner.

"When she approached me and Miriam, we were . . . shocked."

I'd been wrong. *That* had to have been the most awkward conversation. "Wow."

"Your brazen side is all Pederson, by the way." He winked. "Her request was the subject of a rather intense family debate. I didn't want to hurt your mother . . . Miriam."

I held up a hand. I'd called Miriam "Mom" for so long, he didn't need to change his words. "She's been Mom to me for years. I never understood why she didn't have me call her Miriam."

"Miriam is the one who convinced me to be the donor. She loved your mother like a sister. To her this was just a clinical request, like blood or bone marrow. The bigger issue was your grandparents. They didn't want to set a precedence for creating new family members."

Bart and I steered clear of family politics—Bart because he hated conflict; me because I was part of those arguments. "I never thought of that."

"Neither had I until they brought it up. Finally, your grandmothers resolved the issue with a legal contract. In a sealed document, my parental rights were terminated. Your grandparents put funds in a trust for you and the court abolished your right to any future claim of support from the family."

My brain couldn't process all the new information. "When . . . Why didn't you tell everyone the truth? It had to hurt Mom for others to read you cheated on her."

"Tonya wasn't the first person to ask to have a Hollen as a donor, she's just the only one who had Sally Pederson as a mother. When Tonya died, there was another intense family debate. There was no doubt I'd raise you as my son, the only question was what we told the world. I wanted to tell them the truth. I love Miriam with all my heart; I didn't want to see her hurt. Your grandparents, however, didn't want to open Pandora's box and refused to budge. Miriam said she didn't care as long as you came to live with us."

I'd always known Miriam loved me, just not why. "Wow."

Dad smiled. "Her big heart is one reason I love her so much. She's also very logical. In her mind, she was the only other person who could be your mother, since she'd approved the idea. Miriam is very secure in who she is. People's opinion of her didn't matter; she wasn't going to let you suffer." He closed his eyes and shook his head. "You are the result of so much love."

Tears rolled down my cheeks, and I started to hyperventilate. I forced myself to take and hold a deep breath. Somehow, Mom knew I needed to hear this today. She would want me to find a way through my pain. "Thank you. For coming here to talk, for telling me about Mom, and for loving me so much."

I hugged him until my stomach rumbled. My feet were also cold and wet. "I suppose we ought to change shoes and have lunch. I just hope Bart cooked. Cael's hopeless in the kitchen."

Chapter Thirty

CONALL

The sharp pain woke me from a fitful sleep. Jan hurt so badly, he was going to break. He projected such strength, but it masked the broken heart of a five-year-old that had never fully healed. His family had bandaged the wound, but our bond ripped that away. Now Jan couldn't keep it together anymore.

Every day, it got worse and his despair grew. Tears rolled down my cheeks.

Someone knocked on my door.

"Yeah?"

"Hey Con," Nik said. "Can I come in?"

I wiped my eyes as best I could. It wouldn't hide the puffiness. "Sure."

He walked in and without looking at me, shut and locked the door. I probably should have been anxious about that, but nothing he said or did could hurt me more than Jan's pain.

"I came to help." He held up his hand. "Mom asked me to talk to you. Dad has no idea. He's as clueless as ever."

We stared at each other for a second. Nik was the closest I came to bonding with a brother. If Mom asked him to come, my shitty poker face was worse than I thought. I closed my eyes, breathed deeply, and nodded.

"When did it happen?"

I didn't need to ask what he meant. "Twelve days ago, when he came to find out who's taking the kids."

"Is it a full-on mate bond?"

It should have terrified me that he knew. Knowledge of our bond gave others power over us. The way things were going, however, there wasn't going to be an "us" much longer. I nodded. "He's hurting so much, Nik. So much. I . . . can't block it anymore."

Panting, I bowed my head so I couldn't see how repulsed he was by my weakness. He came closer and I braced for the blow, the admonishment to stop being so pathetic. I flinched when he put his arms around me. I collapsed into him and sobbed as he pulled me tight. "He's going to kill himself."

"You can feel that?"

I swallowed twice and sniffed. "Yes. I blocked most of it at first, but it's . . ." I needed several breaths to control the grief. "I don't know how he can bear it."

"Then why aren't you there?" Nik put his hands on my head and tilted it back.

The genuine disbelief set me back. Surely, he knew. "If Dad finds out . . ."

"Right." Nik filled his lungs and held his breath for a few seconds. "He'll pervert it for his benefit."

His words suggested this was about more than my situation. "If I go, Dad will want details."

"Where's your mate?"

Nik said it with more compassion than I expected. I wanted to trust him, but . . . No, that was Dad talking. Dahlia had been right. This was how Dad kept us divided. "The beach."

"Which beach? Do you know where?"

I didn't. Jan wouldn't give me his location. I shook my head. "I'm not sure. I think somewhere in New England?"

"I need a package flown to New England. Can you take it for me?"

I lifted my eyes and stared. How did we go from my mate to flying something to New England? Had this all been a setup? "You want me to do what?"

"You need to go to him, Con." Nik's jaw set. He pulled a package from his back pocket. "This is a fake contract for an imaginary house I'm not thinking of buying, but if Dad asks where you went, I'm going to tell him you flew this to the lawyers wherever you end up."

It took my foggy brain time to process what he'd said. He was risking everything to help me. I couldn't let him do this. "Nik. If he finds out—"

"Call his family and find out where he is." He waved the envelope at me. "Let me know the closest big town. I'll deal with the rest."

It wasn't that I didn't trust Nik, but our family didn't risk the alpha's wrath to help each other. "Why?"

"He's ruined everything that's good in our family. I refuse to let him destroy you." He dropped his free hand onto my shoulder and squeezed. "You're the only one who pushes back. He ridicules you because you want to help kids. I look at my children and know that if anything happened to me, you'd defend them with your life. I've never been as brave as you, but it's about time I do what I can."

My brother had never been a coward. He and Warin were good at reading things and steering clear of the storm. Something had changed. "What happened?"

"Dad is trying to marry Melissa to some shitbag drunk whose support he's trying to shore up." Nik shook as he spoke. "Warin's ready to spit fire. Mel just turned twenty and this creep is over a hundred. He's put Dad off until she turns twenty-one but that's less than a year. We're not going to let him do this to us . . . or you."

He was talking about opening an intra-family fight, but if it meant saving my niece, it was time we threw down. "Let me get my phone."

Jan had programmed his siblings' numbers into my phone in case I needed them; Avie's name came up first, so I hit the green call button. Two rings and she picked up.

"Deputy Inquisitor General Hollen."

"Avie? It's Conall Arawn. Jan gave me—"

"Christ on a sparkly skateboard, Conall, thank God you called. Jan won't give us your number. You need to get to him."

Jan had said she was the most capable being he knew. For all our sakes, I hoped that was true. "I know. That's why I'm calling. I need a favor."

"Whatever you need let me know. Just get there asap."

Avelina Hollen was nothing like the cold, efficient inquisitor who only cared about the work. "I'll let my brother explain. He's helping me."

"Good. I probably don't need to tell you it's that bad. Bart and Cael called Dad in to help. He's flying there now."

I fluttered between relief and fear. If the Mage Chancellor dropped everything to rush to Jan's side, it might be worse than I knew. "I know. I can feel him."

"Let me talk to your brother; you need to get there yesterday."

I handed Nik the phone and went to the kitchen. Mom was at the counter making food. Her brow was furrowed, and her eyes were puffy red. "We need you whole, Con. The family can't live through another generation of pain."

The outpouring of love and concern was so foreign, I wasn't sure how to handle it, but there was one person who deserved more than anyone else. "Thank you, Mom. For caring. For calling

Nik. For everything. Nik's talking to Jan's sister. She's the best there is."

"You need to eat if you're going to fly half the day." She picked up a tray of sandwiches and motioned to the long oak table the family had used for generations.

I opened my arms and gathered her into a hug. As a family, we needed to be closer to heal. "I love you, Mom."

"You two were brought together for a purpose. There's a reason it's called fated mates. It's time to ignore what holds us back and do what's right."

Since Jan left, I'd been all alone. Now that my family was rallying together, I felt a glimmer of hope. "That's what Nik told me."

"He's right." She kissed my cheek. "You and your brother will bring change for the better. Now eat while he works out his details."

* * *

My feathers sparkled at the edges as I passed through the ward surrounding the island. The detour to see Avie had added an hour to my flight time, but it had been worth the delay. Not only did I get the paperwork, I also got a chance to rest and eat. Avie gave me a fake contract to bring home and a charm to get through the defenses surrounding the house.

By the time I reached the coast of Rhode Island, I was glad I'd stopped. The island was farther off the mainland than I expected. Nothing would have stopped me from getting here, but falling on my face wasn't how I wanted to surprise Jan.

The lights from the main house were the only illumination in the moonless night. Jan was inside. His sadness hadn't been displaced, but the pain had been muted. I circled and set down behind a shed and shifted. I dressed quickly as I heard someone leave the house.

I was tying my second shoe when a tall, blond mage with the glow of a fully mated being stopped at the edge of the building.

"Thank you for coming," Bart said. He didn't need to introduce himself. "He's better, but it's fragile. Dad had to beg him not to leave us. Whatever your father might do, it can't be worse than this."

Unfortunately, this was just a taste of what would happen. Soon even Chancellor Hollen wouldn't be able to keep his son alive. "This is exactly what he'd do, but with no end in sight."

"He's made a powerful enemy. My father is prepared to go to war to save Jan."

I didn't like where this was going. Neither Jan nor I could live with the deaths that would cause. "He can't. No matter how much the Assembly doesn't like my father, they won't let him be bullied by the Chancellor of the Mage Council. Gryphons need to police ourselves without human interference."

"You're right, but Dad won't care." Bart held out his hand to help me to my feet. "Principle is expensive, but sometimes you need to pay the price."

Nik had said almost the same thing. "There needs to be another way."

"This isn't the time for that conversation. Front door, turn left, and follow the music. He's playing out his sorrow. It fucking hurts to hear. I can't imagine what it's like for either of you."

If he was lucky, he never would. "Thank you for taking care of him."

I followed his instructions as a second person—an elf—left the house. He nodded to me and headed toward Bart. The stone steps led to a large, wraparound porch. Someone stood in the shadows, hands on the railing, staring into the waves. The most powerful being in the world left his home and his job hoping to save his son. Their love had kept him alive this long, but even that had a limit.

I heard a soft melody. Bart hadn't lied; Jan's pain floated

through the house. It affected everyone, but they were too afraid to ask him to stop. Following the sound, I saw his reflection in a window. The music was hauntingly beautiful. I didn't know he could play, much less with this much passion.

I stepped into the room. "Every Breaking Wave."

Chapter Thirty-One

JANNICK

My fingers danced slowly over the ivory. The melody was sad and poignant, but it called to my soul. The four of us had a good day after my meltdown. Dad made the most of his first full day off in years and we enjoyed having him around. Turns out Bart isn't the only one in the family who can cook. How did we not know that?

I convinced them I wouldn't dash headlong into the surf and let the riptide take me out to sea, and they stopped circling me. Their concern came from the heart, and it reached me just before I gave in to the pain.

I kept playing the opening over. It spoke to me. Conall's absence still nearly crippled me, but I refused to let it blot out all the good life had given me. Dad's promise reminded me that as desolate as the future seemed, hope only died if we gave in to despair.

"Every Breaking Wave."

My head shot up and my hands flew from the keys. "Conall?" I stood so fast, the bench slammed onto the floor. I rushed over and pulled him into a bear hug. "You're here? How?"

"You were in so much pain." Conall brushed his soft lips against mine. "You . . . I thought I'd be too late."

I put my hand behind his head and pulled us tight. His scent calmed my fear. I leaned into him. "Oh, babe. I should've been stronger. I couldn't see a way out."

"I know." He swallowed loudly. "That's why I came."

He said it like we weren't hundreds of miles away on a private island miles out to sea. "How?"

"I flew," Conall said. "Packed my clothes in a bag and came straight here."

The feeling of being whole I'd last felt on the mountain near Hagerstown pulled me from my lowest point and nearly overwhelmed me. My heart was so full, I expected it to burst any second. Tears welled in my eyes. "What about your father?"

"Shh. Let me hold you for a minute before we talk about that."

We stood, heads tucked on each other's shoulder, without moving. I heard the music in my head. It went from sorrowful to jubilant; he'd come, and with just his touch, the hopelessness in my soul receded. "I tried to fight it," I whispered. "Didn't want you to feel it. I almost gave up on us."

"But you didn't, Jan. You fought through the pain. Now I'm here."

He was, but I knew he couldn't stay long. "Won't you get in trouble?"

"I doubt it. My brother Nik and Avie came up with an alibi for the alpha. Most of my family is rallying to help me. Mom, Warin, Nik, my brothers' wives, my sister Dahlia, they all want change." He rubbed my back gently. "I had hours to think this over. If it comes to a fight, as my mate you wouldn't be a human intruder. I think that was what my mother and brother were trying to tell me."

If they tried to harm Conall, I'd defend him to my last breath.

"You're going to rebel against your father?"

"Change needs to happen. Gryphons were once among the most noble of beings. Powerful, wise, and honorable. Now we're scorned for our lack of compassion and insular ways."

I framed his face with my hands and kissed him. "You need to eat, and then I need to hold you until morning."

"Both of those sound wonderful."

We turned to leave, but Dad stood in the doorway. He moved closer and held out his hand. "Wilhelm Hollen. A pleasure to meet you. Welcome to our family."

"Conall Arawn, sir." They shook. "The way Jan speaks of you, I expected you to be twelve feet tall."

"I hate to disappoint you, but I'm not." Dad smiled and I knew that compliment meant more to him than any other. "I reserve that for my children and grandchildren."

"They're lucky beings to have you."

"Thank you." Dad breathed in and nodded. "I'm sorry to do this, but you both need to go back to Hagerstown."

I blinked but couldn't make sense of it. One minute he's giving Conall his blessing, and the next he's telling us we need to leave. "Tonight?"

"It's too late to leave now. Tomorrow."

I swallowed my irritation. Dad had dropped everything to save me; this wasn't something he'd ask on a whim. "What's wrong?"

"The most pressing thing is Conall's excuse won't last past tonight. The other is there's been another abduction. Two days ago. I wouldn't send you back, but it's an excuse to keep you two together until I can figure out what to do next. I'm sending you back with Leo and a strike team. Hopefully you can use this house to find all the missing children."

Wallowing in my own self-pity, I'd forgotten about the children. "Understood. Can we fly back with you?"

"Of course, but let's feed Conall before we discuss this further."

* * *

The sound of the waves had been my companion the last few days. Before, I'd waited for them to take me. Now, they soothed my soul. Under the full moon, Conall and I sat on a blanket, leaning against each other. It was wonderful to be ourselves without fear someone would see us and report back.

After dinner, Dad had set up a Zoom call with Cael's mother. Using my stone and hers, we conducted an "in person" therapy session to repair my damaged psyche. The colorful language she used to describe my childhood psychologist lightened the mood and left me wondering if Cael was adopted. He wasn't as staid as Bart, but he was nothing like his mother. Dr. Reinhold reminded me of Granny Pederson.

We had a lot of work left to do, but we had a plan and a way to make it happen. Most of all, it bought us time to find a permanent solution.

Conall had been quiet after the call. I didn't need a mate bond to know why, but it confirmed what I "knew." Being that connected would have scared me before I met Conall, but now it felt right. It also let me head off this disaster before it got rolling.

"It's not your fault."

"What?"

I tapped my temple. "You can't hide from me—well, you *can* but that's the same as announcing you're hiding something, which is bad all by itself."

Conall's confusion swept into a smirk, and he closed one eye to stare at me. "That was insane, even for you."

From the moment we met, I'd had to suppress my immaturity. Hopefully I didn't annoy him. We'd be together a while, and I'd hate it if my personality grated on his nerves. "Sorry?"

He leaned in and kissed my cheek. "Don't be. It's you. And yes, I feel like this was my fault. I caused you to lower your guard and it nearly killed you."

Guilt was an issue Dr. Reinhold said we'd need to address. I thought she'd meant mine, but clearly, we both had things to work through.

I took his hand in mine and held on until he faced me. "If it were that simple, we'd turn this off until we got things sorted. But we can't, so we need to think with our heads and not our emotions. You can't blame yourself, or we won't be whole. Neither of us chose to hurt the other, intentionally or unintentionally. I'll always miss her, but together I can still love her without falling apart. No one else could give me that. Only you. Please don't take that away."

Conall used his free hand to cover mine. He stayed quiet, but I felt his anxiety fade. After a few seconds, he squeezed my hands. "You're right."

The old me would have wanted him to say more, but we didn't need words. We were together, and that made us strong.

Resting my head on his shoulder, I closed my eyes and remembered her. And for the first time since she left, I smiled.

Chapter Thirty-Two

CONALL

My "flight" home was shortened by Chancellor Hollen securing a landing for his plane at a small airport in central Pennsylvania. That left me less than an hour's flying to get to Nik's house with his contract.

"How is he?" Nik asked while I got dressed in his barn.

I didn't think I'd ever loved my brother more than I did at that moment. Despite the risk to himself and his family, he'd asked about Jannick first. "Better. His brother's mate's mother is a mage psychologist. We did a video session with her to start the healing."

"That's convenient."

In many ways, it was awkward. Dr. Reinhold had probed every inch of our relationship. "It was extremely helpful and exactly what we needed."

"So he's going to be better now?"

I nodded and laced up my boot. When I'd finished, I walked over to hug him. "I owe you so much, Nik. I'll never be able to repay you. Are you sure you won't get in trouble?"

"Everything is legit. The lawyer his sister referred us to took care of everything. If Dad asks—"

"And he will," I said. Anything he didn't have a hand in would frost his nuts.

"Yeah, he will. But the contract you brought back gives me all the cover I need. I should thank you. The Hollens bought me the house."

That fit with who they really were. Up close, Jan's family were so different from what they showed the world. "That's awesome."

"More than you know. It gives me a place to send Jane and the kids when she needs to get away."

I'd never considered how Dad treated anyone except me and Dahlia. Our other siblings had moved out, and I assumed he didn't interfere as much with them. "Damn, Nik. I didn't know he was such an asshole to you and Warin, too. I thought he reserved most of that for me and Dahlia."

"It's different. He's not as nasty with us, but he micromanages everything. This house won't be something he'll approve of because I didn't talk to him first."

My good feeling disappeared faster than ice in the summer. Dad was going to drill down into this as far as he could, looking for something nefarious. "What about the money? Won't he wonder how you could afford it?"

"According to the contract, I only put twenty thousand down. The rest is mortgaged to a bank owned by the Hollens. They'll swear to whatever's in the contract." Nik stared at the documents I'd given him. "It's disturbing, comparing his family to ours. They rallied around Jannick to save him. We're trying to hide everything from Dad and our brothers. You shouldn't be worried he'll destroy you and your mate. That isn't how a family should behave."

Until then, I hadn't realized I'd contributed to the decline of gryphons. I saw everything through the prism of my life. Jan and his family used a much wider lens. "If there's a way, I'm going to fix things. You deserve to raise your children without fear."

"Seeing how the Hollens mobilized to help Jan gives me hope." Nik gripped my shoulder and squeezed. "Come in and say hi to Jane and your niece and nephews before you go home. I want them to know you better. Show them what family means."

They already knew what it meant. Nik lived it for them every day. "Of course."

* * *

The car pulled away, and I walked up the long drive to the house. I'd been warned he was home and in a foul mood. I used the ride home to prepare.

I saw movement in the kitchen window; a few seconds later, the door opened and the alpha strode down the steps with a purpose. If I didn't pass his test, one way or another, I'd never see Jan again.

"Where were you?" he shouted across the yard. His hands flexed and I waited for him to release his talons. "I've been calling you all morning."

It wasn't hard to look concerned for my safety. I was scared. But this was how Dad always treated me, so I had practice. "Nik asked me to fly a contract to Rhode Island yesterday. I just got back this morning. Did I forget to do something for you?"

"If you had, you'd have known it. Where in Rhode Island?"

Two questions in and calling Avie saved Nik and me. In the span of thirty minutes, she'd had an address of a house for sale, an attorney who would vouch for us, and a simple, airtight story for us to memorize. She truly was the most competent being I knew.

"Charlestown. What's wrong? Did I do something wrong?" I asked with just enough fear in my voice that I came off as cowering.

"Why'd he ask you?"

Dad was probing for something, and it wasn't about the house.

"He came over yesterday, said I wasn't doing anything important, and he needed me to fly his offer to this lawyer in Charlestown, Rhode Island."

"He got that part right. You weren't doing anything important."

Studying for a PhD to help children was more important than anything made at the factory, but to the alpha it was nothing.

"No, sir. That's why I did what he asked."

"Why'd he need you to fly a contract? He could've emailed or faxed it."

This was the flaw in Nik's plan we didn't see. Avie did, and she'd prepped us with an answer. "I asked the same thing. The lawyer handling the sale is a three-hundred-year-old shifter, and he still thinks fountain pens are high tech."

"What was his name?"

Fear bubbled inside me. My answers weren't what the alpha had expected. Had he figured out Nik and I were up to something? I kept my focus on our cover story. "Jensen J. Johnson. The address was on the folder I handed to Nik." Dad frowned. "Was I not supposed to do this?"

"You're a shit liar. You got no poker face at all. It's why I keep you from the casino."

His eyes narrowed, and my heart pogoed in my chest. I'd prepared for a different reaction. "I only did what he asked."

"I know, I believe you. You're too weak to lie."

He only made these kinds of personal attacks when he was stressed. I was right about there being more. "Is there something I can help you with?"

"Oh, look at you. Do one productive thing and you think you can help the pack."

I knew better than to answer his insult. He wanted an excuse to lash out, but I didn't. Instead, I waited for him to tell me or dismiss me.

"Someone's trying to make me look like a fool. They took another kid."

Losing another human child wasn't why he was upset, but I had no idea what had put him in this mood. "Hardly your fault the humans can't protect their own."

The hint of smirk started before he stifled it. "Chancellor Hollen, his high mighty self, called me personally. He's sending his sons back. He thinks they can find who's behind the kidnappings if they examine one more house. Since you have time to fly to Rhode Island for your brother, you can babysit them again."

I raised my hand to protest. He would expect it.

"Stuff it, Conall. You asked if you could help. This is what I need you to do."

He took some of the shine off working with Jan, but I was still grateful. "Yes, sir. When are they arriving?"

"Later today. The chancellor is preparing a strike team in anticipation of finding the kids." He pointed a finger and looked me in the eyes. "If they find anything, anything at all, you make sure to call me immediately. And don't let them go without me. I'm not letting them take credit for being invited here to help."

I wanted to know what made him so angry, but you didn't ask him for information. You provided it when he asked. "I agree. You need to be there. This is gryphon territory."

He sneered, and I wondered if I'd overplayed my hand. "I don't need you to agree, just to do what I tell you."

Our meeting was over, and I needed to leave. "Yes, sir."

"Now go inside and see your mother. She was worried when I couldn't reach you."

Mom deserved an Oscar, but now I was worried about my brother. Dad would take his shit mood out on Nik. I hadn't made it up the stairs before I heard Dad raise his voice.

"Do you think you're the alpha? Conall's mine to order around, not yours."

If that was the reason the alpha was mad, Nik would be fine.

Plus, we'd prepared for my being missed. Nik and I rehearsed our story before I left.

Mom was by the door, listening. She put her finger to her lips and motioned to move around her. She stayed there for another minute, but then I heard Dad's truck start.

"Is Nik going to be okay?" I asked when she left the door.

"He'll be fine. Avelina's plan was much tighter than the one Nik came up with. All those details matter because your father will check."

The alpha was overmatched. Avie handled the day-to-day operations for the world's most effective investigative body. "She could teach the FBI or KGB a few things."

"It's good she's on our side." She put her hands on my cheeks. "You look better. How's Jannick?"

Without his pain, my aura had improved, and I could talk about him without falling apart. "Much better. But what's wrong with Dad? Did Chancellor Hollen chew him out for the missing kid?"

Mom let go of my face. "No. Why would you think that?"

"Jan's father is so angry, he's ready to use the full might of his family to fight the alpha."

Raising her eyebrows, she shook her head. "That wouldn't be a wise move."

The problem with our family was the alpha warped everything. Wilhelm didn't care about logic or politics. He wanted to save his son whatever the cost. "He believes Jan is worth the risk."

"That's just posturing. He won't risk a war between mages and the Assembly."

Mom's instincts were usually right, but she'd been isolated by the alpha for too long. The power Chancellor Hollen wielded was far greater than she believed. "I agree. No one wins if this comes to a fight. But if the chancellor didn't insult him, why is the alpha so mad? I know it's not me flying the contract for Nik."

"Not that he tells me much, but from what I've heard,

someone has started to manufacture harnesses. According to your father, only another gryphon could create them with quality to match ours. Not only are they as good or better, whoever is doing this is making them faster and in greater quantities. He also suspects they're using mages, but he has no proof. Without evidence, the Assembly won't take up his complaint."

Dad's paranoia grew every year. Typical tyrant behavior. "That explains why he wanted me to babysit Jan and the others."

"I think he's going to ask the Mage Council to help him root out the culprits."

So much for the alpha progressive reaching out for help. Not that I ever believed that of him, but I had hoped. "Dad just wants to get in good."

"I wish his intentions were more altruistic, but I fear you're right. But . . ." She wagged a finger in my direction. "Everything comes at a price. The Mage Council's help for your freedom."

Interesting concept, but I wanted a more certain outcome. Jan's idea to fight the alpha in court would allow him to save face by making a deal. "How do we make sure Nik's okay?"

"I'm sure he is, but I can do it without getting either of us caught."

Of course she could, but if he wasn't, I wasn't going to let the alpha hurt my brother or his family. "If he needs help, let me know immediately."

"It won't come to that, but I promise I will."

Mom didn't sound as confident as I'd have liked, but I knew she'd tell me if she was wrong. "Thank you. And with that, I'm going to go rest. All that flying has tired me out."

Mom called bullshit with her look, but at least she didn't voice her doubts.

Chapter Thirty-Three

✥

JANNICK

"Avie, you can't." I was glad we'd stopped at a pit stop. "He's not ready."

I paused before responding for a change. Avie had her reasons, and they weren't cruel. "He's been a big asset. You acknowledged that."

"He has, but he's not ready if this comes to a fight. He'll get hurt or worse."

Leo would be crushed if they pulled him from the mission. He'd worked his ass off. He wouldn't take it well. "Please don't."

"He needs more time in the field before something this dangerous."

I didn't know how to respond. I understood her concern—Leo wasn't battle-tested. But who was at twenty-four? At least this way he'd get some experience. "I'll watch over him. I promise."

"I appreciate your willingness to help him, but you can't protect him if you're leading the mission."

She made a good point, but Leo had earned his spot on the team. "There has to be a compromise."

"Let me appoint a field commander, and I'll let him stay."

"You can't be serious." So much for thinking before I responded.

"Totally. If I'm being honest, you'd benefit from the team I want to send."

Something felt off. She came up with that "solution" too quick. "What's really going on?"

She sighed. My instincts were right. I hated being right sometimes. "Yesterday you were barely functioning, Jan. I'm not saying you're unstable, but you're distracted. The team I want to send is the best. Not only can they teach Leo, they'll keep you both alive."

Despite telling Conall my sister was the most capable being I knew, I meant apart from me—and Bart, but he was a freak. The list of people ahead of her just went down by one. "I'm fine."

"If you weren't fit, I'd have told Dad to remove you. Agent Foggerty is the best field commander on the East Coast, maybe in the whole agency. You might think I'm being cold, but I'm doing what's best to ensure you both come home."

I'd always thought she put work over family, but the last few weeks had upended every notion I had of my older sister. Meeting Conall had forced me to face a few things I had wrong about the family lately. "I understand."

"Listen, I know you're a very good fighter, but you haven't led others on a field mission. It's always been you and Bart taking on the world back-to-back. This is different." She paused. "And no one knows how you'd react if Conall was in trouble. We need a field commander who will be dispassionate when making decisions. Agent Foggerty is that being. She's had almost eighty years of field work."

"I said I agree."

"No, you said you understood."

"True, but I meant I agree with you." If I didn't agree, I'd have continued to argue. "The only problem is my orders come from Dad."

"What did he tell you to do?"

Anyone but Avie—or Bart—and I'd have ignored the question. "If I have the chance, I'm to take someone alive. He wants to interrogate them."

She went silent. I wasn't sure I wanted to know what she was thinking. "Would you be mad if I asked Dad to allow me to put Foggerty in charge? Before you freak out, hear why I'm asking."

The fact she asked my permission before just doing it was a good reason to listen. "Okay. And just because we're getting along so well, I'll even keep an open mind. Or as much of my juvenile mind that isn't obsessed with my mate as I can spare."

"Oh, Jan. We were doing so well." I could hear the amusement in her voice. "Like I said, Foggerty is the best field commander I've ever worked with. If I were going into a situation, I'd defer to her."

I'd already agreed to her proposal, but this shocked me. I didn't think she'd let anyone order her around, maybe not even Dad. "Really? You'd give her control over you?"

"Of how to achieve an objective? Yes. She's that good at real-time processing. No offense, but neither you nor I are that good. Bart, maybe, but that's because he's a freak."

I barked out a laugh and then scanned the rest stop to see if anyone was watching. Thankfully, the place was deserted. "Who are you, and what did you do to my sister Avie."

"I have a sense of humor, Jan. You've never seen it because you liked to push my buttons. And before you say it, I know I have more than a few to push."

Bart was never going to stop saying "I told you" when he learned Avie and I had worked things out. Unfortunately, most of the acrimony had come from me, not my sister.

"Can you let Dad know I agree with you, and then text me

when he gives the thumbs up? Also make sure Foggerty knows that we need somebody alive."

"Will do."

I closed my eyes and took a deep breath. I was going to owe her so much after this mission was over. But there was still one thing I had to do before then; I had to talk to Leo. "Thanks again, Avie. For everything."

"Of course."

She hung up before I could say more. No doubt she wanted to hurry up and take care of what we had discussed, but part of me thought it was just to avoid talking about feelings and stuff.

"Are you two finished talking?" Leo asked. "I'd like to check in before we eat."

I didn't turn around. Instead, I put my phone away and prepared myself. "We need to talk."

"What did she say?"

I pointed toward the car, hoping this conversation wouldn't take too long. "She's appointing a field commander to take charge. And . . ." I held up my hand before he could interrupt. "I need you to stay focused. That means no hooking up tonight."

Leo's muscles twitched and his eyes narrowed. "You're one to talk."

He was calling me out, but he was three weeks too late and yelling at the wrong person. "I'm just the messenger. The order comes from Avie."

"What the fuck, Jan. Why would you toss me under the bus like that?"

I understood why he was hurt. We were wingmen, not father and son. Unfortunately, shit was about to get real, and he needed to grow up. "I didn't tell her anything. *She* wanted to pull you from the mission because you don't have enough experience. You're still on the team, but it comes with conditions."

When we'd pulled out of the rest stop, I glanced over. "I was almost pulled, too. She's afraid I'm not stable enough."

"That's bullshit, Jan. We wouldn't even have this chance if not for your skills."

I loved Leo for his loyalty, but he was making Avie's decision look better by the second. "She's right. I'm not well enough to assume command."

"What happened? Mom said Dad left a meeting and flew off to Rhode Island to see you."

Gripping the steering wheel, I exhaled in a whoosh. The familiar tingle in my nose warned me I needed to get a grip on my emotions. "Finding Conall tore down the walls I put up to deal with my mother's death."

"Conall did that?"

The suggestion Conall was to blame made me want to snap at Leo, but I held it back. This was the kid who'd had my back before he was old enough to understand. "Not him, but the mate bond. You can't love someone when you shield your heart. When we couldn't be together, it amplified the pain.

"Conall felt my despair and it freaked him out. He couldn't help me from Hagerstown and he panicked. That fueled my breakdown, and I got worse every day. Bart called Dad because he was afraid I'd do something stupid. He . . . I was waiting for the riptide to form when Dad showed up."

He sucked air through his teeth. "Shit, Jan."

Telling someone made me realize how close I'd come to succumbing to my grief. "Conall showed up and we're both better. Not good, just better. Avie, however, doesn't want to trust me with command since this all happened just yesterday. Agent Foggerty would be the better choice under optimal circumstances. She has eighty years in the field; we don't have sixty years on the planet."

Leo nodded. "I guess that makes sense."

I hated riding herd on him, but he was twenty-four. Frontal lobe development was a thing and his hadn't finished maturing.

"Listen, I won't tell you what to do tonight, but if you give off the slightest vibe you're tired, Foggerty will bench you."

"It's okay for you to sleep with Conall, but I can't hook up?"

This was Leo being Leo. He probably wasn't even planning to try, he just hated being told what to do. "First, this isn't a test you can recover from if you fail. Our name and money won't save you in a fight. And second, Conall won't be with me tonight. Feel better now?"

"Oh."

Seeing him be so reckless, I wondered if this was how Mom and Dad saw me. If so, I'd never be able to face them again. I wasn't, however, letting Leo do what he wanted. If we found what I expected, we'd probably be in a fight by afternoon. We both needed to be rested and ready.

"When we fought the demon—"

"Is this where you tell me you walked uphill both ways barefoot in the snow?"

Leo and I were too much alike: both smartasses who didn't take things too seriously.

"No. This is where I tell you my stupidity almost cost me my life. If Bart wasn't so amazing, I wouldn't be here."

"What do you mean?"

I had always known Bart was special—different from everyone else—but seeing it in action drove it home. "I thought I'd show up, throw some spells at the demon to help Bart. But what we found was far worse than I expected. If Bart hadn't created a glyph to contain the demon, I would've been the first to die."

"Holy . . . How'd he do that?"

Months later I still didn't understand it, I was simply glad he knew what he was doing. "No idea. The scary part was it was more powerful than even Bart anticipated. Lucky for us, he had a backup plan. Me? I thought I'd run in with my stone out and fire at whatever bad thing was there."

Leo snorted. "I might've done the same thing."

It's what most people would do. Ask Cael—it was his plan we'd followed. "And you would've died too without Bart. Which brings me back to why I brought this up. Bart isn't here, and I'm not near as good as him. No one is."

"Got it." He sat back. "I need to be at my best."

I did, too, and mentally I wasn't one hundred percent yet. "And to be sure we both stay on our game, Avie sent us Agent Foggerty."

"Thanks for not being a dick about this."

It pays to know your audience. "You're welcome. But now for the really bad news," I said, keeping my eyes on the road. "You and I are sharing a room."

"No fucking way."

One downside of our upbringing: we didn't rough it. Ever. Time to rip the Band-Aid off for my little brother. "You're an adult and can pay for your own room if you like."

"You're such a douche nozzle."

I laughed. Such brotherly love. "It has two beds, you little fuckwit."

Leo crossed his arms and looked out the window with a huff. "You better not snore."

Knowing my luck, *he'd* snore and keep me awake. "No promises."

Chapter Thirty-Four

CONALL

Thank God for Avelina Hollen. The alpha had gone straight to Nik's after he left home. He wanted to see the contract and the nasty old bird called the lawyer. Jenson J. Johnson could run circles around Dad and evidently convinced him in short order that the offer was legit, asked if he wanted to make an offer himself, and if not, was he interested in other properties?

The hour it took for that to play out left my stomach tied in a pretzel knot. I'd never expected we'd be sneaking around, trying to hide things from our father. Since he was also our alpha, it was akin to treason.

Except he'd stopped working for the good of the pack a long time ago.

"Conall?"

I searched my room, and then the windows, but they were shut. Had I imagined his voice? "Jan?" I whispered his name in case the alpha was around.

"Not sure if you can hear me, but I'm trying to talk mind-to-mind."

Leave it to a mage to find a way around forced separation.

"*Jan!*"

"*Hot damn! It works.*"

Hearing his voice calmed me immediately. I wanted to hold him and feel him next to me, but this was about as intimate as two people could be. "*How are you doing this?*"

"*My power stone. You touched it. Leo suggested this should work.*"

"*Thank him for me.*"

"*I know I saw you fourteen hours ago, but I miss you.*"

Would it be like this every time we were away from each other? It was crazy how much I missed him. "*Miss you too, babe. How are you?*"

"*Believe it or not, this really helps. I don't feel so alone when I can hear your voice.*"

The sensation filled my soul, pushing into the tiny bits of emptiness I tried to wall off. It was incredible. "*How far away can you do this?*"

"*I'm not sure. In theory, there's no limit, but that's between mages who each have a stone. I think it'll work when I'm home. If not, Bart and Cael can help us make it work.*"

He wasn't back to normal, and he wouldn't be until we completed our bond, but Jan sounded so much more hopeful. "*This is good for me too, babe. If I close my eyes, it feels like you're here with me. This is so much better than a phone call.*"

He didn't say anything, but he was still there. His presence permeated me. It wasn't real, but I could smell his scent, and the way his fingers touched me. "*How long can you keep this open without tiring yourself?*"

"*I don't know, I've never done this before. But keeping the link open isn't taxing.*"

I wanted it to stay open all night, but he needed his strength for whatever happened tomorrow. "*We probably shouldn't push it then.*"

"I'm not. This relieves my anxiety, which improves my energy. I think once we fall asleep one or both of us will sever the link."

Connected to him mind to mind, I felt how true that was. He was vibrant; his core thrummed with positive energy. "*As long as you're sure you aren't draining yourself.*"

"I'm not. I promise if it feels like it's sapping my strength, I'll end the link."

The crushing sadness in his voice was gone. He'd rediscovered the hope he needed, and I planned to help him keep it. "Then I want to fall asleep together."

* * *

I woke feeling like we'd held each other all night. In the back of my thoughts, he was there, and I had a panicked moment. Had we stayed connected all night?

"*Good morning, handsome. I hope I didn't wake you.*"

Jan's energetic, upbeat tone allayed some of my fears, but not all of them. "*Did you keep this open all night?*"

"*No. It shut down at some point. I just got up and at the risk of sounding like an obsessed stalker, I grabbed my stone to see if you were awake.*"

Tossing back the sheets, I indulged in a long stretch. I felt as rested as I had those few days we slept together. "*I don't know if you woke me, but if you did, it wasn't jarring. It felt normal.*"

"*That's good. When will you be here?*"

He was just as eager as me. "*I'm going to jump in the shower and get something to eat. Meet you soon?*"

"*Can I take you to breakfast?*"

Take me? As in use one of his free passes? I chuckled; did he hear that? "*At the hotel?*"

"*I wish we could go somewhere else, but the mission leader is expecting me. I said we would meet her for breakfast. You should join us so you know what's going on.*"

Jan might want me there, but it wasn't to discuss the mission.

"*Are you sure?*"

"*You're part of the team. If you can't make it, I'll link you in mentally.*" The total trust shouldn't have surprised me as much as it did. It wasn't that he trusted me—I'd do the same for him—but how it already felt normal. "*I'll try to get there on time, but don't wait for me to start.*"

"*I'd say we'll wait, but Foggerty is going to start whether I like it or not.*"

It didn't sit well that he wasn't in command this time. He'd done an amazing job the first time.

"*You're bleeding emotions, love. I'm not upset. Foggerty has ten times more experience than I do. I'd be a fool to think I'm better than her.*"

Growing up as the alpha's son, I was taught not to defer to anyone else. "*I'm glad to hear you're practical as well as smoking hot.*"

"*I had good teachers.*"

"*Okay, babe. Let me shower and get moving.*" I was about to end the link, but I held it open a moment longer. "*I love you. Keep that in your heart always. That will never change.*"

"*I love you, too. Now go before I perv on you and stay with you while you shower.*"

Laughing, I closed the link, but not before I wondered what that would feel like.

Chapter Thirty-Five

JANNICK

Tall, athletically built, with short brown hair and incredible gray eyes that took in every detail, Foggerty was exactly the type of leader I'd expected. She could probably kick my ass in a physical fight, but magically I was confident I could take her. Maybe.

The thing that impressed me most was how she *listened* before she made her decisions. I liked her, despite how often we disagreed.

"What do you think, Jan?" Foggerty asked. "I don't understand half of what you did or how you expect this to find a location."

She understood more than half. We'd talk later about my less-than-fragile ego. "This time we got lucky. The house is far enough from the other two that Leo and I should be able to pinpoint the location."

"Yes, but will you both have enough strength to join us?"

Despite how well my sister and I were getting along, I was going to kill her. She must've told Foggerty to protect me. "Commander, I'm the strongest mage you have, by a decent amount.

My combat magic is alpha two. Leo probably has the second highest ranking."

"All true, Jannick, but we are not a team of tenderfoots. I need you to answer me, or I won't permit you to join us."

Conall and Leo both tensed, but I silenced them by raising a hand. This was on me. "My apologies, Commander. I was out of line. We'll need to assess that question when we're done. Having done this before, it *shouldn't* be taxing. Theory and reality, however, don't always see eye to eye."

"Thank you. For both." She smiled and it was as real as any she'd shown since we'd met. "That was a test and you passed. Had you tried to bluster your way through my question, I'd have sat you without a thought. Even though we lack someone of your talent, our training and team cohesion allow us to punch above our weight limit."

Sitting us would be a mistake. The mages who planned these abductions had above-average talent—or at least one of them did. Foggerty would almost certainly need us. "Understood. How do we support your team?"

Look at me, I was adulting again.

"By following orders," she said with a wink. "I'm pairing myself with Leo, and you with Frank. Teams meet after breakfast; we'll talk more once you're familiar with each other."

After fighting the demon, I had a new appreciation for the power of planning and working in tandem. "Thank you. I'm reasonably sure we'll find the kids today, so I'm glad you're here."

"You're welcome. Now, I need you and Leo to walk me through one more time what you did and what you plan to do. I'm not too old to learn something from superior mages."

* * *

Agent Winston—Frank—was less intense and easier to work with, so I finished before Leo. As second in command, he was the good cop to Foggerty's bad. Not that she was bad, she was just absorbed in the mission. Like Avie. Must come from having lives depend on your decisions.

I'd wanted to catch up with Conall, but he stepped out to call his father while the mission partners got to know each other. He hadn't come back by the time I'd finished. Rather than sit and wait anxiously, I headed for my room to make sure I had everything.

"Jannick Pederson?"

I turned toward the voice. Two older males sat in the lobby. When I made eye contact, they stood and approached me. They were an interesting pair. One was a mage of some power. He was a few inches shorter than me. His snow-white hair was cut short and neatly styled to accent his fine-boned features. In his day, he'd have been a total twink. Blue eyes watched me carefully, and I noted his hand strayed near the pocket of his khaki slacks.

Typical mage behavior when heading into the unknown.

The second male had to be a shifter. I couldn't tell for sure, but he reminded me of Conall. I hadn't been good at spotting shifters before he and I met, but now I saw a faint aura of magic. His iron-gray hair framed a strong jaw and wide cheeks. I didn't know if he'd ever been handsome in the classic sense, but he was commanding. His thick body oozed strength that age hadn't diminished.

I resisted the urge to slip my hand into my pocket. In the middle of a hotel lobby, with a strike team in the area, these two weren't here for trouble. "Can I help you?"

"Anso Hollen and my mate, Leifr Cormaic." He held out his hand. "Can we speak to you in private?"

My jaw hung open for a second. Shutting it, I blinked twice. "Um..."

"I told you this would happen," Leifr said. "We should have snuck into his room."

His medieval accent was kinda hot. It sounded Scottish, or

maybe Welsh, but not quite either. I wondered if Conall could talk like that—which, given my guests were staring at me, was entirely inappropriate. "I'd prefer you didn't. Leo might attack you and someone would get hurt."

Anso made a face at his mate. "Stop playing."

If they were legit, and it was a possibility they were the Guardians, I had no idea *how* to verify their identity. Either way, I didn't have time. "Not to be rude, but Anso and Leifr? I'm supposed to accept your word that you're the Eastern Guardians? Nope. Not today. If you'll excuse me, I need to get ready for a meeting."

I turned, but a hand gripped my wrist. Something smooth and cool was placed in my palm. Glancing at Anso first, I looked at the object my fingers now clutched. A brilliant green power stone.

Lifting my gaze, I met his stare. "That is my power stone. Ask it who it belongs to."

Either he was crazy, or he was telling me the truth. No mage willingly handed over their power stone. The man staring back at me didn't look crazy.

I stared into the emerald. *"Who owns this stone?"*

{Anso Hollen.}

I handed it back to its owner. "Let me tell Leo I need five minutes alone in the room."

"Make it ten," Leifr said, his eyes twinkling mischievously. "He won't believe you if you ask for five."

* * *

I didn't see the pair in the common area as I left the dining room. Their behavior made no sense. It was possible the mage changed his stone to give a fake name, but it wasn't something you did just to prank someone.

Checking my watch, I shrugged. Probably better they left. If they were really Anso and Leifr, that didn't bode well for me and

Conall. They were the only known mage gryphon pairing in history. Math wasn't my best subject, but even I could solve that equation.

Time to forget them and focus on the mission. I wanted to find those kids, and I was certain if we could track the mage, we'd find them. I slid the key card into the door and pushed when the light turned green.

"Holy shit!" I dug my stone out and pointed it at the two intruders sitting on my couch. Anso and Leifr looked up. "How did you get in here?"

"You can come up with all manner of useful spells in twelve hundred years," Anso said.

"I pinched your brother's key earlier." Leifr held up the white rectangle of plastic. "You can come up with any number of useful skills in twelve hundred years."

"Holy shit." I was going to kill Leo for being so careless.

"He's fond of that expression," Anso said. "Is someone blessing excrement?"

Leifr flicked him off. "Ignore him. He's still stuck in the ninth century."

My head spun as I tried to make sense of it all. "I need another coffee. Would you like some?"

"I'll make it," Anso said. "We're particular how we like it."

He was up and out of his seat before I could respond—like he was thirty, not twelve hundred and thirty. I plopped down in a chair with a thump. This was unbelievable. A pickpocket and a coffee snob. What next?

"Are you well?" Leifr asked. "You look pale."

Was I? I didn't know anymore. "Fine. Just a bit out of sorts." I glanced up at him quickly. "You *are* a gryphon, right?"

Leifr laughed. "I am. You *are* a mage, right?"

I shook my head apologetically. "That was stupid. Obviously you are, you're Leifr Cormaic . . . Guardian of the Eastern Point."

He raised an eyebrow skeptically and then turned to Anso puttering about in the kitchen making coffee for us both.

"Anso, are you sure he's okay? He sounds confused."

"He's fine. As he said, he has a lot on his mind."

He wasn't wrong. I needed to find out what they wanted and get back to the others. "Maybe we should skip the coffee. Leo will be here in a few minutes."

"Since he's lost his card, that is unlikely," Leifr said.

I laughed. Poor Leo would be embarrassed as fuck in front of Agent Foggerty. "I shouldn't laugh. Commander Foggerty is going to think he's careless."

"A small price to pay, I fear," Anso said, handing me a cup.

Easy for him to say. He hadn't met Foggerty. "Thank you."

Anso set a second cup in front of Leifr. "Your point is still valid. We should talk while I wait for mine to finish."

I took a sip and eyed Leifr. There was nothing weird about sitting across from a twelve-hundred-year-old gryphon who happened to be the Eastern Guardian while his mate made coffee in the tiny kitchenette of the "King Deluxe" suite. Nothing at all. "What did you need to talk to me about?"

"We come with a warning," Leifr said. "You must bond with your mate."

I didn't see that coming. "I'm not sure this is any of your business."

"Surely you understand the significance of our coming to you," Anso said. He sat on the couch next to Leifr.

People in China could see the significance of their visit, but that didn't give them any right to intrude in our personal life. I raised an eyebrow and took another drink. The coffee helped me perk up. More than it should. I picked up the cup and sniffed. "What did you put in this?"

"A pinch of mage mince." Anso pulled a small leather pouch from his pocket. "It's made from roots and herbs and helps restore magical balance. Don't worry, it is harmless, non-addictive, and has no ill side effects, but it will make sure you're at your peak today."

"Thank you? I think." I eyed the cup warily and drank more. "I understand why you're here—you want Conall and me to complete the bond so we can train to take your place."

"Your assessment of why we are here would be on the . . ." Leifr tapped his index finger to his nose.

I laughed. Had to give the old guy credit for lightening the mood. "I haven't seen anyone do that since middle school."

Leifr shrugged. "Why change a good thing?"

Funny or not, I still wasn't going to discuss this with them. "It's still none of your business."

"I felt Conall mate with you, but you haven't completed the bond."

I was mildly irritated. Leifr was acting as if I hadn't told him to butt out already. "That has to be a bitch, if you feel all gryphons when they find their mate."

"Not all of them, just the one who is going to take my place."

Credit for being honest. They were still out of line, and not going to get what they wanted, but I appreciated hearing the truth. "Thanks, but I'm not interested."

"Unfortunately, kid, the world picks who it wants," Anso said. "When Katarina Hollen and Adelais FionnLach created the Great Ward, they tapped the earth power we believe creates mate bonds. It chose the original four pairs of Guardians, and now it is choosing our successors."

Bart and Cael talked about this enough that I knew my chances of refusing were small, but I hadn't even had a chance to spend time with my mate. "If the earth is sentient, tell it to pick someone else."

"Earth power isn't sentient like beings," Leifr said. "It's more akin to instinct in animals, or how some plants know to follow the sun. And like either of those examples, you can't tell it to stop."

The childish part of me wondered if the earth got mad when people pissed on her when they couldn't find the loo. Which just proved Avie was right about me not being the right person to lead the mission. Speaking of which, their time was up. "Got it. If there's nothing else, I have some kids to find."

"This is going well," Leifr said with a frown. "Why am I not surprised one of your descendants is difficult."

"Really, Le? *Your* descendant is an autocratic cabbage head who's destroying the gryphons from within. Why am I not surprised?"

The back and forth amused me at first, but I had kidnappers to catch. I got up and walked to the door. "I have an appointment, so I need to cut this short. Thanks for the chat and coffee, but I need you to leave."

They looked at each other, their arms over their chests, and in unison said, "No."

Leifr struck me as every bit as childish as me, but Anso was totally unexpected. "You can't say I'm difficult when you do that."

"Is this where I say 'I know you are, but what am I?'" Leifr rolled his eyes. "The things aren't mutually exclusive. You're still difficult."

Anso put his hand on his mate's chest. "Enough. This is serious."

Great. Now they were playing good cop/bad cop. "I see you've worked on your routine, but it's not working. I'm still not doing it, and you need to go."

"We didn't plan how to convince you," Anso said. "We expected you'd agree once we explained."

Explained? All they'd done was talk around things and make demands. "Maybe if I knew what you wanted, I could consider it."

"If you two don't bond, the new Ward can't be created." Leifr raised an eyebrow. "Is that clear enough?"

The old guy was gruff and direct, and if he weren't trying to force me to do something I wasn't going to do, we'd probably get along great. "I hope you have a backup plan because we're not completing the bond any time soon."

"But you plan to?" Anso asked.

What was it with these two? "Again, not your business." I checked my watch. "Wow, look at the time. It hasn't been lovely seeing you, please don't stop in again if you're in the area."

"Mature," Leifr grumbled.

I should've just thrown them out, but my snarky side wouldn't let well enough alone. "Is this where I say 'I know you are but what am I?'"

Leifr smirked. "Now you can say you heard it and used it since middle school."

"Two records in ten minutes. Must be a record of some kind."

"If you two are through pretending to be eleven, can we get back to Jannick and Conall mating."

What part of "not your business" led them to think I wanted to talk about this? "We can't get back to it because I never agreed to discuss it with you."

"Surely you of all people understand what will happen if the Ward fails," Anso said.

I shook my head. We were talking in circles. "Unless the Ward is in danger of failing any time soon—and because Bart and I talk every day, I know it's not—I've got to deal with something now. Come see me next week. This time make an appointment instead of breaking and entering."

"Jannick, this is more serious than you realize," Anso said. "Events are happening that have the eight Guardians concerned. Someone, or a group of beings, is focusing their efforts on breaching the Great Ward. It's under constant attack."

"Really?" Sarcasm dripped from the word. "So that demon my brother, his mate, and I fought is a threat to the Great Ward? Who would've thought?"

"I realize I'm part of the problem, but sarcasm isn't helping us," Leifr said. "Anso's point is we may need to act quickly. To address your other question, for good or ill, you and Conall are going to replace us when the new ward is created. I think that makes it our business."

I still didn't agree they had a right to ask about the status of our bond, but at least we'd stopped playing games. "Thank you for answering me directly. The reason we haven't bonded is Conall's father is an asshole. If we mate, he'll use our bond against us. Before we complete the bond, we need to extricate Conall from his father's reach."

"Thank *you* for answering." He gave Anso a told-you-so face. "Not picking a fight is sometimes the easier path."

"One time. One time he helps in a situation like this, and now he's giving me pointers."

Watching them bicker left me wondering if this was my future with Conall. Something to ponder another day. I stood and slapped my thighs. "I really need to get back to work. Besides, you came to the wrong half of this couple. Conall controls if we bond or not. And right now, he's refusing to let it happen."

"Then you must force it," Anso said.

Had he forced their bond on Leifr over his objection? That would explain their love-hate relationship. "You can file that suggestion in the dumpster of nope. I'm not going to force something he doesn't want."

"Let me give you one last bit of information before you kick us out," Anso said. "The bond makes the sum of pairing greater than the individual parts. Being mates makes both of you stronger. And if one of you was in trouble, the other could aid them through your link. At least let me tell you how you can force the bond if he were in trouble and needed your help."

I didn't like the idea of forcing my will on Conall's, but seeing him hurt or dying was worse. I took out my power stone and held it out.

"Send me the information."

Chapter Thirty-Six

CONALL

I'd looked forward to the drive to our destination, but it didn't live up to my hopes. First, we spent twenty minutes putting wards on the cars to avoid detection. I didn't understand it, but anyone more than fifty feet away wouldn't be able to see or hear us. Next, Leo was stewing in the back seat about something to do with his room key, and Jan was quiet. Last, I'm not sure why I built this up in my head. We were driving to another abduction site and then probably—hopefully—saving the children. Those kids would almost surely be guarded by several mages. Neither of those places screamed party time with your mate.

Other than Jan was pensive, I didn't pick up much from our link. He wasn't closed to me, but I didn't get the same level of emotion. The mission consumed him.

Except this didn't feel like anxiety over the mission. We'd ridden together to other sites after I bonded with him, and he hadn't been this focused. Something else was weighing on him.

We were only two days removed from him wanting to drown his sorrow in the ocean. Had it been too soon to thrust him back into work? I didn't know a lot about magic, but I knew he needed to be clear-headed or he wouldn't be effective.

Agent Foggerty had been concerned enough that she'd asked. She might have couched it as "would locating the wizard tire him," but the question was broader in scope. I'd tried to have a private conversation with her when Jan was upstairs, but she and Leo had talked for a while.

"You okay?" Jan asked. "You're quiet."

I smiled and nodded. "I'm thinking about what's going to happen next. You're quiet, too."

"Thinking here, too."

"Me three," Leo said from the back. "I still can't figure how the one and only time I lost my key it had to be when Foggerty was watching."

If only Jan would explain his mood. I didn't want to press him, but it seemed important given what we were going to be facing. I put my hand on his thigh. "Can I help?"

"This is all I need." He smiled and put his hand over mine.

The change was small, but noticeable. Whatever bothered him, it wasn't related to me. I shouldn't have been so relieved. Something was still wrong, and I wanted to help. Maybe if we'd completed our bond it would help, but we hadn't—and couldn't—until things changed.

His skin on mine sent frizzles through me. Would this continue when we were fully mated? In a hundred years? Or was this typical new-to-each-other wonky emotions?

I wanted to believe it would always be like this. Our connection was strong; maybe it would.

When we reached the house, I knew what had Jan in a knot. I chastised myself for not making the connection sooner. A full mate bond shouldn't have been necessary to put his mood together with visiting another family.

"I'm here for you to lean on, babe."

"I know. I'll be okay."

He lied well, but you couldn't lie to a mate bond. The potential for another emotional collapse weighed on him. Even with me there, it was possible.

"I got the parents, Jan," Leo said. "Focus on finding these bastards. If anyone can do it, it's you."

He glanced in the rear-view mirror, and I knew he and Leo made eye contact. "Thanks, Leo. I appreciate it."

"All for one."

They laughed and I joined them. They were a pair. I wished I could have seen the four brothers band together and take on their older sister. Or anyone else. Nik coming through for me gave me a taste of the connection they shared. I might not have realized it, but it was always there. Nik had watched out for me since I was a little kid.

We waited until the three SUVs came to a stop. Jan was first out and went to the passenger window to speak to Agent Foggerty.

"With your permission, I'd like for just the three of us to go inside," Jan said. "The parents are already upset. The more we bring in, the harder it will be for them."

"I would like to send Agent Winston with you, if you think it won't be too much."

Jan didn't want the inquisitor, but he stifled the emotion. "I think that will be fine."

Not being in charge was a struggle for Jan. As much as he respected Foggerty, he wasn't used to being told what to do by someone not of his family. It made me proud of him for doing the right thing instead of what he wanted.

The parents of the latest victim were divorced, and they hadn't noticed their daughter was gone for almost two days. They shared custody, and each had worked a late shift on Monday. Given the hour, they'd assumed she was with the other parent.

Jan's anxiety increased with each step. Leo took point with Agent Winston on his tail. The door opened before we knocked, and the anxious parents—who'd set aside their issues to work together—greeted us.

Leo and Winston talked to them while Jan led me down the hallway the father indicated to the girl's room. Stuffed animals sat arranged perfectly on the bed, and the walls had the expected tween posters. We stood at the door, as if going in would disturb important evidence.

"The magic here is more like the first houses," Jan said. "But now that I know what to look for, I can see what they were trying to hide."

I understood only a little of what he'd said, but he sounded confident. "Does that mean it will lead us to the children?"

"Maybe? The spell tracks the mage, not the kids." He looked away from the girl's room. "And there's no guarantee these bits will connect to the other two. Without that, we don't have much."

I had more questions, but everything was speculation until he tried. "I'm sure it will work."

"What's taking Leo so long?" he asked.

Feeling his angst building, I rubbed his back. "Relax. He's dealing with parents who lost their only child. If it helps, we can wait outside."

"Inside or out doesn't matter." He shifted until his back touched my chest. "If this works, we're one step closer to finding the kids. I'm anxious to see what we find."

He might be able to fool others, but these abductions ripped at his soul. Finding these children had become personal. "You're not alone. I'm here. I'll always be here."

He reached back and squeezed my hand. "Thank you for reminding me."

Tension washed away the longer we stayed in contact. It wasn't a perfect calm, but he was better. "Always."

"But I don't want to let this drag out. Whoever is behind this, they're going to act soon."

This time, his concern was just as he said. He was worried we'd be too late. "Why?"

"Twelve is a significant number in many religions. Twelve tribes of Israel, twelve Olympian gods, twelve disciples of Christ, twelve zodiac signs, twelve major demon clans. In theory, the number is irrelevant; there shouldn't be any significance to a number. But you can make anything a foundation of spell casting. Demon worshippers made their most powerful glyphs with twelve points.

"Twelve points, twelve kids, twelve sacrifices, and April twelfth is two days away. I can't prove the date matters, but I don't think it's a coincidence."

Jan was talking faster than usual, but it eased his pent-up anxiety. "Let's hope we learn something that will help."

"I can't say I'm one hundred percent certain, but I'm pretty sure this house will lead us to the mage responsible for the abductions. I've only felt two different mages, and given how hard it is to cast the spells they used, it makes sense. If we're right and this has to do with raising a demon, they won't let the kids out of their sight. That's my theory at least."

He'd obviously thought about this way more than he'd told me. "It's sound logic."

Leo and Agent Winston finished with the parents and made their way toward us.

"You ready?" Leo asked.

Jan squeezed my hand again and released it. "Let's do it."

Chapter Thirty-Seven

JANNICK

The benefit of working with Leo was we were close—we could connect seamlessly to handle complex magic. We weren't as tight as me and Bart, but it was a close second. He protected, while I engaged.

Building on the success of the second house, I knew how to isolate what I needed without fear of destroying the evidence. I quickly got the trackers we needed, and we left the room with minimal disruption.

We combined the marker with the pair we recovered from our last visit, and we triangulated a fixed point. Things moved quickly once we had our answer. Leo promised the parents we'd be in contact while I transferred the location to a map, and Winston updated the field commander on our results.

Back at the cars, all Conall could tell us was our destination was an old farm. He didn't need to spell out how good that would be for hiding twelve kids.

"I need to call the alpha and let him know what we learned," Conall said.

After he'd stepped behind the SUV, I approached Agent Foggerty. "Alpha Arawn is not a pleasant being. He won't be helpful if he tags along."

"I've been briefed, but this is squarely in his territory. He has a right to come with us if nothing else." She watched me closely. "Are you certain your close connection to Conall hasn't biased you against his father?"

I wasn't sure of much where father or son were concerned, but Aodhan Arawn *was* an asshole. "I'll admit to being biased, but he was difficult to deal with before Conall and I realized we were mates."

"I'll tell them," Conall said as he rounded the SUV. I didn't need to hear what he was going to say to know my response would be a not-so-polite, "Fuck no."

"The alpha said we're to stay here until he arrives. He will accompany us to the location."

The *alpha* could go fuck himself with his orders. "Not happening," I said, loud enough for Aodhan to hear me. "*Tell him* he can meet us somewhere along the way to the farm or go right to the location."

Aodhan started yelling so loud Conall had to hold the phone away from his ear. I motioned for it. "I'll tell him myself."

"No, Jannick," Agent Foggerty said. "I'll take care of this."

She motioned and Conall nodded. "Dad? The mission leader, Agent Foggerty, would like to speak to you." He handed her the phone without listening to his dad's response.

As much as I wanted to light up Aodhan from nape to toes, Foggerty probably had a better chance of swaying Conall's father. God knows he would never listen to me.

"Alpha Arawn? This is Colonel Foggerty of the Mage Inquisitors."

I didn't know she was a colonel. That was one step below a director, which made sense given all her time in the division.

"Absolutely sir," Foggerty said. "However, these are human

children. The treaties clearly spell out who has jurisdiction if their people are wronged."

She wasn't amused but she fake-smiled into the phone.

"I understand this is your territory, but the law clearly gives the Council the authority to track down human children."

"Your father is never going to win," I whispered.

"If he'd shut up and stop always trying to be right, he might have achieved something lasting for our pack," Conall said. "Instead, he's going to make a new enemy."

"That's a very interesting position," Foggerty said without any deference, "but we're going to do what we came to do. You can file a formal complaint with the Council. I look forward to answering questions for the review committee in six or seven months."

She listened and her smile grew. "Let me ask." She tapped a button on the phone.

"Your father wishes to know where a good place would be to meet the convoy. He said to tell you he is at the factory."

"Tell him Miller's Farm. That's about the same distance for each of us to travel."

Reconnecting the call, Foggerty stepped away. "I have a location for you, Alpha. Your son said to meet us at Miller's Farm. We should arrive about the same time."

* * *

I let Conall drive so I could focus on our destination. Once I'd made the connection, it stayed with me, and I could tell we were getting closer. Foggerty wanted us to work in pairs the moment we arrived, so Leo switched to her SUV and Winston came with me and Conall.

Conall was more stressed than me. Whatever his father had said after Agent Foggerty gave him back his phone had upset him. There wasn't any privacy, so he couldn't tell me. I could've used magic to keep the conversation private, but that would've sapped my strength. Not a lot, but heading into a potentially fierce fight, I needed to conserve my energy.

The drive also gave me time to think. I'd decided that once this mission was over, I would try to convince Conall to let me complete the bond. Foggerty telling Aodhan to file a complaint opened my eyes to the right solution. Conall could leave his pack once we mated. His father would file a formal complaint with the Assembly and the Council, but it would be years before either would get around to hearing that complaint. More, if Dad successfully delayed the hearing.

By the time the complaint was heard, we'd have been mates for long enough that we could petition to have Conall formally removed from the pack. Docketing our request would take more time to be heard, giving us more evidence to present in support of our petition.

If all that failed, my final ace would be for Conall to challenge his father. Leifr and Anso said our mate bond would give Conall greater strength. More than enough to defeat his father and take over the pack.

No matter what happened, we'd be together long enough to ensure the result we wanted. Provided I stayed focused and didn't get myself killed in this raid.

We pulled up to Miller's Farm and Aodhan had brought a small army. If he thought a show of force was going to cower us, he was more of a fool than I thought. Any one of us could incinerate the whole lot of them. The question was, did we want to set off that level of animosity this close to finding the children?

I stayed in the car while Conall got out to introduce Colonel Foggerty to the alpha. It required a lot of willpower not to confront the pompous asshat. Oddly, he had less animosity toward Colonel Foggerty than to me. Our authority derived from the same source—the mage chancellor—and without a doubt, my report would reach the chancellor's desk much quicker than hers.

"He's an interesting being," Winston said. "He likes to live dangerously."

Winston's description of him was a lot kinder than I'd use. "That's one way to refer to him."

"That's your mate's father, correct?"

Behind my shades, I watched Aodhan glance in my direction every few sentences. "Sadly, yes."

Leo and I had sealed the car, so he couldn't hear me. Seeing my lips move without hearing what I said probably frustrated the hell out of him. Good.

"If he doesn't like you, I'd keep my wards up around him. He doesn't have a great reputation in the shifter community."

I'd kept them up since our first meeting had gone so well. "I don't plan to be around him without all my protections in place."

The meeting broke up, but Conall said something to Foggerty and she followed him back to our car. In a surprise move, she opened the back door and sat next to Winston.

"That was pleasant. No offense, Conall, but I feel like I need a shower after speaking to your alpha."

"I wish I could say I didn't understand." Conall heaved in a breath. "In case you hadn't noticed, he's on edge over this whole incident."

"I did." She was a mage of few words.

"My father thinks another gryphon, or a group of them, are plotting against him. He thinks the missing kids are connected. Basically, the family business is manufacturing harnesses and other accessories for gryphons. It requires gryphons to make them accurately. Someone is making better quality ones faster than we can. Ours are very good, so someone who knows the trade is working against him."

"I don't see the connection," Foggerty said.

"Our family has been making these for two centuries, almost as long as he's been alpha. Undercutting the family's finances weakens the pack, in his mind at least. He's also convinced the only way they can make superior goods faster than him is by using magic. Magic is being used to abduct the kids. The fact these are all happening in our territory is, in his mind, meant to embarrass him. Taken together, he sees it as a prelude to someone challenging him for the position of pack alpha.

"I'm telling you this because he's coming with us for his own reasons. He's going to be hunting for traitors. You can't count on his gryphons to help you."

"Do you think they will oppose us?" Foggerty asked.

"Maybe. If what you do conflicts with his agenda, then yes. Everything revolves around him."

Not that I was Aodhan's biggest fan, but he might be right. "Avie and I discussed these kidnappings. She thinks it could be related to the incident at Utrecht last October. If someone wanted to raise a demon away from prying eyes, helping someone become alpha would be a very good carrot to dangle in exchange for local assistance."

The car was silent for almost a minute. "Thank you for sharing this information. We should proceed as planned. Make sure the team extends our cloaking spell to include the alpha and his cars."

"Understood, Commander." Winston practically saluted before she got out of the car.

Chapter Thirty-Eight

CONALL

We stopped at the entrance to the farm and in the rearview mirror I saw Dad jump out of the car.

"We have trouble," I said. "Dad's got a red-hot iron up his ass."

"What fucking game are you playing?" he shouted as he walked up to the passenger side of our car. Yanking on the front passenger door handle, he staggered back when it didn't open.

"Agent Winston," Jan shouted. "Someone needs to get that asshole out of my face, or I'll do it myself."

Jan had his stone out and it pulsed. When Dad stormed toward us again, he slammed to a stop two feet from the car. He pushed in vain against the invisible barrier. Jan used the space to exit the car.

"You want me? Come and get me." He raised his stone and Dad had the smarts to step back. Winston grabbed Jan's arm.

"Stand down, Pederson."

From what I knew about magic and mages, Jan could easily

have repulsed Winston's hand. He was mad, but not beyond reasoning with.

"What is the meaning of this?" Foggerty had her stone out, and it was glowing a fiery orange. She glared pointedly at Jan.

"Ask him." He nodded toward Dad with his chin. "He stormed up screaming obscenities and tried to rip my door open."

"Alpha Arawn, what were you thinking? I command the mission, but if you pick a fight with the chancellor's son, I have no authority to intervene."

"I'm not afraid of that weak little human."

"Then you are a fool, because you should be very afraid right now." Her words hit Dad and he flinched.

Foggerty stood still as the other gryphons surrounded Dad. Twelve inquisitors plus Jan and Leo would make quick work of fifteen gryphons.

"Are you playing a game?" Dad asked with spittle coming from his lips.

"If you would explain the basis of your anger maybe we could have a civil conversation." She crossed her arms over her chest, but her stone was still visible.

"This is my son Braylen's farm!"

"Oh shit," I muttered.

"Then you really have a problem, don't you Aodhan?" Jan's snarky voice only egged Dad on. Which might have been his goal.

"Enough." Foggerty shot Jan a withering look that had no effect.

"No, not even close," Jan said. "He has no authority over me, and I refuse to let this third-rate bully try to intimidate me."

Dad snarled, but it was pointless. Jan could destroy him with a thought. Ignoring everyone, Jan pointed toward the farm. "That is where the missing kids are. If your son owns this property, he's knee-deep in this shit."

Braylen being involved made total sense. Dad had played him off Kelton for years, but it was always a false hope. Who better to undercut Dad than his own son? The son he thought was a loyal soldier? Mom said Braylen had tried to blame the Mage Council. Clearly, he'd been trying to send Dad down an empty mineshaft.

"I'm going to get to the bottom of this," Dad said. He pointed to the others and headed for the house.

Three steps in, he collided with another invisible wall. He spun around, talons out. "I will gut you for that."

Foggerty stepped forward and her stone flashed in her right hand. "*I* stopped you. This is a Mage Council investigation. You will not interfere."

Dad's eyes bulged. "You dare? This is *my* property. I forbid you to enter."

"Then you're going to be disappointed when we do exactly that." The mages all paired off, with Leo coming to her left side. "If you wish to come along, you may, but I'll not let you jeopardize the lives of those children."

"This is—"

"An official inquisitor investigation," Foggerty said. "If you persist in interfering, I'll restrain you as a probable suspect."

"What?"

"Your son's property? You want to storm in and leave us outside? Why? So you can warn your offspring? No, Alpha Arawn, you will not compromise this raid. Am I clear?"

"There are at least a dozen mages in there," Leo said.

Everyone looked his way. "How can you tell?" Foggerty asked.

Leo shrugged. "It's one of my weird talents. Some people have an ear for sounds or an eye for details. I feel the unique signature a mage leaves when they work their power. There are at least twelve who've been active recently."

"Alpha?" Joe Davis, one of the pack's most loyal betas, stepped closer. "It would be wise to let them deal with their own first. If there are any gryphons involved, we can deal with them once the mages are neutralized."

The voice of reason in a tense storm. He'd be a good beta for someone other than Dad.

It wasn't like he had a choice. Foggerty wouldn't let him go ahead and if he balked, it was clear the mages had the power to restrain him.

"I don't mean to interrupt, but does your cloaking spell hide us while we're out here having this big snarl fest, or is it going to warn everyone we're here?" Jan asked. "Because if not, we need to charge in now, before they have a chance to prepare, retreat, or worse—kill the children."

"We extended it out from the cars when we arrived," Winston said. "But Pederson is correct, the longer we sit here talking the more chance we have of being detected."

Dad was never going to submit to these mages. None of them knew him like I did, but inserting myself in the conversation was dangerous. "May I suggest something, Commander."

Dad shot me a nasty look. No doubt because I was addressing her and not him. When Foggerty nodded, I continued. "The alpha has every right to show up at his son's farm. If he and I and two others go first, Braylen may not suspect there's more. It'll allow us to get closer and keep them off guard. We can take his car, that way it'll appear like we're here for a regular visit."

Dad's scowl turned into an almost smile. Nothing like getting him what he wanted to make him happy.

"Your idea has merit, but what reason will you give him for the visit?" Foggerty asked.

I glanced at my father first this time, and he nodded at me. "The alpha could tell Braylen he wants me to work on his farm since I'm not working at the factory."

It was a dangerous game. I'd just planted a seed in Dad's head he might use after this was over. I couldn't worry about later, and Dad was smiling. It totally fit his personality, and he wouldn't have to fake it much to convince Braylen he was serious.

"I like it," Dad said. "You can follow in your hidden cars and prove or disprove your allegation."

The mages remained silent until Winston nodded. "I agree, Commander. The alpha's suggestion should be followed."

I should have been miffed they gave Dad credit for my idea, but they'd clearly studied psychology and knew who needed to be praised.

"It was your idea," Jan said.

I stifled a laugh. *"True, but he needs to take credit to save face."*

"He's not improving his standing in my eyes." Jan laughed in my head. *"That's a great suggestion. It also helps us because we don't have to cloak you four to get you close."*

Jan's praise meant more than anyone else's. I wanted a hug, but now was not the right time. *"I love you, so be careful."*

"Love you, too," he said.

Dad motioned sharply to get in his car. I wondered if he'd round on me for speaking out of turn; he'd have an audience, so I braced for it.

Beta Davis got in the driver seat, and I took the back seat with one of Dad's toadies. We'd barely shut the door when Dad turned in his seat.

"Good job putting that college degree to good use. I'm glad you put the pack first."

Even when he tried to compliment me, he couldn't hold in the insult. "Yes, sir. That's what you taught us since we were born."

"Glad to see one of my sons learned that lesson."

We drove toward the main house, and I checked out Bray's land. It looked like he raised horses and cattle. Neither were in the pen or pasture.

"You don't think Braylen is behind this, do you?" Davis asked.

If he didn't, he was a bigger fool than I expected. Of his five sons, Braylen was the most like Dad. He was hands down the most likely to plot to overthrow him.

"That's what we're going to find out."

His refusal to say he didn't suspect Bray was telling. Bray was easily his favorite, but that didn't mean he'd bare his neck to his son.

"That barn's new," Dad said. "So's that second bunkhouse."

A perfect place to house twelve kids and almost as many mages. Davis stopped the car between the house and the barn, and we all got out. The kitchen door swung open, and Bray trotted down the stairs. Two big guys stood on the landing, their eyes following Bray as he jogged to meet us.

"Dad?" Bray kept a wary distance. "What are you and Conall doing here?"

"Made some major improvements I see." He glanced in the direction of the barn. "Expecting to bring in a big herd this season?"

"Hopefully," Bray said. "I had the contractor here to build a new bunkhouse, so I asked him to do the barn as well."

"It's empty right now?" Dad thought he could read everyone's mind and was testing Bray.

"Um . . . mostly, yeah."

Even I could tell that wasn't a topic Bray wanted to discuss.

"Can I see the inside?" He didn't wait for an answer before heading toward the barn.

"Dad, wait." Bray ran to get ahead of us. "Why are you here? It's certainly not to see my new barn."

"In time, boy. In time."

"What is he doing?" Jan asked. *"He's leading them right to us."*

"Dad?" He turned to face me before I could find the right way to tell him without giving Jan and the others away. "You have that meeting with Foggerty and Winston soon. Maybe we should tell Bray why we're here."

The forced scowl meant he got my point. "You're probably right." He turned and headed back toward the main house. "I want to leave Conall here to work on your farm. He's spending too much time reading books and studying for a worthless degree."

"Here?" He shook his head. "I don't need any more help."

"I didn't ask you, did I? For the good of the pack, Conall works here until further notice."

"That's not going to—"

The door to the barn blew off its hinges and the inquisitors became visible. Energy flew around the open area, and Dad's jaw tightened.

"You were distracting me?" Bray stared a hole through Dad. "You worthless excuse for a being."

His talons replaced his fingers and he swiped at Dad's midsection. Clutching his wound, Dad barely had time to open his mouth and scream before Bray struck again. This time he swiped with his left hand and tore half of Dad's face off.

The body dropped before my stomach revolted. Shots rang out from the house. Davis was killed mid shift and the other goon who I didn't know fell next. If Bray hadn't been between me and the house, I'd have been next.

"You got a choice, baby bro. Serve me or die." His sneer had a darker feel than any of Dad's.

Bray took a step to the side, and I dropped to the ground to avoid being a target. A second later the front of the house exploded, and my brother joined me on the ground.

"Get out of here!" Jan screamed into my head. *"There're more in the house."*

I turned; Jan still had his stone pointed at the house. Swinging it toward Bray, he was hit by a blow that rocked his wards.

Bray looked over my head and his eyes narrowed. I spared a glance—the rest of Dad's entourage had shifted and were charging our way.

"I can't believe you chose him over me," Bray said. "I'll kill you, too."

My clothes shredded as I shifted a half second before my brother. I roared in anger and defiance. *"You're welcome to try."* Bray squawked in contempt. He was bigger than me and could easily take me out on the ground. I remembered my training with Nik and swept dirt into his face with a flap of my wings. Using the moment that bought me, I launched myself skyward where my smaller frame gave me an agility advantage.

"Run, little coward. I'll find you."

A lifetime of ignoring my father's taunts served me well. I focused on an attack plan instead of responding. Gaining altitude, I circled back as Bray flapped after me.

Below us, a dozen gryphons rushed out the back of the house. They charged the ones loyal to Dad, leaving me and Bray to settle this ourselves.

Despite his furious attempts to catch me, I increased my distance from him. I knew he thought I was fleeing, so I planned to use his overconfidence to my advantage. When I'd gained enough height, I executed a tight turn, tucked my wings, and extended my talons. I was rewarded by a hitch in his flight.

Now I'd gained the air above, his options were few. He struggled with his next move as I bore down on his head. At the last second, he dipped his beak and began a dive. He was a second too late.

My talons tore into flesh, etching deep gashes in his back and hindquarter. He roared in pain and anger.

Snapping my wings out, I caught the draft and soared up. Pumping hard, I put distance between us.

"I'll kill you!" His scream exploded in my head. *"I'm going to make you suffer, you little shit."*

Knowing it would fuel his rage, I refused to engage him. An angry gryphon made mistakes.

Bray circled and his wings beat hard and fast. His efforts were powered by anger and adrenaline. I twisted once, hoping to shake him, but it only bought me a second. I swooped up and he matched my move.

"*You got lucky that first attack. I won't underestimate you again.*"

My considerable lead slowly narrowed. Banking left, I earned a second, but he quickly came after me. Fear pooled in my chest. I couldn't shake him. I was about to try a series of twists when my body exploded with energy.

My core thrummed and I felt Jan's energy flow into me as he forced our bond. He gave me his strength. Propelled by a burst of speed, I twisted left, dropped down, and circled under my brother. My wings pumped furiously, and I moved faster than I thought possible. He'd barely reacted to the first move, and I was executing a third turn.

I climbed, until I was above and behind him. Bray didn't see me until after I'd begun my attack. Gryphon bloodlust took over and I sank my talons into his neck. I maintained my grip until I felt his body go limp, then I released him. If my attack hadn't killed him, the fall would.

Moving in a tight circle, I followed his body down until it crashed in the field to the right of the driveway. The few remaining gryphons loyal to Bray disengaged from the fight and flew away. The next alpha would need to track them down. You didn't leave traitors in your midst.

Flying over the field, I searched for Jan. Mage duels raged in the space between the barn and the house. Foggerty's team appeared to hold the upper hand, but I didn't pay too close attention. I needed to locate Jan. I found him and Winston fighting a trio of mages, but my relief quickly turned to fear. His inner glow had dulled. My fear turned to horror when I realized I caused his condition.

He'd given me too much of his power. I needed to give it back, but I wasn't sure how. Flying lower, I remembered how my core had hummed when Jan gave me his strength.

I focused on our link; the connection was stronger now. Jan

struggled to maintain his defenses, and his determined refusal to yield wouldn't last long. Without help, he'd be overwhelmed, but the other inquisitors still engaged a superior number of enemy mages.

I didn't know how transferring energy worked, but I pushed my will into our link like I was talking to Jan. The extra jolt I'd received from him faded, and his glow increased. Shoving again, I sent more energy to my mate.

The effect was immediate. I felt his renewed hope as he focused his stone on the enemy.

My vision blurred. I felt wobbly. Flying became almost impossible; my wings refused to move fast enough to create lift. I extended them as wide as I could but my attempt to slow my approach failed and the ground rushed up to meet me.

Pride and love for my mate filled me as the world went black.

Chapter Thirty-Nine

JANNICK

I'd given Conall too much of my energy. He'd have died without it, but now I needed it back. There were more mages than we expected. The strongest of the group must have felt my power and he and two others attacked me and Winston. They were good, but not nearly good enough.

I'd set them up for a killing strike, but then Conall needed me. Our advantage quickly turned into a deficit as they easily withstood my depleted attacks.

I switched to defending us, but Winston didn't have the firepower to take them out. Worse, even my defenses were failing. Unless Conall returned some of my energy, my wards wouldn't last much longer.

Digging deep, I willed myself to hold on long enough for one of the other pairs to come to our aid. The enemy unleashed a new assault, and I knew I wouldn't survive.

But I could save Winston.

He didn't deserve to die because I prioritized Conall's life over his. I tethered my life force to my stone and unlocked a life ward.

It would last until it drained every erg of energy from my body. By that point, someone would be free to help Winston.

I turned to tell him what I'd done, and a surge of energy left me pulsing with power. *Conall.* A second burst followed, and I had the strength to use my deadliest spells.

Aiming my stone at the strongest of the three, I fired a massive strike. The smarmy asshole, who'd smirked a second ago, looked like someone had walked over his grave. My attack rattled his wards. The wide eyes and shaking hand mirrored the wobbly defenses he had left. I fired again and my blast swept away his flimsy protection.

He was dead before I could turn on the other two.

"I'm not sure what just happened, but I'm glad you're back," Winston said.

Flattening the second mage with a brilliant ball of blue energy, I saw the terror on the last mage's face. "Let me try to capture him."

"Can you do it safely?"

Not for our enemy. My blow would either leave him shaken or dead. "I'm going to break his shield. If that doesn't kill him, stun him when he's defenseless."

"Copy."

I used what I hoped would be a non-lethal pulsing, concussive shock wave. The hard part was ending the attack before the energy struck the defenseless mage. "He's buckling," I whispered.

Upping the force a fraction, I sent a last wave. Hopefully it would be dissipated when it shattered the mage's protective sphere.

"Now!"

Winston sent a stasis spell the moment the mage's ward failed. Our foe seemed to collapse inward and slowly toppled over.

"Yes!" I shouted, pumping my fist.

Winston attacked the three mages fighting with Foggerty and Leo, and they quickly dropped their stones in a sign of submission. A cascade of surrenders followed and a minute later, we had twelve captives.

My adrenaline faded, and I searched for Conall through our link. When I couldn't raise him, I froze. I had violated his trust by forcing our bond. Had he shut me out?

I searched frantically and saw his body splayed on the ground. Three gryphons shifted and ran to his side.

"Stop!" I shouted. With my stone extended, I ran toward them. "I'll incinerate the first being who touches him."

"He's the alpha's son. He's hurt."

I reached Conall's body and shifted my stone from one gryphon to the other. "How do I know you're not with his brother?"

Winston appeared at my left elbow. "They're with us. The tall blond one is the other beta who came with Aodhan." I turned and Winston nodded. "I promise you, they're with us."

Lowering my stone, I knelt next to my mate. His chest moved and his breath, though soft, moved the dirt near his nose. I swallowed my worst fear and examined him.

"Is anyone here a healer?" Winston asked.

"I'm not a full healer," a dark-haired older gryphon said. "But I can heal minor scrapes and cuts."

Did he think this was a minor injury? Conall was unconscious, barely breathing. "I don't see any sign of injury."

"There's no blood on the ground," the beta said. "He shouldn't be down."

I turned to the healer, who shook his head. "I can't find any sign of injury. It feels like his life is draining away."

I choked back a sob. Conall needed me to be strong, not fall apart and fail him. Touching his face, I severed our link and glanced at the healer. He had his hands on Conall's side, just below his heart.

"Whatever you did, it helped, but he's still slipping away."

I wanted to scream in rage. I knew what had happened, but

not how to undo the damage. Following Anso's directions, I reached out to Conall and found our mate bond. It was faint, like Conall's life force. Bile burned my throat and my chest hurt from the pounding of my heart. If I messed this up, I'd kill him.

Imagining myself outside the door to his soul, I put my shoulder against the barrier in my way and pushed. It opened a crack and I imagined my foot wedged in to keep it from closing. Instead of pushing everything into him at once, I sent a tendril through the opening. Something tugged and I let it pull energy from me into him.

"He's stabilizing," the healer said.

The demand from Conall increased, but I kept the flow steady. Until the door opened wider, I couldn't send more than this tiny stream. Too much too fast might destroy his organs. He needed to stay with me until I could restore his balance.

"Conall? Stay with me, babe. We've got a lot of living to do."

The gap inched further apart, and I doubled the amount I sent him.

"That's it, babe. Take back what you gave me."

A door that wasn't there before burst open behind me, sucking me backward. I fought against the receding tide, but I was dragged toward oblivion. Staggering under the unyielding pull, I teetered on the edge of a precipice. I clutched at the doorframe and resisted with all my strength.

Like Sisyphus, every time I clawed back an iota, another sharp yank drew me toward the dark maw below. Bracing myself, I struggled to step back from the edge.

"Stay with me, Conall. We're free. I'm never leaving you again."

"His life force grows stronger. It's working."

Easy for him to say. He wasn't one slip away from both of us falling into the abyss.

"Please help me, Conall. I love you so much. Fight for us."

I heaved and my grip weakened. Battling against the relentless pull, I felt my strength failing. *"Conall, please!"*

The door to his soul flung open wide and I was enveloped in a warm, comforting embrace that drew me away from the void. When I glanced back that hole shrank rapidly, until it winked out of existence.

Conall's essence swirled around me, pulling energy from me and then giving it back. The gyrations grew smaller until we were in perfect balance.

I was finally whole, for the first time since Mom died. A calm, peaceful feeling descended and the turmoil I kept locked away melted before the brilliance of our bond.

When I opened my eyes, I was staring into Conall's amber raptor eyes. *"That's twice you saved me today."* In my mind, Conall was smiling. *"I love you, babe."*

The wave of giddy relief surged through me, and I leaned forward to hug him. *"Let's never have a third?"*

"Sounds like a plan." He lurched unsteadily to his paws and talons. Steadying himself, he pulled his wings back and rose on his hind paws. Magic blurred the transformation, and a second later Conall stood naked on the hard dirt. "Hey, babe."

His thin smile seemed to take all his energy. I rushed forward and grabbed him before he fell. The gryphon beta steadied him on the other side.

"Let's get him inside," I said.

Before we moved, someone ran from the bunkhouse in our direction. The inquisitor's sprint had her in front of me in seconds. Beads of sweat glistened on her dark skin, and her deep purple power stone hummed with energy.

"Special Agent Pederson. Commander Foggerty needs your help." She gulped air and added, "We found the children. All twelve are alive."

There was so much to unpack in those four sentences. When did I become a special agent? Foggerty admitted she needed my help? Someone needed to record that. The children were alive;

that made everything worth it. Especially now that Conall and I were fully bonded.

"Let her know I'll be there when I can. My mate requires my help right now." I could get used to that word, especially when it applied to the hot being letting me hold him.

"This was an order from the commander," the agent said.

I wasn't a special agent and now that the kids were safe, my job was finished. Avie might have something to say about that, but I didn't care. Conall's needs and mine took priority. "My part of the mission is over; I'm not Foggerty's to command. See if Leo can help her."

She opened her mouth, but I set my jaw and shook my head. Snapping her jaw shut, she looked to Winston. I readied my rejection of his recommendation to do as asked.

"My three associates and I will personally guard your mate until you return," Winston said. "As you pointed out, you're the best mage by a lot."

He smirked and I liked him even more. I still wasn't going, but that was nothing to do with him. "Leo's almost as good."

"Maybe better," Leo said with a shrug. "You don't know."

I pointed to my brother. "See? He's better than me."

"You should go," Conall said. "I'll be fine."

"I will personally guard him," the beta said.

If that was supposed to comfort me, it missed the mark by miles. These were Aodhan's hand-picked associates. The alpha was dead, and as the gryphon who killed the alpha's killer, Conall was the inside favorite to be the next alpha. That he had no interest in the position didn't matter. To the pretenders who would be vying for a chance to be the next bull of the woods, Conall was a threat.

"I trust Beta Olson, and Agent Winston and his teammates can handle a few angry gryphons. I'll be fine."

I wanted something a lot more positive than fine, but I couldn't be with him every second of every day. Leaning in, I kissed him on the lips. It was a prelude to what I had planned once I was sure he was up to it.

"Thank you," I said to Winston. "I appreciate it."

"Thank you for today. You were every bit as good as advertised."

He and Beta Olson led Conall toward the house. I turned to Leo. "Okay, Mister 'Better Than Me,' let's see what Colonel Foggerty needs."

The moment I stepped into the newly built dormitory, I knew something was wrong. I blocked the door with my hand to stop Leo and the agent from entering. "Don't. Something's wrong."

"Indeed," Foggerty said. "I triggered the spell. I'm holding it still for now, but you must get the children out. They're held in place by separate glyphs."

That was a big problem. Maybe I could disarm it. Who was I kidding? Bart could do it, but I wasn't him. "What can you tell me?"

"The children first. Then we can talk."

I swept the room for other trigger points and didn't see any. Leo and I disrupted the glyphs holding the children, woke them, and sent them to the agent at the door.

When the last kid made it out, I turned to Foggerty. "What happened?"

"In my zeal to free the children, I didn't do a complete search."

My initial reaction was to point out that she was supposed to be the best field commander, but everyone makes mistakes. The more pressing issue was how did we fix this without Foggerty dying or worse, summoning a demon.

"Any ideas?" I asked Leo.

His eyes opened wider and he shook his head in tight, short movements. "I was kidding about being better than you."

He was scared and he should be. If this went belly up, we were in deep shit. "I know you were. Any ideas anyway?"

"Call for help?" he said. "Didn't Bart write something about glyphs that won some award?"

I nodded. He'd had me proofread it before he submitted it for editing. I probably wouldn't have skimmed it if he hadn't asked for my help. It was a brilliant piece. Unfortunately, he wasn't here. Hopefully he didn't need to be physically present to help. "See if Bart's available. If not, call Avie."

Leo pulled out his phone and I pushed it down. "Use your stone."

"Oh, right." He blushed.

Pointing toward the door, I motioned for him to leave. I wanted to speak to Foggerty alone. "Link us all together when you reach him."

Once Leo left, I made eye contact with Foggerty. Her breathing was shorter and the muscles in her face were tight. She hid most of it, but she was afraid. "What can you tell me about the spell?"

I only half listened as she explained things I could observe for myself. There were twelve points, one for each of the smaller glyphs under the children. The larger spell was an elaborate array of several different elements. I wasn't an expert, but the smaller glyphs were meant to contain whatever the larger spell summoned.

"Should I stop?" Foggerty asked. "You seem to be deep in thought."

Busted, but she'd probably done the same thing countless times. "I'm trying to confirm your observations in real time. How hard is it to hold the spell dormant?"

"It's not. I have no proof, but I believe the plan was for someone to stand where I am as the main sacrifice before they killed the children to summon lesser demons to serve the main one."

I could see why she said that, but I didn't agree. "That's too obvious an explanation. And not necessary. The twelve points are significant. Look at how they're arranged. This is a rectangular room, but they organized the children in a circle. They also didn't need to create different glyphs to hold each child."

"Then what is the purpose of this elaborate design?"

"I'm not sure, but it appears to be one of two possibilities. The first is once they summoned the demon, they'd use the kids as bait. Each child the demon consumed would feed the prison, not the demon."

"You must see something I don't."

Did I? Since I met Conall, I saw magic differently. If he wasn't so tired, I'd ask him to help. "The key is the glyphs under the children. If their purpose was to summon new demons, they could use the same pattern. It would be easier and more effective.

"Plus, they're all linked to the main drawing. I'm speculating of course, but the different spells would work together to contain the demon. Those twelve glyphs gain power over the demon when it consumes the sacrifices. That's why the mage linked the children to their glyphs."

"That's a fascinating theory." She stared at a smaller glyph a few seconds longer. "You said you had two ideas?"

I wished I didn't, but I couldn't ignore the threat. "It's worse than the first."

Chapter Forty

CONALL

Winston and his inquisitors stayed close with their stones out. Olson wasn't happy, but for some reason he didn't try to force the issue. Instead, he went to find me something to wear. Braylen's clothes were big on me, but it was better than strutting around naked. Only one being got to see that now.

"Conall, may I speak to you?" Olson asked once I was dressed. He eyed the inquisitors standing on either side. "Alone."

I felt Winston edge closer, but I put my hand out to stop him. Olson wasn't one of the sadistic fuckers who did whatever Dad said with a smile and a giddy spring in his step. Yes, he supported Dad, but outwardly so did Nik and Warin.

"Is this pack business?" I asked, hoping he was smart enough to say yes.

"It is."

I held his gaze, looking for any sign of deception. Unfortunately, I wasn't great at reading people. Dad thought he was good at it, but people totally played him. Like Bray had.

"Agent Winston, can you give us a moment, please? Beta

Olson has known me since I was born. He was loyal to my father and not Braylen. I'm in no danger."

I didn't turn away, still checking for some hint he'd lied to me. There was concern, sadness, and a hint of shock. In the background, Winston and the others left the room.

"Thank you for trusting me," Olson said.

This wasn't the conversation I'd expected. He was the beta of the pack—I owed him my loyalty, at least in public. "You don't need to thank me, Beta. I serve you and the pack."

His brow furrowed as if I'd said the wrong thing. "You don't know, do you?"

That was ominous. Had I violated some rule Dad never told us about? "Know what?"

"Braylen killed the alpha. He became the new alpha. You killed him minutes later." He bowed his head. "You are the alpha now."

That was never happening. Not only did I not want it, but there'd also be an endless string of challenges. "I didn't challenge Braylen for the title. I killed him for murdering the alpha."

"Whatever your intention, once you bloodied him, he challenged you. You *are* the new alpha."

There wasn't a chance in hell Kelton would accept any solution that didn't end with him being alpha. He'd also be better at instilling order. "I'll relinquish the title to Kelton."

"Permission to speak in confidence, Alpha?"

I raised an eyebrow. That rule hadn't been invoked in decades. You didn't tell Dad something you didn't want repeated. He wouldn't honor the rule if he could use the information to his advantage.

"You may."

"The pack doesn't want Kelton as alpha."

"You think they want *me*?" That was a joke. Most of the pack barely knew I existed.

"The pack has been in decline almost since your father took

over. The good of the pack meant whatever was best for him. Kelton isn't as cruel as Braylen, but he reminds me of your father when he was that age. He embodies the worst traits of an alpha." Everything he said was true, but that didn't translate into the pack wanting me. "My father raised me, too. How do you know I'll be any better?"

Olson smiled and it softened his features. There had been too few smiles among our kind since I could remember. "We watch and listen. You'd put pack over self."

That was precisely why I couldn't be alpha. "No, I won't. I can't."

His smile faded, and it hurt to disappoint him, but I couldn't be the alpha he wanted or the pack needed. "Mage Pederson is my mate. He isn't part of our pack, and the politics of the world ensures he'll never join."

I also wouldn't ask him to sacrifice himself for me. Not when there were many other good options.

"Shit!" Olson's eyes opened wider and his mouth hung open like I'd proven the world was flat. "Did the alpha know this?"

Jan's thoughts intruded through our link. Whatever Commander Foggerty wanted, his mood had turned apprehensive. "Of course not. My father would have perverted Jan for his own ends."

"You can't go in there!" Winston shouted.

Olson turned and we faced the door.

"Like hell I can't," Kelton yelled. "Move out of my way before I gut you."

"One more step and I'll turn you three into a pile of ashes," Winston said.

If Kelton had half the brains I credited him with, he'd know to stand down.

"Kel, stop," Nik said. "Just wait for him to come out."

"They're serious," Warin added. "If you charge in, we're not with you."

Olson turned to me. "He's here to challenge you. For the good of the pack, you must not concede to him."

Jan's emotions jumped and I closed our link. Whatever he was doing, he didn't need to be disturbed by my feelings.

Olson was right. Kel might not be as big a bully as Dad, but he was still young; the pack needed better. But I couldn't be the alpha.

"I'm here to champion Alpha Conall Arawn." The thick Scottish accent was one I hadn't heard before.

Could this day get any crazier?

"Did you . . .?" Olson asked.

I shook my head. How could I call for a champion. I didn't know I could. "Is that a thing? Champion for an alpha?"

"It is," Olson said. "The alpha may have a champion, but if he loses to a challenger, the alpha has to step down and the winner takes his place."

Alphas were supposed to be the strongest in the pack. Having a champion defeated that purpose. "How does that work?"

"When an alpha grows older, he can select a champion. If the alpha was wise and well-liked, said champion would accept to keep a well-loved alpha in power. If the elder alpha was not leading well, no one would agree to be his champion and he would either concede or die when challenged."

In a perfect world it sounded great, but I didn't even know who was taking my place. "I get to decide if I want to use a champion, correct?"

"Indeed, Alpha. Even if you have a champion, you can still accept a challenge if it is made."

I motioned toward the front of the house. "Let's go see who else is here."

Nik and Warin had positioned themselves in front of Kel, who was glaring at someone standing in the ruins of the front of the house. The newcomer was an older man with steel-gray hair. His thick body radiated power.

"No one is challenging Conall without going through us first," Winston said. "I have orders to guard him until Commander Foggerty returns."

"Don't interfere in pack business," Kelton shot back. "I've a right to challenge him."

"Not until you get through me you don't," my "champion" said. "In twelve hundred years I've defended the alpha eight times. None lasted longer than forty-five seconds. You won't last ten."

"Hold on," I said, announcing my presence. "I haven't . . . Wait. Did you say twelve hundred years?"

He crossed his arms over his chest. "Indeed."

Holy fuck, this was Leifr Cormaic. Or at least it was if he was telling the truth. "Guardian, why are you here?"

"You've bonded with your mate. It's time we talked."

How could he know that? And why?

"You two are the only gryphon/mage pairing since Anso and me before the Great Ward," Leifr said as if he'd read my mind. "We were aware the moment you bonded with Jannick. Now that bond has been completed, we should speak."

"Stop ignoring me!" Kelton shouted. "I've issued my challenge. I demand it be accepted or Conall concede."

"If you are so eager to die, you can step outside now." Leifr stepped to the side to make room for Kelton to leave.

This wasn't what I wanted. We had a chance, as a family, to start over—to be better. Our pack didn't need to live in fear. To reclaim our mantle, I needed all my brothers.

"You won't win, Kel. This is Leifr Cormaic." I let that sink in. "You also can't beat me now that I bonded with Jan. It gives me power you can't hope to match."

Seeing the effect this had on my brother, I realized I'd tossed down a gauntlet and dared him not to pick it up. His pride required he press his claim. "Please don't, Kel. We lost Dad and Braylen today. Do you really want to add to that total?"

"You think you can talk your way out of a fight?" Spit flew from his lips; he had an unhinged glint in his eyes. "I did *everything* he asked because I was next. No baby brother is taking what's mine. Don't hide behind an old gryphon who thinks he's a legend. Face me yourself."

I wondered if he had a death wish. He clearly saw the power Cormaic had, or he wouldn't have demanded I face him myself. Did he want to be alpha so badly, he'd prefer death to letting someone else take that role?

"No. I'm not going to fight you. I nearly died keeping Braylen from destroying us all. That's enough for one day. You have two choices: revoke your challenge or have us bury a second brother today. I'd prefer you work with me to rebuild our pack, but I won't give in to your whims like we did to Dad's. The pack deserves better."

I really wanted Kelton to help rebuild the pack, but it was clear my words hadn't penetrated beneath the crazy. His fingers twitched and I braced myself for him to lunge at me with his talons. Winston's stone pulsed and time seemed to slow to a crawl.

Kelton flexed his muscles and his hands morphed into claws. He tried to rush past Nik and Warin, but they grabbed him by the arms. Struggling to get free, he didn't see Leifr approach until the last second.

I tried to shout not to hurt him, but his left hand lashed out before I could speak. Kelton's eyes bulged and I waited for the fountains of blood to shower everyone.

Nothing happened.

Kelton relaxed, but Leifr never released his grip. Finally, he met the older man's gaze and nodded. "Understood."

Leifr let go and spun on his heel. Four long strides and the legend stood in front of me. "He has yielded his challenge, Alpha."

Chapter Forty-One

JANNICK

The room seemed smaller and the air thicker. I didn't tell her I thought the "worse" idea was the more likely. "If you were on this side of a barrier but wanted to bring over something from the other side, you'd need a way past the barrier. That's what this could be."

"A permanent rift? Is that even possible?" Foggerty asked.

Someone had already found a way to break the Ward twice, so anything was possible. "If this is a permanent doorway between worlds, it would be an incredible feat of magic. One none of those mages we fought should be capable of creating."

Leo ran into the building, and I had to remind him to stop before entering the main room. "I couldn't reach Bart, so I called Avie. She's pulling him from his class."

I explained my ideas to Leo, and he listened closely. Neither were good options. Avie had wanted him to get real-world experience, and she got her wish. He'd lost a lot of his frat boy frivolity seeing Foggerty standing in the middle of her death sentence.

A familiar tingle alerted me that Bart had received the

message. Leo's head snapped toward mine and my pulse hammered in my ears. I touched my stone, praying Bart had some idea how to solve this.

"*Can you show me what you're dealing with?*" He didn't bother with small talk. As kids we'd shared our thoughts so often it had become a game. We'd do it just to see what the other was doing. No one suspected because even for siblings, that level of trust was rare.

I walked around the room, pausing at each alcove to give him a better look. Then I made a second pass, showing him the main glyph.

Through our link, Conall's anxiety rose. Before I could isolate what was bothering him, he shut me out. I pushed back to reconnect, but Bart yelled in my head.

"*Stop! A bit to your left.*"

"*What part?*"

"*By her right foot.*"

I focused where he said, but I didn't see anything particularly remarkable. There was a patch of crossed lines, but nothing atypical of magical ley lines.

"*Step back to where you started and show me the whole room again.*"

Walking backward, I swept my gaze slowly around the room. When I reached the door, I continued to scan until he told me to stop.

"*I need you to go back to the intersection by her foot.*"

"What is it?" Leo asked.

I ignored the question and moved back to the spot.

"*That's where you unravel the spell.*"

Like our younger brother, I still didn't understand the significance. "*Explain.*"

"*All the spells are connected at that point. There are three components: the twelve smaller sites; the outer ring, which likely creates a power containment circle; and the inner one that summons the demon. They criss-*

cross other places, but this is the only point where lines from all three elements touch."

"How do we use that to free Commander Foggerty?" I asked.

"Dissolve the lines at that point, and the glyphs will all be useless. Then you can erase them completely once she is free."

Having read his article, I knew basically what he was talking about, but reading and doing were very different things. I glanced up. I'd forgotten Foggerty wasn't part of the conversation. She looked like she had ice in her veins. We'd just discussed a spell that trapped her and would cause a very painful death if we didn't prevail, while she stayed silent to let the "experts" talk.

"You'll need three strong wizards in addition to yourself. They'll each need to hold a line while you dissolve the knot. Otherwise, it almost surely will trigger some adverse reaction."

"Define adverse," Leo said.

"Either it will explode, taking out the entire building and then some given its size, or it will activate the whole spell. Without the twelve sacrifices, the containment won't hold a puppy, let alone an adult demon lord."

Wonderful. My choice of death was to have my bits scattered across Western Maryland or to be an afternoon crumpet for some hungry demon lord.

"We're one wizard short," I said. "I need to go find Agent Winston."

"Hold on," Bart said. "Make sure he's an alpha-class creative. The other three will need to basically keep the spell open until you sever the connection. Once you touch the knot with magic, it will react. I'm not sure a beta-class creative can handle it given the complexity you're dealing with."

By my estimate, Winston was an alpha five class mage in combat and defensive magic only. This was creative. "Colonel, what's your rank in creative magic?"

"Alpha four."

I didn't need to ask the next question to know, Houston, we have a problem. "Are any of the other inquisitors on your team alpha-class creative?"

"No." She shook her head. "We focus on combat and defensive and overall rank. Why?"

It would take hours for another mage to get here. I hoped Foggerty could hold out. "We need four alpha-class creatives to unravel this. We're one short."

"Perhaps I can help."

My head whipped around. Anso Hollen stood in the doorway, mage stone already in his hand.

"Holy shit, you scared me." Leo lowered his stone, which he'd instinctively pointed toward the voice.

Anso rolled his eyes. "Another of my descendants who is fond of blessing excrement."

And he said I was immature? "What are you doing here?"

"You completed your bond; Leifr and I want to talk to you. My mate is dealing with the oldest brother who thinks he should be alpha after his father because they shared a nasty streak. Leifr has appointed himself Conall's champion. All challengers will need to fight him and not Conall. He's hoping he gets a few before word spreads he's too strong."

That sounded like something a gryphon would dream about. Especially a twelve-hundred-year-old gryphon who grew up during the Great Species Wars. "He has no room to talk smack about us."

Anso smiled. "No, but we are not so lofty his comments aren't valid as well."

"Commander Foggerty." I waved a hand from Anso to her and back. "Anso Hollen, Guardian of the Eastern Point."

Foggerty's eyebrow rose a fraction. It was the closest thing to surprise she'd registered. "An honor, Guardian."

"The same, Commander." Anso bowed. "Before we begin, Jannick, I assume you are in contact with your brother?"

I nodded.

"Good. Ask him to contact Darius. He's the expert on demons and the Great Ward. I'd like his input if you don't mind."

I'd rather not fight a demon today, Leifr and I have dinner plans."

His casual attitude didn't fool me. He knew how serious this was. I hadn't thought to ask Bart to consult Darius, but it made sense. *"Bart?"*

"On it, Jan. Give me a minute and we'll all link up."

Leo looked a bit frazzled. Poor kid, my first mission was nothing like this. I put my arm around him. "You got this, Leo. Compared to what you've done today, you won't break a sweat on this."

"I'm good." He looked me in the eyes. "Thanks, Jan. For everything. You've been a great mission buddy."

I felt Bart's touch a moment before I heard his voice. *"Jan? Leo?"*

"We're here," Leo and I said at the same time.

"Can you link Foggerty? Darius is linking in Anso."

"Commander, I need to link you into the conversation."

Foggerty held up her stone and I linked us together. The first five minutes rehashed what Bart and I had discussed. Anso did another scout for Darius, and after they were done, the plan remained the same. I might have crowed a bit that Bart had it right; Anso's "need" to get Darius's input hadn't been needed at all.

Not that it mattered. Darius and Bart carried on like they'd known each other for years, which was nice and all, but I had a mate to see. *"We good?"*

A chorus of yeses rang out through our link.

"Easy peasy," Bart said. *"Stay focused and this won't be an issue."*

Easy peasy for him to say. In Bart's mind, the difficult things he did so effortlessly were just as simple for everyone else. If only life were so simple. *"Is it okay if I wish you were doing this instead of me?"*

"Nope. Cael and I don't fancy a visit to Hagerstown."

He'd succeeded in calming me. I'd wondered if we'd still be

close after he found Cael, but he was still Bart. The love was different, but no less strong. We'd always be tight and that made me happy. "*Fucker. You two are such homebodies.*"

Bart laughed and it soothed my last few fears. "*Talk to me in a couple of months.*"

Anso stepped outside to clear the area. No one doubted this would work, but taking precautions was prudent. Everyone but Bart and Darius dropped off the call. They wouldn't be able to help if I screwed things up, but maybe they could stop me from making a mistake.

"Let me know when you've isolated the three lines." I shifted my eye contact from Foggerty to Anso and finally rested on Leo.

They each raised a ward around themselves and nodded. "We're set," Anso said.

I was glad Anso was taking charge. It would also help Leo's confidence to be working with a mage of Anso's power and reputation. I pulled out my stone and knelt in front of the knot. In theory, this was simple—dissolve it before it could trigger a release. The demon was in the detail. We didn't know what would set it off. And I'd be the only one not shielded.

I built an invisible wall around the three lines and strengthened it as much as I could. Holding the point of my gem just above the lines, I held my breath and pushed a burst of energy at the black mark.

Outside the range of my regular vision, magic attacked the dark spell. Resistance flared and as expected, the glyph tried to go fully active the moment we tried to erase the spells.

My wards held and the command stopped well short of its target. What I hadn't expected was it wasn't a single pulse. It continued to send the order. We had it contained, but we couldn't let our concentration slip.

Working out from the center, I used Bart's spell to erase the lines and the magic embedded in them. It was slow work. The pressure on my containment wards remained constant but didn't increase. I reached the last bit of the intersection of the three lines and felt confident. The undoing of many a man was confidence. With the end in sight, I quickly erased the last bit of black on the concrete and I heard a snick, like a clicker had been snapped. A small bit spat from the last erg of ebony and divided into three; each speck landed on one of the lines I'd detached from the core.

"Oh shit!"

A white flash sent me flying into blackness.

Chapter Forty-Two

CONALL

Leifr blocked the sun, but his energy shone brightly. "What did you say to him?"

"I asked him to help you and me return gryphons to our former glory, and then I let him see my full power."

There was no way Kelton had accepted that as a reason to back down. Dying on an anthill was preferable to backing down. "What did you really say?"

"I told him your time as alpha would be short because you are needed for greater things. If he wants to be alpha, he needs to prove he is better than Aodhan. Until such day, if he ever ascends to the title, I will challenge him the first chance I get and make sure his reign is the second shortest in recorded history after your brother Braylen's."

Despite Leifr's belief Kelton had changed, I'd have to keep a close watch on him. He wouldn't attack me like Bray had our father, but working against me would be almost as bad. "You're sure he's on board with this?"

"You'll need to demonstrate your new strength once this

current crisis has passed, but your brother is smart. Aodhan wasn't leaving soon and when he did, Kelton knew he'd need to fight Braylen. Today's events made his path quicker and easier. He'll wait until you and your mate leave."

I'd been so focused on Kelton and Leifr, I forgot to check on Jan. I stopped before I opened our link; I didn't want to break his concentration. "What are they doing?"

"Anso went to see if he could help, but he didn't explain why he thought they required his assistance."

I looked out the front; a group of inquisitors were herding people away from the bunkhouse. A chill raced up my back and through my body. Jan was in there.

A thick hand landed on my chest before I could move. "You can't go to him. Whatever they are about to do, if you can't ward yourself, you need to stay clear."

Jan had been apprehensive before I cut him off. I'd thought it had to do with him feeling me. "I need to get to him."

"No, Alpha. You need to stay here. My mate of twelve hundred years is in there, so I know the need is strong. You won't be able to help. More likely you will cause him to falter at a critical time."

"Con," Nik put his hands on my shoulders. "You're the alpha. The good of the pack must come first if we're to heal."

In that moment I cared nothing for the good of the pack. It was wrong. It was why I shouldn't be the alpha. I looked up and Kelton was staring at me. Pushing Nik's hands gently aside, I approached my brother. I could feel the eyes of the room on us, but this needed to be as public as his challenge.

He bowed his head and waited for me.

"Kel? Look at me please?"

I waited to see what he'd do. If he fought me on this, there would never be a time for reconciliation. He swallowed and looked up.

"I need you. I need your experience, guidance, and support.

The pack needs you. We let Dad poison us against each other. You're my brother, not my enemy. I don't expect you to bow to me. That doesn't serve anyone well. If I screw up, and I will, I need my brothers to walk me back so I don't make it worse.

"Please. Be my brother and not an adversary."

Kelton blinked. He opened his mouth, but an explosion rocked the compound before he could speak.

Part of the bunkhouse roof shot into the air and pain flashed through my link with Jan. I staggered under the onslaught of impulses from my mate.

"Conall!" Kelton shouted and steadied me.

Through the haze, I heard Leifr roar.

"What happened?" Nik asked.

My link was quiet. "Jan!"

I ripped free of Kel's grip and pushed my way past the others in my path. An inquisitor tried to stop me, but I shouldered him aside as bits of the roof rained down on the courtyard.

"Jan?" I called softly through our link. He was alive, but our connection was faint.

I stormed into the room and pulled up. Jan was crumpled against the wall, blood everywhere. Leo was on his left and a white-haired wizard I didn't know was to his right. The older man turned when I entered.

"You should stay back. It's bad."

I ignored his warning. No matter how bad it was, my place was at his side. "I felt it happen to him."

His body was torn open in a dozen spots. Leo's stone glowed, and the blood flow stopped.

"Where's your fucking mage healer?" he screamed, his voice one notch below hysterical. "I can't handle this alone."

"She's coming," Foggerty said. "Do what you can to maintain him."

I wedged myself between the older wizard and the wall. Jan's beautiful face was sliced in too many places to count.

"Anso, I need help," Leo said.

"I'm not a healer," Anso said.

"You don't need to be. Use your stone to apply pressure to the cuts on his chest. We need to stop those, or he'll bleed out."

"Out of the way!" someone shouted and an inquisitor I'd seen during the planning squeezed through the people between her and us. "Move. Medic coming through."

She knelt to Leo's right and sucked breath between her teeth.

"You need to save him," Anso said. "The fate of the world depends on you."

"No fucking pressure, old man." She pulled out a pair of green stones. "I need Reynolds."

"He's coming," Foggerty said.

The mages worked, but I could feel him slipping. "Jan? Stay with us, babe. Just a bit longer."

"Con . . ." His voice was barely a whisper. "Hurt. . . . Love . . . you."

I reached for our link and coiled myself around it. *"Jan. You said you wouldn't leave me. Stay with me."*

"Need . . . to . . . sleep," he said in between tiny breaths. "Hurts."

If I let him go, he'd never wake up. "I know it hurts, babe. Just stay with us. They'll make it better."

"Go now." It was so faint I might have imagined it.

A tug on our link almost cost me my grip. I closed my eyes and dug in. *"Don't you leave me!"*

"You need to let go," Anso said. "If he goes, he'll take you with him."

An empty threat. If Jan died, a huge part of me would, too. "You'd better make sure to save him, because I'm not letting go." Never again.

I imagined I held a rope around him as he slid down a steep slope. My heels dug in, but the ground crumbled under our weight.

"We're losing him," Leo said.

"Goddamn it, where is fucking Reynolds?" the healer shouted.

"He isn't here," Anso said. "Tell us what to do."

"I need someone to stabilize the smaller injuries so I can work on the ones that are killing him. But there are too many."

"Which ones are the worst?" Leo asked.

"Here and here," she said. I didn't look. If I let my concentration slip, he'd slip out of my grasp.

"Conall . . ." Anso whispered.

I ignored the warning in his voice. I'd go with him before I released my hold on his soul. *"Jan. I'm here. Fight babe. Fight for us. Fight for our future. Just hold on a bit more."*

"I . . . love you. . . . Need . . . to . . . let . . . go."

Our slide down hastened, and I held on with everything I had left. It wouldn't be enough, but I wasn't going to let him go alone.

We jerked to a halt, and I felt someone holding me. *"I have you, little brother."*

Nik wrapped himself around my core; he slowed the descent. A moment later, Warin and shockingly Kelton joined him. Others I couldn't name joined my brothers.

"What are you doing?" Anso asked. "If we lose him, we'll lose all of you."

"He's our alpha and our brother," Nik said. "We won't let go."

More gryphons wrapped their lives around us. We weren't sliding anymore, but Jan was growing heavier by the second. Another presence joined us, strong and steady; an anchor that held us firm.

"Leifr!" Anso sounded panicked. "What are *you* doing?"

"He's my alpha, too," Leifr said. "We're using our power to save a member of the pack."

"If he dies—"

"Then we're all dead anyway. Use the time we're giving you to work a miracle."

"Babe, you have so many people who love you. Fight. Don't give up."

"*Conall. I'm ... cold.*"
"*I know. Come to me and get warm.*"
"*Too ... tired ... move ...*"
"Why don't you put him in stasis?" someone asked.
"It would sever their link," the healer said. "He'd die before we could save him."
"Incoming medic!"
"Fucking time," Leo growled.
"*Just a little longer. Please. For me.*"
Jan didn't answer, but the downward drag seemed to ease. Rather than ask me to let him go, now he'd wrapped himself around my core. He'd snuggled in like when we clung to each other on the mountain. I was his safe place, and we'd ride this out together.

How long we stayed locked together was murky, but my body was numb when I realized the pull had stopped altogether. I inched us up the imaginary hill until it flattened, and I flopped onto my back. The danger had passed, but I kept a tight grip on his core. I enjoyed how tightly we were entwined; I wanted to stay with it another few moments.

"You did it, Con," Nik said.

My eyes flew open, and I sagged into his arms. I didn't do it. Everyone did. "He's okay?"

"They got him stabilized and in stasis. You saved him."

My head drooped and I could barely keep my eyes open. "Thank you." I searched until I found Warin and Kelton standing over Nik's shoulder. Behind them, the room was crowded with gryphons. "Thank you all for saving Jan."

I steadied myself and stood. The room was packed, but I headed for Kelton. "Kel. I . . . This means everything to me."

He pulled me into a hug, and we were joined by our brothers. Wrapped in their arms, it felt like I was surrounded by their wings. It was comforting and filled with love I'd missed for so long. People would say I saved Jan, but it was Nik, Warin, and especially Kelton. He broke through his pain and anger and by his example, did something only he could do. He united us again.

Someone entered the space near us. I already recognized his scent. He wouldn't interrupt if it wasn't important.

"The medivac will be here in three minutes," Leifr said. "You need to go with him, Alpha."

I nodded and pinched my eyes shut. My brothers let go, but I grabbed Kel.

"I need to . . . I can't . . . Will you act in my place until I get back?"

"Of course, Alpha." He pulled me close and whispered in my ear. "Go. We'll take care of things."

Nik shooed me away, and Warin put his arm around the two of them. For the first time in my life, I felt like things were going to get better. I just needed Jan to heal.

Chapter Forty-Three

JANNICK

I woke from a nap still stuck in the fucking hospital I'd woken up in three days prior. By all accounts, I should have died, but the gryphon community rallied to Conall and saved us both. Coming as close to death as a being could and still be alive gave me a new appreciation for living. I didn't want to spend any more of my time in the hospital.

Leo had stayed with Conall for nearly two days, until I opened my eyes. He should've gone home once he'd helped save me, but he'd ignored even Mom's strongly worded suggestion to leave. I owed him and I'd never forget.

Mom and Dad had arrived within hours and tried to move me to Hollen Memorial in Philadelphia. Much to their consternation, once I woke up, I refused. Restoring the gryphon pack to full health would take time. Conall had a lot of work ahead of him; he was the new alpha, and I wanted to be near him. Mom's complaint about no one listening to her might have been more forceful if she hadn't smiled.

Not that Conall needed me. I didn't know everything, but I'd heard Kelton put pack over personal ambition and the family had come together to heal. Kelton's actions set the tone for the family and the pack. Conall's family took turns sitting with me, Dahlia more than any other. I smiled every time she and Beta Olson came in together. None of us wanted to hope for too much, but Conall had told her to follow her heart. He would support her decisions.

"Prodigal son two point oh is awake."

I rolled my head and snapped fully awake. "Roderick! You're here?"

"I seem to be making a habit of visiting my brothers in the hospital." He smiled and I swear he looked just like a young Grandpa. "After this, the Terrible Twosome will be renamed the Terrific Twosome. You and Bart are quite the talk of the mage world."

The late-night show must've had fun comparing us. "They're wrong. Bart wouldn't have screwed up like I did."

"No one's saying anything negative. Colonel Foggerty has credited you with saving everyone. No one expected what was hidden in there. Not even Bart."

Bart might not have expected it, but he'd have planned better. "I didn't ward myself properly."

"Everyone makes mistakes. Learn from the ones you walk away from."

He moved a strand of hair from my face. It was surprisingly tender, and something I would never have expected from him. "Thanks for coming, Rod. Do you think you can spring me soon? Dad said he wouldn't help, Avie thinks I need a month, and Bart can't leave the school. Help me Roderick Kenobi, you're my only hope."

He snorted and rolled his eyes. "You're certainly a princess, but I'm not saving you. I had to sneak in to see you, so technically I'm not really here."

Growing up, Roderick had only showed up sporadically, but he was always kind and full of warmth. Something pushed him away, but if anyone knew what, they never told us. "Whatever happened, Rod?"

"Not today, little bro." He squeezed my hand. "I wanted to make sure you're okay. And having satisfied myself you'll be back to your old self, I'll head off."

"You could stay." I shrugged. "Bart and I have room in our houses."

He laughed and it softened his face. "No offense, Jan, but I'm not the roommate type. I mean, next you'll suggest I live with Leo."

It wasn't a terrible idea. "He could use the guidance."

"He's in good hands." He smiled. "You three and Owen are special. Most of the family tries to carve out space; you four created a kingdom. And the family is better for your example."

There was a message there, but my brain couldn't parse it out. Something to think about when I was better. "Thanks for coming, Rod."

"You bet. And congrats on the new mate. Conall's lucky to have you."

I lost the ability to speak. Roderick had always been an enigma. This visit cleared up nothing. He opened the door and he nodded. A calming presence filled me, and I knew Roderick was speaking to Conall.

"Thanks for letting me in," Rod said, and they shook hands.

"Thank you for coming." Conall stepped aside and let my brother out.

Shutting the door, he smiled as he walked over. "Hey, babe. You look almost healthy."

It was a proven scientific fact that I was exponentially better whenever he came near. "I'd be so much better if I could get out of here."

"I'm sure, but nearly dying is not something to rush back from."

For most of my life, I'd tended to avoid dwelling on hard things like nearly dying. I would need to change that if I wanted to be a better mate, but I'd deal with that once I got released.

"No, but these gowns that have your ass hanging out, having to use bed pans, and disgusting but supposedly nutritious food are things you run away from as soon as you can."

"I'll help you escape but only if you promise to run in front of me wearing the gown."

Conall laughed, and it was the second-best medicine for what hurt. The best would be to hold him all night.

"Seriously, have you heard when they'll let me go?" I had visions of Dylan and his two-week stay. My injuries were arguably worse, but not really. Healers could mend physical trauma much easier than they could reverse Gallows' Hex.

"Yes, I've heard things," he said coyly. "Your parents requested a medical team from Hollen Memorial, which is where you should have gone, to examine you."

I'd expected Conall, of all people, would understand. If they'd moved me, he would've had to choose between me and his pack. He had enough on his plate. "If I had a shifter's healing power, it wouldn't have been an issue."

He sat on the side of the bed and stroked my hand. "If you'd been a shifter, you wouldn't be my mate."

Three weeks ago, I wouldn't have known how barren my life would be if that were the case. Now even the suggestion left me achingly empty. It also didn't answer my question. "You were saying about my parents and doctors?"

"Was I?" He leaned over and grazed a kiss over my lips.

The effect went right to my cock, which, if you're stuck in a hospital bed, isn't nearly as much fun as it should be. "Yes." It came out a frustrated growl.

"They're coming this morning. They want the specialist to clear you before you're released."

I knew they were doing this from a place of love, but I didn't need their approval or to be seen by those doctors. "You realize I can sign myself out anytime I want?"

"But you won't." He smiled and ran his thumb over the back of my hand. "Patience, babe. Better to be sure than do harm to yourself. Besides, your boss isn't expecting you back anytime soon."

It wasn't work I wanted to get back to, but he knew that. He was also right; I wouldn't leave before they arrived. "Fine, but if they don't clear me, I am leaving this afternoon."

"Jan, they're not doing this to punish you. Neither of us are doctors. There might be more we don't know about."

If the doctors were keeping things from me, I was leaving without signing myself out. Let them try to stop me. "In the past twenty-four hours, they've done nothing but monitor me. No more IVs, no pills, no laying of hands by the healers, and I don't need rehab. That's the definition of good to go."

"Then I assume you'll be able to go home once they see you," Conall said, appearing amused. "I know you want to leave. If they don't see anything out of the ordinary and they still refuse to release you, I'll help you leave. But please wait for them to do one more evaluation."

After all he'd risked, there was nothing I'd refuse him. "I promise."

I pulled his hand to my lips and breathed deeply. His touch, feel, and taste were the best medicine for my remaining injuries. With my head clear, I focused on the next problem. Where I would go when I was released.

"Whatever has you anxious, you need to let it go," Conall said. "If you sabotage your release, my offer to help you escape is null."

Conall sensing my emotions on such a granular level was scary and wonderful. "I was thinking about where I'll go when I leave."

"Home with me, obviously."

I swallowed a snarky, "No shit, Sherlock" and rolled my eyes. "Which will be where? In case you forgot, I live in one place, and you live in another. And just so we're clear, all options are on the table. I'm not opposed to anything."

"What do you want?"

The easy answer was the obvious one. I wanted us to be together. The details, however, hadn't been hammered out. "Ideally? To keep working and still come home to you every night."

"Me too. What's the problem?"

He looked totally confused, as if living almost two hundred miles apart didn't complicate things. "Let me see. You live here, and I live and work in Philadelphia. Unlike you, I can't fly. It's at least two and a half hours each way."

"Yes, but neither of us have to go into an office every day. We can live here or there, depending on the circumstances."

Could it really be that simple? I'd spent the last two days thinking about how to make it work. "As the alpha, don't you need to be here?"

"There are gryphons all over the world. I can be alpha anywhere. There's nothing special about Maryland other than my family lives here."

Maybe my brain was more damaged than I thought. I took something simple and made it hard. "Oh. Right. I forgot."

"Jan?" He waited for me to look at him. "You're making this too hard. When we leave today, we're going to my house for a few days. Then we'll drive to Philly, and you can show me around."

Conall had changed in the five days since he'd become alpha. It changed him. Or maybe it allowed his true nature to shine.

There was something else I'd spent my idle time thinking about.

"What about your degree?"

He smiled and I felt his joy, but there was also indecision. "I'm going to finish it, graduate, and see if I can fit working with kids into my new responsibilities."

I knew this weighed on him, and I wanted to shoulder the burden. "I have an idea about how you can do both."

"Great, let me hear it."

I struggled to find the words, which was ridiculous. He might not like it, but he wouldn't scoff at me. Exhaling, I dove in. "The biggest impediment to being a social worker is your duties as alpha. They would almost surely interfere."

"That's what I fear will happen, yes."

Identifying the correct problem made me confident I'd found the right answer. "What if we started our own agency? The government outsources most of these duties to contractors, and the result is less than optimal. We could create a nonprofit, hire the best people by paying top dollar, and have a program to encourage good people to go into the field by offering scholarships and other incentives.

"Before you wonder about how we'd do it, *we* have more than enough money to seed the program. My family connections will enable us to fundraise and ensure the foundation we create starts its existence with a large enough endowment to support everything you want it to achieve."

I waited to hear his response. The reality was, as alpha, there was no way he could carry an active caseload. But the goal was to help the kids, and this would allow him to do so much more. Finally, he smiled.

"I love it. Especially that it will be something we create together."

Joy bubbled inside me. I wanted him to be happy so he could be the best alpha possible. He hadn't grown up a Hollen; he didn't understand the resources we had to throw at good ideas.

"Of course. I'm going to support everything you do. I know how much this means to you—can't let a little something like being made alpha derail your big plans. We have the money and connections to make it a reality. How can the Assembly refuse to work with us when the Mage Council has thrown its weight behind the idea?"

"Is this what you've been thinking about while you were here?"

Heat burned in my cheeks, and I wiggled my eyebrows. "It's *one* of the things I thought about."

He barked out a laugh. "You'll need to ask the doctors if you're well enough for *that*."

If he thought I'd be too embarrassed to ask, he didn't know me quite as well as he thought. "Stick around and hear for yourself."

Conall leaned in and kissed me. "You've never seen the house. Everyone will hear us."

Two things hit me at once. The first: Despite being his mate, I still knew almost nothing about him or his life. The second: I didn't care if they heard. "We can be quiet."

Epilogue

Growing up, family get-togethers had never been joyous events. No one wanted to be there, but Dad ordered us to show up and we did. There was always an ulterior motive, and we spent most of the time trying to avoid Dad's notice.

It was funny how I'd stopped thinking of him as the alpha now that he was gone. I was the gryphon alpha now, and part of the family healing required we discontinue old bad habits. Dad was a shitty alpha and a worse parent, but he'd been our father.

Flying along the coast, I remembered my frantic flight six months earlier. My sole focus had been getting to Jan as quick as possible; I hadn't had time for something so mundane as admiring the stunning beauty of the ocean crashing against the shore.

This trip, I took the time to memorize every detail—the colorful array of homes perched on the stony cliffs, their windows reflecting the glassy water below. I'd missed a lot but gained so much more.

Jan dangled below my talons, adrenaline coursing through him. The air rushing around him was a thrill-seeker's drug, but for him this was our thing. Our mate bond allowed us to share the experience on a level I'd never imagined. It made flying feel new and exciting again.

I pulled up and glided over the center of the village. The house was on an inlet at the north end of town, but we needed to approach from the east to land.

The other homeowners were a bit apprehensive about having gryphons for neighbors, and I didn't blame them. Apart from the terrible reputation we suffered from under Dad, there was the whole "naked people walking around the yard after shifting" thing. My brothers and I put Jan and Bart's time working for Habitat for Humanity to good use building a solution. The small structure at the edge of the property allowed us to shift and change out of sight.

I shifted and dressed quickly in the chilly November New England air. Jan handed me a scarf, not for warmth but for style. Evidently, as a Hollen, I had a look to uphold. Compared to Jan, I had a ways to go, but I was learning.

Despite the spell he cast to ward off the cold, Jan's cheeks were red with windburn. His hair was a mess, too. "How many times do I need to remind you, it's not just the cold. It's the wind."

Jan moved to the mirror and turned his face side to side. "I thought I'd compensated for that. Guess that spell failed."

Sliding up behind him, I took the brush from the small table and fixed his thick brown hair. "If you'd admit defeat and ask Bart, you could protect your skin *and* keep the feel on your face."

"Or I could figure it out on my own. I'm getting closer."

He smiled and my heart skipped a beat. Even with all that had happened, there were times when I was still blown away by him. He was handsome, intelligent, talented, and stubborn, but in a good way. I'd been given the most amazing gift, and nothing could replace the joy he brought me.

I finished taming his hair and kissed his cheek. "I love you."

"Love you, too." After a peck on the lips, he fussed with my scarf and shirt. "Ready?"

Was I? Probably not. This was my first family holiday as the gryphon alpha. It was also the first one that everyone *wanted* to attend.

Laughter, missing for so long in our family, filled the house and carried to the outside. I couldn't hear everything, but Kelton's deep baritone filled the night, regaling the family as befit his status. He'd not only accepted his new, temporary role, but he also excelled at it, giving the pack a taste of the bright future we had ahead.

A familiar flurry of wings announced a new arrival. A pair of boots appeared before Anso dropped the last two feet to the ground. Unlike my mate, this mage had perfected the spells needed to keep warm *and* keep the wind off his face and his hair.

"Greetings, Alpha, and thank you for the invitation," Anso said as he made room for Leifr to land. "I trust you both had a pleasant trip."

I couldn't tell if he was making small talk or trolling Jan. Before either of us could answer him, Leifr's massive body shook the ground as he landed. Jan and I left the small space to give the Guardians room.

"We'll see you inside," I said, nodding to the elder gryphon as we passed.

We were halfway to the back door when it flew open, and several small beings rushed into the night. They barely greeted Jan and me as they ran toward the shed, squealing about meeting *the Leifr Cormaic*. It was hard to be upset when playing second fiddle to a living legend.

The next two out the door were the most surprising. Mom had briefed me on this, but to see it, and feel how accepted it was, made the entire flight worth the effort. Kelton's youngest son Maxwell and his *boyfriend*, a mountain lion shifter, made a beeline for me and Jan. Max was twenty-three and finally living his life.

He'd started college earlier in the fall and was going to lead the next generation of gryphons.

"Uncle Conall, Uncle Jannick," Max said. "This is Ashlen, my boyfriend."

There was more to this rush out to greet us than just saying hello. I had an idea, but I wasn't going to press my nephew. I extended my hand. "Pleased to meet you, Ashlen."

"It's . . . it's an honor to meet you, Alpha Arawn." Max elbowed him. "What? I've never even met our alpha."

Jan chuckled. "He is pretty cool but wait until you meet Leifr Cormaic. *He's* truly impressive."

Ashlen's eyes almost popped, and Jan barely controlled his laughter.

"C'mon," Jan said. "I'll introduce you." He winked as he put his arm around the gobsmacked young man and led him back the way we came.

Max stared after them with a lopsided grin. "That worked out. I wasn't sure how I could get Ash to give us a minute."

Jan must've sensed what I had. "He's good that way. What's on your mind?"

"I just wanted to say thank you." Before I could blink, he had me in hug.

I didn't need an explanation. Dad would never have allowed him to mate with a "lesser" shifter, let alone earn his degree. I wrapped my arms around him. "You're welcome."

When I looked up, Kelton stood in the doorway. He nodded and gave me a thumbs up.

I'd never known how much Kel had hidden from everyone until Dad died. He loved his children every bit as much as Nik and Warin. He'd risked a lot hiding his son's happiness, but removing that weight freed him from his shackles.

I liked this version of my brother. Now he led by example, and the family and the pack had never been happier.

Releasing my nephew, I grabbed him by the shoulders. "If you need anything..."

"I know. Just ask." He nodded behind him. "I'm good; I have Dad."

He had a whole pack, but Kelton was a great start.

I heard Jan returning.

"You may want to rescue Ashlen," he said. "Leifr is asking him about his intentions, and he can be intimidating."

Max gulped, looked at me, and walked as quick as he could to rescue his boyfriend. I took Jan's hand in mine and headed for the house.

Nik and Warin had joined Kelton. Free from Dad's manipulation, they'd bonded like real brothers. Whatever plans Anso and Leifr had for me and Jan, the gryphons would thrive under their leadership.

"You did that," Jan whispered, squeezing my fingers gently. "You gave them the chance to be who they wanted, not who they needed to be to survive."

I shook my head. I hadn't saved them, and they hadn't saved me. "Actually, *you* did that and so much more. You made me believe in us and from there, the rest was easy."

"We believed in each other." He tugged my hand to his lips. "There is no me or you. Just us."

Leifr's booming voice caused an eruption of squeals. They'd be out soon, and I had a family to greet. "Then let *us* go inside and see Mom and my sisters before Leifr turns the house upside down."

We hit the stairs and were engulfed in a blanket of love. Jan was right—we didn't survive alone. We needed each other.

Judging by the first few minutes of this holiday, we were all going to be just fine.

* * *

Thank you for reading! I hope you enjoyed this second book in the Mages and Mates world.

Jan and Conall are on their path, but the Great Ward still needs two more pairings. Pre-Order *Under a Spell* and read how Leothius finds his mate and has to fight to keep him.

Available March 26, 2024.

Under a Spell: Mates and Mates Book 3

And, if you haven't done so already, sign up for my newsletter to learn more about the next books in the series, cover reveals, and other news.

Gallorious Reader News Sign Up:

Acknowledgments

It takes a village to do so many things and writing a book is no different.

Macy Blake - my younger big sister who has encouraged me and given me her most precious gift - her time. Thank you for everything.

Meghan Maslow - I owe you too many thank yous to list, so I'll go with the most important - thank you for being an amazing friend.

Lynda Lamb and Lorraine Fico-White - thank for your wonderful editing skills.

Kitty Munday - for being a great proof reader and a better friend.

Alexandria Corza - your talent brought my cover to life and makes me smile every time I look at your work.

To Mike and kiddo - I don't want to know a world or a day without you both brightening my life. It is my great joy to spend my life with you both.

About Andy

Andy Gallo prefers mountains over the beach, coffee over tea, and regardless if you shake it or stir it, he isn't drinking a martini. He remembers his "good old days" as filled with mullets, disco music, too-short shorts, and too-high socks. Thanks to good shredders and a lack of social media, there is no proof he ever descended into any of those evils.

Married and living his own happy every after, Andy helps others find their happy endings in the pages of his stories. No living or deceased ex-boyfriends appear on the pages of his stories.

Andy and his husband of more than twenty-five years spend their days raising their daughter and rubbing elbows with other parents. Embracing his status as the gay dad, Andy sometimes has to remind others that one does want a hint of color even when chasing after their child.

A World Away: Learning to Breathe
Book One*

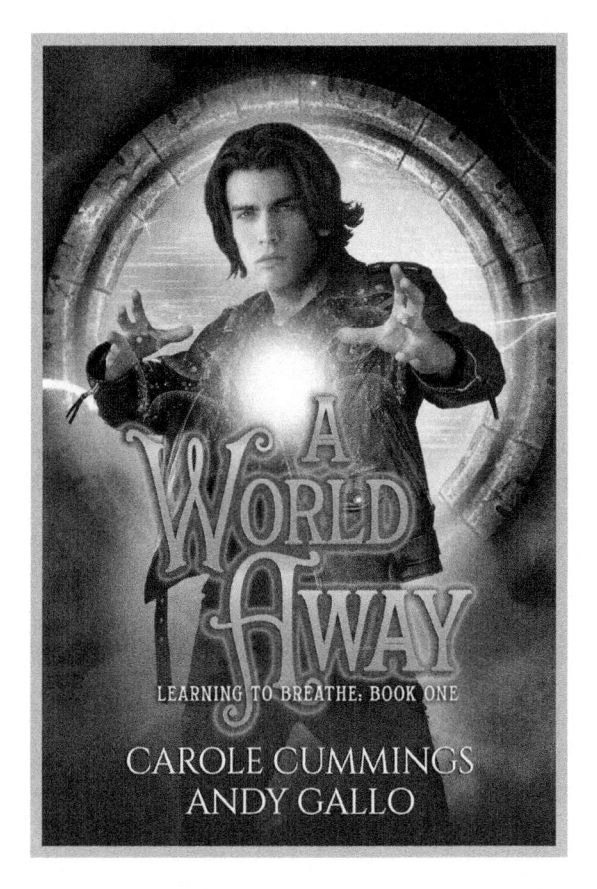

**Please note, *A World Away* was previously published as *Relativity*, by Carole Cummings and Andrew Q. Gordon. There is a new epilogue for this version, but if you purchased the original *Relativity*, email me to read the epilogue for free.*

Available July 11, 2023: Pre-Order now.

Nathan Duffy knows how to keep things locked down so tight even he doesn't know they're there. Like his childhood trauma over the near-catastrophe he almost caused when his power manifested. His adolescent resentment over the near fatal injury he still hasn't really accepted. His futile not-so-platonic love for his best friend Cam. And that one pivotal moment when the love and the power had merged to save Cam from the accident that left Nathan unable to walk. Nathan figures losing the use of his legs was a fair exchange for Cam's life. He just can't ever let Cam know why.

For Cam Almenara, life has been an ongoing cycle of questioning reality. What if his mother hadn't died when he was ten? What if that drunk driver hadn't almost killed him and Nathan? What if Nathan's powers hadn't protected Cam at the cost of Nathan's ability to walk? What if Nathan had never convinced himself that Cam's feelings for him are nothing more than attachment and survivor's guilt? And what if Cam can never convince Nathan otherwise?

When Nathan is suddenly stricken by seizure like nightmares, his power slips its leash—*again*. Fearful his rogue abilities will hurt—or worse, kill—Cam, Nathan comes to the conclusion that it's him or Cam. Nathan knows who he'll choose. Trouble is, so does Cam. And he's just as willing as Nathan is to make the ultimate sacrifice to save the best friend he loves… and prove they belong together.

Available July 11, 2023: Pre-Order now.

Also by Andy Gallo

If you enjoyed *Break the Spell*, be sure to check out my other stories.

Mages and Mates:

Spell it Out: A Mages and Mates Prequel

Break the Spell: Mages and Mates Book 1

It Spells Trouble: Mages and Mates Book 2

Harrison Campus: A contemporary MM Romance series:

Better Have Heart: Book 1

Better Be True: Book 2

Better to Believe: Book 3

Better Be Sure: A Harrison Campus Novel

Better For You: A Harrison Campus Holiday Novella

Harrison Campus Box Set

Harrison Campus Box Set Collection
AN MM COLLEGE ROMANCE SERIES

[Buy it or Read it on KU:](#)

This box set includes all five books in the Harrison Campus series (four novels and one novella). These slow-burn, low-angst stories prove opposites do attract, and follow the emotional highs and lows of five couples falling in love and finding their HEA.

Better Be Sure: An Out for You MM Romance (Harrison Campus Book 1)

Jackson Murphy bet his legacy that he can bring a guy to his fraternity formal. The guy he loves, Ed Knowles, isn't out and won't come to the dance. Does Jack follow his heart or hold onto the last link to his deceased father?

Better Have Heart: A Rivals to Lovers MM Romance (Harrison Campus Book 2)

Isaiah Nettles counts on winning the Gage Scholar program to help his family. The only thing in his way is Darren Gage, the heir to the Gage fortune.

Darren Gage plans to become the Gage Scholar to win back his father's affection. Then he meets the competition and things get complicated.

Better Be True: A Fake Boyfriend, Roommates to Lovers MM Romance (Harrison Campus Book 3)

Nico Amato is in love with his roommate. His all-American, jeans and t-shirt roommate who thinks Nico is too much. When Luke needs a fake boyfriend, does Nico refuse? Nope. He's in so much trouble.

Luke DeRosa has it bad for his roommate. His flamboyant, oversized personality roommate who does everything big. They kind of guy who finds Luke boring. When Nico needs a fake boyfriend, Luke should refuse. How does yes come out of his mouth?

Better to Believe: A Brother's Best Friends, Nerd/Jock MM Romance (Harrison Campus Book 4)

Coury Henderson has it all worked out: Pitch well his senior year, get drafted, play pro baseball. Falling for, Liam, his best friend's super smart, younger brother, isn't compatible with those plans.

Liam Wright has crushed on his brother's best friend, Coury, since he was twelve years old. Not that he'd ever have a chance. Jocks don't dig nerdy guys like him and Coury barely knows he's alive. So why can't he stop hoping for more?

Better For You: A Nerd/Jock, Forced Proximity MM Romance (A Harrison Campus Novella)

Charlie O'Leary agrees to work at the library before going home for Christmas. He needs the money. Staying with his secret crush, Evan, is a bonus. But hot, rich jocks don't go for nerds like him.

Evan Turgon needs help. He has five days to finish a paper he can't wrap his head around. Lucky for him, his cute, straight-A, fraternity brother Charlie is staying in the house. Too bad smart, cute guys always think he's stupid.

ಜಿಕ್ಕಿ

Buy it or Read it on KU:

Fantasy by Andrew Q. Gordon

Do you like epic fantasy? I invite you to check out my non-romance fantasy and urban fantasy books penned under my Andrew Q. Gordon author name.

Champion of the Gods

A Mother's Love - Prequel Short Story

The Last Grand Master:

The Eye and the Arm:

Kings of Lore and Legend:

Child of Night and Day:

When Heroes Fall:

Champion of the Gods - Box Set:

Stand Alone Books

Purpose:

Champion of the Gods
BOX SET

It took the Seven to create the world, each to rule their own. Until one wanted to control it all.

Buy it or Read it on KU:

In the Great War of ancient times the God of Death sought to rule the world. He almost succeeded, but the Champion of the Six, destroyed the bridge into the world and closed the Eight Gates of Neblor. Some thought forever.

But he returned.

His servant, Meglar, surprised his enemies and all the great wizards who opposed him. The Six chose a new Champion to save the world. Young and untested, Farrell struggles to unite those who oppose the God of Death. With each confrontation, however, his task seems ever more impossible.

What readers have said:

If you like beautifully designed worlds, riveting action, and a story steeped in magic, you'll love Andrew Q. Gordon's **Champion of the Gods,** *an epic fantasy series of magic, swords, and sorcery.*

"Mr. Gordon's world-building and character creation are definitely on par with that of Tolkien." -Len Evans, Amazon Reviewer ★★★★★

I am left wanting more details and stories from this incredible universe Andrew Q. Gordon has created. -Brax, Amazon Reviewer ★★★★★

This complete set contains all five books in the Champion of the Gods series. Over 2500 pages of magic, heroism, and fantasy adventures. Save 50% versus buying the individual books by reading the entire series in this special bundle deal!

Included in the Box Set:

The Last Grand Master (Book One)
The Eye and the Arm (Book Two)

Kings of Lore and Legend (Book Three)
Child of Night and Day (Book Four)
When Heroes Fall (Book Five)

❧❧❧

Buy it or Read it on KU:

Purpose
AN URBAN FANTASY THRILLER

But it or Read it on KU:

Forty years ago the Spirit of Vengeance—a Purpose—took William Morgan as its host, demanding he avenge the innocent by killing the guilty. Since then, Will has retreated behind Gar, a façade he uses to avoid dealing with what he's become. Cold, impassive, and devoid of emotion, Gar goes about his life alone—until his tidy, orderly world is upended when he meets Ryan, a broken young man cast out by his family. Spurred to action for reasons he can't understand, Gar saves Ryan from death and finds himself confronted by his humanity.

Spending time with Ryan helps Will claw out from under Gar's shadow. He recognizes Ryan is the key to reclaiming his humanity and facing his past. As Will struggles to control the Purpose, Ryan challenges him to rethink everything he knew about himself and the spirit that possesses him. In the process, he pushes Will to do something he hasn't done in decades: care.

But it or Read it on KU:

Printed in Great Britain
by Amazon

44195051R00159